DANNY BOY

DANNY BOY

Henry Hack

Broadhead Books
Portland, Oregon

This is a work of fiction. All characters and events portrayed in this novel are fictitious and not intended to represent real people or places.

Although the locale where this story takes place is a real one, various liberties have been taken, and this book does not purport to offer an exact depiction of any particular place or location.

DANNY BOY
Copyright © 2009 by Henry Hack

Broadhead Books
Portland, Oregon
www.salvopress.com

Main cover istockphoto images by Iconogenic, The Netherlands
Additional istockphoto by Daniele Gastoldi, Italy

Library of Congress Control Number: 2008938975

ISBN: 1-930486-87-1
9781930486874

Printed in U.S.A.
First Edition

For Lorraine,
Who always believed

Acknowledgments

Many thanks to all the readers of the draft version of this work for their helpful comments and valuable suggestions, especially Jennifer and Rob LaSpina, Richard and Barbara Paul, Jim and Cathy Magee, Frank and Edie Mauro, Carl and Jeanne Moller, Chip and Sue Logan, Charles Jeny, Ruth Hain, Dennis Cahill, Kathy Cunningham and Joe LaSpina. The highest thanks and appreciation go to my wife, Lorraine, who served as my most critical reader, typist, proofreader and detector of verbosity, pomposity and nonsense in general. Finally, I give special thanks to Scott Schmidt, publisher of Salvo Press, for taking the chance and allowing *Danny Boy* to come to life in print.

PART ONE

Prologue

I have to write this book. I need money and this book can make me a lot of money. I know it can. It has all the ingredients of what they call a "page turner." You know—love, lust, obsession, murders, an investigation, a trial, twists and turns, lawyers and liars. Oh, yeah—a lot of liars.

I never wrote a book before, but I figure that since I've written countless police reports in my time on the Force, I should be able to get it done. Of course, police reports can be pretty dull, but this story will be anything but dull. And I know I have to be very careful to avoid lawsuits from the guilty and innocent characters portrayed in the book. I mean, what's the sense of making a million bucks on a best seller only to lose it to the damned lawyers? Jeff Levy, a rare good lawyer, will help me with that.

The beginning of this tale, this horrible nightmare, started about a year after I was assigned to the Nassau Homicide Squad, my dream job. I eagerly awaited my first "big one"—the kind of case that stays on the front page of the newspapers for a month. And when I got it, my big case, I had all the good things in life going for me—a pretty, devoted wife, two wonderful, happy kids and the house in the suburbs with the prospect of a bigger one in the near future. With our recent promotions, Jeanie and I were knocking down $150,000 a year. Not too shabby, huh? So why am I now so desperate for money? I don't want to get ahead of the story, but I'll tell you this much—I need it to pay my lawyers and my private investigators and the bills due are already in the several thousand dollar range. You see, I have all this time to write because I no longer have my job. I've been suspended indefinitely, without pay, pending the resolution of my, uh…situation. Well, you're asking, what about Jeanie? She makes a good salary, right? Yeah, but Jeanie is not too sympathetic anymore. Now you're thinking, what the hell happened here? Danny, what have you done?

The nightmare started with a phone call at 3:38 in the morning on June 10. Let me put it this way—I would have been better off, if on the way home from the office the day before, I had been run over by a big truck and was on a gurney in the emergency room, unable to move, with every bone in my stupid body broken and on life support, rather than home in bed when that telephone rang and changed my life forever.

BREAKING NEWS

Woodmere, Long Island, NY—June 10.

The citizens of the affluent suburban village of Woodmere, located in the southwest corner of Nassau County, were shocked this morning when the body of resident Laura Samuels was discovered by her husband early this morning. It appears that Mrs. Samuels was murdered during the course of a burglary gone wrong. It is not known at this time if Mr. Samuels was injured.

According to Detective Lieutenant Ray Roberts of the Nassau Homicide Squad, it appears that the intruders entered through a side door and escaped with approximately $1,100 in cash and one or more pieces of jewelry which Roberts declined to identify at this time. Roberts also declined to discuss just how Mrs. Samuels was murdered or if a weapon, or any other evidence, was found at the scene.

The lead investigator on the case, Detective Daniel Boyland, who may be reached at 516-555-4200, is requesting that anyone who may have information helpful in this investigation to call him. All calls will be held strictly confidential. Lieutenant Roberts pledged to keep the media informed of further developments as they occur, but an official press conference has not yet been scheduled.

Chapter 1

The ringing of the phone jarred me out of a sound sleep and I glanced at the alarm clock. I picked up the phone just as the fuzzy red numerals changed from 3:37 to 3:38. I wiped the sleep from my eyes and answered, "Yeah?"

"Detective Danny Boyland?"

"Yes," I said, becoming a bit alert now.

"Jack Kernan, over in Central Detectives. I have a request for you at the scene of a suspicious murder in the Nine-Four Precinct in Woodmere."

"Hold on Jack, let me get a pen," I said as I turned on the small night table lamp. "Okay, give me the address."

"Three-seventy-three Sunset, east off Peninsula Boulevard."

"Got it, what do you mean a suspicious death? Is it a shooting? A stabbing?"

"The cops at the scene said the deceased, a Laura Samuels, had some kinda tape covering her mouth and her husband was mumbling something about smelling some chemical, but that's all I know."

"Tape? Chemicals? Sounds pretty weird," I said. "I'm responding in car 1722. Call the scene and tell them I should be there within the hour and you better call out the works on this one."

"Crime scene, the medical examiner and the district attorney?"

"That'll do for starters. Oh, call Sergeant Francis Finn and fill him in on what you told me. Tell him I'll call him from the scene when I get a handle on what's really going on."

"Will do. Sounds as if you got a real mystery over there. I never heard of such a murder."

"I don't think too many of us have."

I looked over at my sleeping wife, Jean, and smiled. She hadn't moved when the phone rang, or during my conversation with Kernan, having long ago gotten used to the late night interruptions enjoyed by a homicide detective.

Woodmere is an upper-middle class village on Nassau County's south shore, not far from the Queens border. It is one of a group of four other similar towns that are known collectively as the "five towns," the term bringing to mind expensive residences with well-trimmed lawns and well-kept wives. Number 373 Sunset Avenue was no exception, although my view of the house was hampered by the darkness as I rolled to a stop at the curb at 4:34 a.m. The morning smelled alive and fresh as the scent of late spring flowers and recently mown grass came to me. I deeply inhaled the aromas knowing that I was about to enter a place imbued with a much different scent—the smell of death.

Two blue and white patrol cars from the Nine-Four Precinct were parked at the curb as well as an unmarked sedan. A uniformed police officer with a clipboard in his hand stood by the varnished front door on a brick stoop. I identified myself and the officer entered my name on the yellow legal pad that would serve as the official crime scene log which recorded the comings and goings of all who would have business here.

I handed the clipboard back to him and he said, "Well, Detective Boyland, I wish you luck with this one. This is one bizarre situation."

"Thank you, Mitchell. If you let me inside I would like to see what you mean."

"Oh, sure," he said, quickly stepping aside. "I didn't mean to block the doorway."

I walked across the slate floor of the foyer into a plush blue-carpeted living room glancing around as I headed for the kitchen. Seated at the kitchen table were Detective Ted Nowicki from the Nine-Four Squad and a thin dark-haired man wearing a white tee shirt, gray sweatpants and black bedroom slippers. I assumed he was the husband of the deceased. Teddy rose as I approached and said, "Hi Danny, long time no see. This is Mr. Martin Samuels."

"Hello, Mr. Samuels," I said. "I'm sorry to meet you under these circumstances. My name is Detective Daniel Boyland. I'm assigned to the Nassau Homicide Squad and I will be in charge of this investigation."

"I'm pleased to meet you Detective Boyland," he said, smiling weakly and extending his hand.

I grasped his hand softly between both of mine and said, "I am very sorry for your loss and I wish to assure you that I and the entire police department will do all we can to arrest the person who committed this terrible crime."

"Thank you," he said, wiping a tear from his eye with his free hand.

"Mr. Samuels," I said, "I'd like to get a few basic details on the record."

"Please, call me Marty."

"And feel free to call me Danny."

I took out my note pad and recorded Marty's answers to my questions. Without asking, I knew Ted was observing Marty's responses—his tone, his gestures, his mannerisms. Marty was 42 years old and employed as a lawyer at a large firm in Queens. He was the head of the corporate tax department at Keenan, Rosen, and Vario and had been in that position for the past eight years. His wife Laura, age 40, taught fifth grade at an elementary school in Levittown. They had two children, Tammy twelve and Jason nine. I stopped writing and looked up.

"Where are the children now?"

"Sleeping in their bedrooms."

"They slept through this incident?"

"Yes. I checked them before I called the police. They were sound asleep and no harm had been done to them as was done to me and Laura."

"I checked them out," said Ted. "They're fine."

"Marty," I said. "Is there anyone close that can take them for the day? I'm assuming you don't want to send them to school."

"I have a brother, Joe, a couple of miles away in Cedarhurst. His wife Debbie doesn't work. I'm sure she'll come get them and watch them for the day."

"Good. Now, let's get into your story. I want you to tell me exactly what happened and when you're done we'll go into the bedroom."

"It's not a story."

"Pardon me?"

"You said for me to get into my story. It's not a story, it's the truth."

"I didn't mean to imply that a story was a fabrication by any stretch. It's only a police term. Let me re-phrase my question. Just give me the facts as best as you can recall."

I knew that Ted was thinking the same thing I was right now—why was

Martin Samuels getting so damn touchy and defensive? And, most likely, Ted concluded what I couldn't help but conclude—the husband did it!

"Around 9:30 the kids went into their bedrooms to finish up their homework and watch TV. Laura and I sat on the sofa in the living room. We put the TV on and read the newspaper a while then got ready for bed."

"What time was that?"

"About 10:45. We checked the kids and made Tammy turn off her TV. Laura turned off Jason's TV—he was already asleep. We shut their doors and went into our bedroom and put on the TV to catch the eleven o'clock news."

"What time did you turn off the TV last night?"

"Right at 11:30. We were both very tired."

"Now Marty—and this is very important—before you and Laura went to bed did you check all the doors to make sure they were locked?"

"I…I don't remember. We don't usually check them."

"All right," I said. "I'd like to pick up your story—I mean the facts— where you left off. You both fell asleep. Now please continue."

"I felt as if I were awakening from a bad dream, a dream where I was suffocating. I tried to sit up in bed, but became dizzy. I couldn't breathe. Something was on my mouth—I couldn't open it. I was groggy. I smelled a strange chemical odor. It seemed to be in my head. I finally was able to sit up and my head cleared a little. I glanced over at Laura and she looked different, strange. I was having trouble focusing my eyes and then when I did I saw she had a wide piece of tape—silver duct tape—across her mouth. I immediately put my hands to my mouth as I tried to suck in some air, but I couldn't do it. There was tape there, too. I ripped it off and then reached over and ripped the tape from Laura's mouth. I tried to wake her up, but I couldn't do it. My God, she was dead! I tried mouth to mouth resuscitation, but it didn't work. I guess I sat there and cried a while."

"Do you know what time it was when you first woke up?"

"No. I don't remember seeing the clock."

"Did you call 9-1-1 right then?"

"Not until after I calmed down. I thought of the kids and ran out of the room and opened their doors, but they were fine and both sound asleep."

"Did you smell any more of the chemical?"

"Not after I came completely around. I only smelled it for a short time. It was like some sort of cleaning solvent."

"Can you narrow that down? Maybe paint thinner or turpentine?"

"Maybe, but more sweet, like benzene."

"Since you woke up have you urinated?"

"No. Why do you ask?"

"When the deputy medical examiner arrives I want you to give him a urine and blood sample. I want to know exactly what that chemical was. It could be cleaning fluid, or nail polish remover, or something that smells like that. The exact identification should provide a good clue."

"I'll do that, but they'll find that out from the autopsy results, won't they?"

"I hope so, but suppose there was a different substance used on Laura? Please continue."

"After checking on the kids I went back to our bedroom and turned the lights on. That's when I discovered the burglary. Some drawers in the dresser were open and the contents were strewn on the floor. Closet doors were open. My wallet was open on the floor and my credit cards were thrown about. When I realized what occurred I decided to let everything alone, just as the crime scene shows on TV tell you to do, and I called 9-1-1."

"Marty, how long was it from the time that you woke up until you made that call?"

"H-m-m, no more than six or seven minutes I'd guess."

Ted said, "The call came in to 9-1-1 at 2:51."

"So you probably woke up at 2:44 or 2:45," I said.

"I guess so."

"From the time you turned off the TV at 11:30 until the time you awakened at 2:45 do you remember anything at all? Was your sleep disturbed in any way? Did you hear any doors opening or closing—anything?"

"Not a thing. Nothing at all."

The Chief Deputy Medical Examiner, William Maguire, arrived and I said, "Marty, it's good that the doctor is here so bright and early because he is the first one I want to check out the crime scene. He's only going to take a few moments to examine Laura. When he's done he'll take those samples from you and by then the Photo Unit and the Crime Scene Search Unit should be here."

I walked with Maguire to the bedroom. This was to be my first glimpse of the crime scene and I'm glad I was able to do it without Marty being present. We entered and put on latex gloves and I closed the door behind us. Laura lay on her back. Her eyes were half open and there appeared to be dried saliva on her lips. Her face was contorted with pain—a violent death will do that. I said a brief silent prayer for her and continued my examination of the scene. I did not see any visible blood stains on her or the bedding. The carpeted floor was strewn with items that matched what Marty had told me, but I paid them little attention as we got closer to the body.

"Smell anything?" asked Maguire.

"No."

"Come closer," he said as he turned down the bed covers.

I smelled it then, very faintly, a sweet, vaguely familiar chemical odor.

"I'm pretty sure it's toluene," said Maguire, pointing to the damp stain between Laura's legs. "She voided her bladder when she died. Make sure the Crime Scene guys package that bed sheet up for analysis so we can confirm it."

"Sure thing, Doc. But toluene? Isn't that the ingredient in the glue that the glue-sniffers used to get high on when that was all the rage?"

"Right you are, but we don't see too much of that anymore."

"Was the toluene by itself enough to kill her?"

"Possibly, but look at her neck. I see some bruising. She could have been strangled, but I'll know better when I do the post."

He rolled Laura on her side and inserted an electronic thermometer in her rectum and placed a room thermometer on her night table. When both readings stabilized after a few moments, Maguire recorded the temperatures in his notebook and checked his watch, noting the time.

"Ambient room temperature is 21.3 degrees centigrade and the rectal temperature is 32.5 degrees centigrade." He punched those numbers into a small calculator and said, "Time of death is approximately 1:00 a.m., plus or minus fifteen minutes, and time of pronouncement is 5:24 a.m. What do you think, Danny?"

"I'll tell you when I see you later. I'm not sure what went on here."

"Baloney. This is the phoniest looking burglary I've ever seen."

I grinned and said, "What are you, a detective? Go get some breakfast and I'll ship the body over as soon as I process the scene. Oh, and Doc, please take those blood and urine samples from Mr. Samuels before you leave."

"Is he the guy, Danny? Did the husband do it?"

"As soon as I solve the murder of Laura Samuels you will be the first to know. Now leave me alone!"

When Maguire left the room I closed the door and resumed my observations, gazing carefully around the room. The doc was right on about the burglary—it was definitely a put-up job. No burglar leaves credit cards—at least none that I've ever encountered. And, most significantly, Laura's huge diamond engagement ring and wedding band were still on her finger. It was all wrong.

I stared at Laura. Maguire had closed her eyelids and I was about to draw the sheet over her face, but decided to bring it just up to her neck. I wanted to see Marty's face when he saw hers. Her face was not a pretty one. Perhaps it was the cruel death she had suffered, but she looked much older than her 40 years and not attractive at all. However, she was a wife, a mother of two, and as I would later discover, a well-loved teacher. But someone wanted her out of the way and I'd bet a month's salary that it was no common burglar. How about it Marty? Why did you do it?

I went back into the kitchen and sat down with Ted. Maguire was just finishing up in the bathroom with Marty. "What do you think so far?" asked Ted quietly.

"I think this is no burglary. It was even obvious to Doc Maguire."

"My thoughts exactly when I saw the scene in the bedroom."

"I could use your help for a few days. I'm going to call Sergeant Finn right now and have him call your boss for authorization, plus I'm going to need a couple more guys from your squad and my squad down here right away. The sun's coming up and I want to get a thorough neighborhood canvass well underway before people start leaving for work."

I called Finn and filled him in. He said he'd make the calls right away and offered to come down to the scene himself. I told him that would be a good idea. I knew his experience and savvy would be an asset.

Doc Maguire waved good-bye and Marty rejoined us at the kitchen table. I asked if he was ready to go with us to the bedroom and he replied that he was. As we entered the room he did not look directly at his wife's body, but pointed to the floor and said, "See? A burglary!"

"Looks that way," I said. I handed him a pair of latex gloves and explained that I didn't want him, or anyone else, to add unnecessary prints to the scene.

"Marty, would you like me to draw the sheet over Laura's face?"

"Yes. That would be fine."

"Before I do, I'm going to remove her rings and give them to you, okay?"

"Sure."

I drew the sheet halfway down her body, exposing her bare arms and gently removed the two rings from her left hand. They came off surprisingly easy and would have been no problem for a burglar whose victim was sedated or dead.

"Does Laura wear other jewelry such as toe rings or an ankle bracelet?"

"No, just those rings and her watch, but she doesn't wear the watch to bed."

"Where does she keep it?"

"Usually on her nightstand, next to her side of the bed."

We looked over and there it was, not quite in plain view, but half hidden under a small handkerchief. The watch had a stunning platinum and diamond band, probably worth well over $10,000. The engagement ring looked to be at least two and a half, maybe three carats in a platinum setting, and the wedding band had at least a carat of diamonds in a platinum setting. Not a very observant burglar for sure. I handed the rings and watch to Marty and he put them in the pocket of his pants. I drew the sheet up and covered Laura completely.

"Here's what I want you to do," I said. "See if you can determine exactly what is missing without disturbing anything, then after photos are taken we'll do a more careful search."

Marty looked around and said, "I had about $150 cash in my wallet and it looks as if it's gone."

"Any other cash in the house?"

"We keep about $1,000 in a dresser drawer for when we go to Foxwood's Casino or Atlantic City."

"Which drawer?"

"That middle one which is out all the way."

"Can you carefully feel around to see if it's still there?"

Marty gently parted his neatly folded socks and handkerchiefs and said, "It's gone, there were hundreds and fifties in a gold money clip."

"Any engraving on the money clip?"

"My initials, M.I.S. It was a gift from Laura several years ago."

"We'll get that information out to the pawn shops. Anything else?"

He scanned the room and said, "No, everything else appears to be in its place."

Just then Officer Mitchell appeared at the bedroom to announce that the Photo Unit and Crime Scene Search Team were here.

"Tell them I'll be with them shortly," I said.

We continued our inspection of the bedroom and I was giving the bed and the area surrounding it a final glance when I spotted something on the floor, on Marty's side of the bed, lying in the space between the bed and his nightstand. I peered at it, bending down to do so. It was a brown woolen ski mask.

"Marty, please come over here and look at this."

He stared at the mask and shook his head saying, "I don't recognize this at all. It's not mine."

"How about Laura or the kids?"

"Well, Jason has one I think, but I'm sure it's a bright red color. I guess the burglar wore that and somehow left it here."

"Maybe it was soaked with the toluene," I said. "That's what Doc Maguire thinks the chemical was." I got down on my knees and sniffed it, but I couldn't detect any odors.

"Any smell?" asked Marty.

"No, but we'll get it tested at the Lab for traces of chemicals and for any hairs that may be adhering to it. Now let's leave the technicians to do their jobs and we'll resume later."

Ted and Marty went back to the kitchen and I suggested he notify his brother about taking care of the kids before they woke up. Officer Mitchell came up to me to announce the arrival of Jake Ellison, the assistant district attorney on call from the Homicide Bureau. I filled Jake in as we watched the photographers and crime scene techs go about their work.

"I'm sorry I'm late," he said, "but I'm glad I got here before things were all wrapped up."

"You haven't missed anything. Were you shacked up with some hot babe and couldn't bear to leave her?" I asked the confirmed bachelor.

"Don't I wish. I was visiting a buddy out in the Hampton's and decided to stay over. It's a long drive from there to here."

"How are things back at the office? Get a replacement for Levy yet?"

Jeff Levy had left the DA's Homicide Bureau about the same time my old mentor, Detective Willy Edwards, retired. The same budget constraints that kept us from assigning a replacement for Willy were keeping Barry Walsh, the homicide bureau chief, from getting a replacement for Jeff.

"No, the opening is still there. Is there anything you want me to do for you? Need any paper? Subpoenas or search warrants?"

"No, not yet," I said.

"When do you think we can sit down on this?"

"I should have a good handle on the physical evidence, medical examiner's results and some interview results by the middle of next week. I'll put it all together and give you a call."

"Danny?"

"Yeah?"

"This is not a burglary, is it?"

"No way, counselor,"

"All right. See you next week."

Things were heating up as more people arrived. Two detectives from the Nine-Four and Tim O'Gara and Rube Wilson from Homicide came in and Ted and I briefed them on what went down. O'Gara told me that Finn was on the way and would be here in a few minutes. "Listen up guys, here's what I want you to do," I said. "Knock on as many doors as possible before people leave for work. The critical time is from about 12:30 a.m. to 3:00 a.m. We're looking for people, cars, noises, lights. Anything and everything. You all know the drill. Hopefully, you'll find an insomniac or two who'll crack this case wide open."

"Dream on," said Rube.

Finn arrived five minutes after the two teams of detectives hit the streets and I informed him what had transpired so far.

"It looks as if things are under control," he said. "What's your course of action now?"

"After I wrap up here, I'm going to attend the autopsy then head for the Lab to see if they can tell me anything about the tape and the ski mask."

"All right. We'll have a squad meeting when you get back and we can have a brainstorming session. Show me the bedroom now."

Sergeant Finn looked around as I pointed out various items as we quietly observed the technicians at work. The technician who had just finished bagging the strips of duct tape walked over and said, "Look at this one piece of tape, guys. It has a tan piece of something stuck under one corner, about a half inch square."

We scrutinized it and Finn said, "Any idea what it is?"

The technician replied that it looked like thin plastic, so I said, "Make sure the Lab gets on this right away. Tell them I'll be over this afternoon to talk with them."

"Will do," he said.

Marty finally called his brother and I heard him say, "Joe, it's Marty. Something terrible happened last night. We had a burglary and Laura...my poor Laura, is dead."

After a long pause Marty said, "Joe, I don't know, but please listen. I need your help and Debbie's help with the kids. No, they don't know yet. I'm going to wake them now. Please, come over right away."

He looked at me and said, "They'll be over shortly. I guess I'd better wake Tammy and Jason. Can you help me with this? I don't know how to say it to them."

"Sure," I said.

He was shaking a bit and on the verge of tears, but was it genuine grief setting in, or a realization that what he had done had resulted in his children being left without a loving mother?

It was just about 7:00 a.m. and the kids were due to wake up anyway when we went into Tammy's room. I had made many notifications of death over the years, but when I saw this child calmly sleeping, the images of Patrick and Kelly flashed through my mind. In two minutes this sweet girl's life was going to be flipped upside down forever as was her brother's in the next room. Marty shook her awake and said, "Tammy...honey...wake up...it's Daddy."

She opened her eyes and sat up and then spotted me. Marty said, "This is Detective Boyland. I'm afraid he has some bad news."

"What, Daddy? What's going on?"

The tears were running down Marty's cheeks and I choked back some of my own as I said, "Tammy, there was a burglary here last night. Someone broke into the house and I'm afraid that your mom got hurt very badly...so badly that she died...I'm very sorry, sweetheart."

She began to cry and Marty hugged her. After a few moments Marty said, "Come on, Tam, we have to tell Jason."

We all went to Jason's room and the heart breaking scene with Tammy was repeated. "Aunt Debbie's coming over to take you to her house for most of the day," said Marty.

"Why do we have to leave? I want to see Mommy," said Tammy.

Marty looked at me for help and I said, "Tammy, Jason, there'll be police all over the house today searching for evidence, so it's best if you leave for the day. And yes, you can see your mommy, if it's all right with your dad."

Marty nodded yes and the kids grabbed their clothes and headed for the bathroom. When they were out of earshot, Marty said, "Thanks for your help, Danny. I really appreciate it."

Whether Martin Samuels was a murderer, or set up the murder of his wife, I felt for him as one father and husband feels for another in the face of tragedy.

"I have two kids of my own," I said, "a boy and girl a couple of years younger than Tammy and Jason. The thought of losing my wife and their mother is too horrible to consider. I truly share your grief and I promise you I will find out who did this."

"Thank you," he said. "I know you will."

Marty and I brought Tammy and Jason into the bedroom and the technicians stopped their activities and stood in respectful silence as the children took turns kissing their mother good-bye. I was watching Marty out of the corner of my eye, but didn't detect any reaction to this farewell scene. Marty took the crying children out of the room and I spent a few minutes with the technicians. They had discovered a few latent prints and were in the process of lifting them. A team had gone outside to search the yard for footprints or other evidence that could be meaningful.

Joe and Debbie arrived a few minutes later and took the kids with them, thankfully, just before the first news truck rolled up. The four detectives that were out knocking on doors had returned and told me they had come up with nothing.

I returned to the bedroom, closed the door, and took one last careful look around for real or false clues, but none were apparently left. Why? What's the motive? Is there a motive or just a reason? If not Marty, then whodunit?

Chapter 2

By noon the scene was cleared and it was now time to talk with Marty and put a little pressure on him. I began, "I'm not going to be long. I have a lot to do today and so do you, unfortunately. Have you called a funeral home yet?"

"Yes, Glickman's on Woodmere Boulevard."

"I will probably be there tonight at the services."

"Why?"

"Just to sit and observe. I'm not sold on this being a burglary."

"What do you mean?"

"It doesn't fit. Burglars don't kill their victims."

"But maybe he didn't mean to kill Laura."

"True. I am not completely discarding the burglary theory, but you must admit the whole thing with the duct tape and toluene is very bizarre. Let's go with another theory."

"Such as?"

"Such as intentional murder. Perhaps the person or persons who killed Laura meant to do just that and used the burglary as a cover-up."

"Kill Laura, but why? She had no enemies."

"Or they meant to kill you, not Laura or…they meant to kill you both, but you survived."

"You have me confused," he said. "And scared."

"I know, but I have to investigate all angles and I need your help. I'm going to ask some tough questions. Please bear with me and don't get upset. Can you do that for me?"

"Okay, but…"

"No buts—just listen and think carefully before you respond. Who would benefit from Laura's death?"

"No one," he answered a bit too fast.

"How about financially? Do you have any large insurance policies?"

I could see that I hit a nerve and he answered, "Well yes, we each have a substantial life insurance policy with each other as the beneficiary."

"What's substantial?"

"One million dollars."

I showed no reaction and proceeded to my next question.

"How about jealousy? Any extra-marital affairs past or present?"

"No! Of course not! Laura was a devoted wife and mother."

"How about you?"

"You mean affairs? Now, wait a minute…"

"Marty," I interrupted, "I told you these would be tough questions, but I must ask them. Please…"

"No. No affairs, past or present."

"Let's get back to finances. Do you or Laura owe any money?"

"Sure, the mortgage and one car payment."

"How about out of the ordinary? Like gambling debts, substance abuse debts, business debts…"

"You know, this is getting annoying. These implications are…"

"Marty listen to me, you are my ally, my only source of information right now to help me solve your wife's murder. Put aside your petty annoyances and please help me—now."

"I'm…I'm sorry. I understand. No, no debts. The extent of our gambling is a few trips a year to the casinos. We don't play the horses. We don't bet on sports. We don't use drugs of any kind and we drink alcohol sparingly. I cannot, for the life of me, think of any reason whatsoever why anyone would want to kill Laura or me—or the both of us."

"Thanks, Marty," I said, grabbing his hand. "I know this is difficult and that's all I'm going to ask for now. I'll get out of here and let you take care of the arrangements, but let me say this once more—I am truly sorry for your loss."

"Thanks. Where do you go from here?"

"Everywhere. I'm going to Laura's school, her jewelry store, her beautician, her manicurist and I'm going to visit your law firm, your barber, your friends and your acquaintances. I have a case of murder and attempted murder and I'm going to find out who wanted Laura and/or you dead."

"Or catch the burglar."

"Yes. Or catch the burglar."

When I got to the morgue it was well past one o'clock and I noticed a shiny black hearse idling in the parking lot with the nameplate Glickman's discreetly set in the side window. The county morgue was one of my least favorite places to visit, but a necessary part of the job. I could handle the sights of the ripped open bodies on the steel tables, but the odors sometimes got to me. The smell of death, whatever it was composed of, seemed to ooze out of the outer doors as I approached the old, gray brick building. I took a deep breath of the fragrant June air knowing it would be the last for a long time and I pulled open the doors and went inside.

Doc Maguire was just finishing up with Laura. He snapped off his gloves, undid his mask, and called an assistant over to sew her up.

"So my good Doctor," I said as we stepped out into the hall, "what is your esteemed professional opinion?"

"She's dead all right, Danny."

"Very funny—and?"

"Not strangled, but there were hands around her neck. I smelled more toluene when I opened her up. Blood and body fluids are already being analyzed in Toxicology."

"Marty's, too?"

"Yes."

"Conclusions thus far?"

"Well, pending the tox report, which I'm sure will come back with lethal concentrations of toluene, I'm pretty sure I'll call this a homicide by asphyxiation due to toluene poisoning."

"Can you tell if this was a one or two man job?"

"I think two. There was definitely a pair of hands around her throat. Perhaps someone else held a toluene soaked rag over her mouth and nose at the same time."

"How about if the toluene soaked rag was in a plastic bag that was over her head and held in place with the tape? Then one person could have done it?"

"Possibly."

"Okay, Doc. I'm going up to the Lab and check on whatever Crime Scene delivered and especially that tape. Please call me at the office as soon as those reports come down."

"I sure will. Looks as if you got a real mystery here—and that was no burglary, was it?"

"It sure wasn't. Even a rookie detective like you figured that out."

"What then?"

"Who knows? Right now your guess is as good as mine. Now let me get out of here"

Maguire chuckled and said, "You really don't like it here do you?"

"Oh, I just love it, especially when I visualize myself on one of those tables someday," I said.

"Don't worry, Danny. I'll be gentle with my incisions. You'll hardly feel a thing."

I made the rounds at the Lab, stopping first at Latent Fingerprints. Detective John Dennison, one of the senior examiners, told me that Crime Scene had delivered 13 latents they had lifted from the bedroom, the tape and the side entrance door.

"I have good news and bad news," he said. "The good news is that I've already identified all 13 latents. The bad news is that eight belong to Mr. Samuels and five to the deceased."

"Damn!" I said.

I went over to the Trace Evidence Section and Detective Frank Mattio called out that he'd be right with me. I took the opportunity to grab a cup of coffee and dialed Jean at work.

"Danny!" she exclaimed. "It's all over the TV! What's happening now?"

"I'm at the Lab and it's still a mystery. I'll give you all the gory details later."

"When did you get called out? I didn't even hear the phone ring. When the alarm clock went off this morning you were already gone."

"Typical," I said. "Sleep on as usual while my butt gets dragged out of bed at 3:30 a.m. to go out and earn a living."

"Will you be home for dinner?"

"Yes, but then I need to head out again for a couple of hours. I want to go to the wake."

"Okay, honey," she said. "I'll see you soon. This is it, isn't it? Your Big One?"

"I believe it is. Bye."

Mattio called me in to a small lab room where he had the tape placed on a plastic sheet on the table. "It appears to be ordinary two inch silver duct tape as you would find around a workshop at home," he said. "I ran out at lunch time and was able to find four different brands at local stores."

He pointed to the four rolls on his desk and continued, "I'm going to contact all four manufacturers and see if they have any way they use to determine if an unknown piece of tape can be specifically identified as their brand. That's going to take at least a week, maybe more. What I can tell you for sure right now is that the pieces of tape were once joined together and were partially cut and partially ripped. The piece from the mouth of the deceased is eight and a half inches long and a small piece of tan plastic is adhering to one corner. The piece that Mr. Samuels says was on his mouth is seven and three quarter inches long."

"What can you tell me about that bit of plastic?"

"It's two millimeters thick and could come from a plastic garbage bag or sheet of plastic wrapping."

"Frank, if I could locate the roll of tape that these pieces came from could you match the ends up?"

"Sure, assuming that that specific end is still there—you know, no more tape removed since these pieces came off. Also, if the manufacturers come through, I might be able to chemically or microscopically make a match."

"How about the plastic?"

"Find me the bag or sheet that it came from and I think I'll be able to jigsaw match it up for you."

"Great, now if you'll just tell me where to look for those two items…"

"That's your job Danny Boy," he laughed. "Not mine."

I checked in with the Chemistry Section and they were still analyzing the vapors from the bed sheet and the ski mask on a complicated-looking machine they called a gas chromatograph. Detective Vince Jordan told me that the Biology Section had pulled a couple of human hairs from the inside of the mask and were analyzing them now.

"Preliminary analysis shows no vapors from the mask, but definitely toluene from the bed sheet," he said.

"Tell me all about toluene, Vince."

"I don't want to bore you with chemical formulas and such. Basically, its primary use is as a solvent and it's very common in most labs."

"Do you use it here?"

"Occasionally. It's the solvent of choice for extracting certain substances out from complex mixtures."

"Where do you get it?"

"From a chemical supply house."

"Could I buy some?"

"Sure, in your local drugstore."

"Do I have to sign for it or show identification?"

"You have to show ID and the pharmacist is supposed to record your name, address and date of purchase in a log book."

"Supposed to?"

"I'm sure most do, but it's no big deal. I mean the DEA rarely checks log books for the sale of small quantities of common chemicals."

"How long does it take to put someone under if you put a rag dosed with it under their nose? And how long to kill them?"

"Better ask Doc Maguire or Doc Pomerantz that one."

"Damn, I was just with Maguire. I must be getting tired."

"How long have you been at it?"

"Since before 4:00 a.m."

"Listen, I'll go talk with them and have Maguire call you at the office."

"Thanks, Vince, you're a real pal," I said. "Let me go see about those hairs."

Detective Mary Riggins in the Biology Section showed me the two long dark brown hairs she had removed from the mask and placed in a plastic bag.

"Definitely human, probably female," she said.

"Probably?"

"A guess from their length. Hair analysis is not an exact science, but the DNA contained therein is much better for exact comparison, as you already know."

"Mary," I said, taking out a pen, "please give me the name and address of the female whose hair this is and I'll get you a DNA sample from her."

"That's your job Danny Boy, not mine."

"Seems as if I heard that one before. You Lab types are a pain in the neck."

"Good hunting," she said. "I'll keep these hairs safeguarded just in case you get lucky and find a suspect."

•

I arrived back at the office at 3:45 and went right to the coffee room.

"Fresh pot's coming down," said Tara Brown, "and you look as if you need it, Danny Boy."

"I sure do, it's been a long day."

"I can't wait to hear about this one," she said. "Tape, toluene, a real mystery."

"You'll hear all about it in a few minutes and I expect some good advice and direction from you and everybody else. Now I gotta go see the boss."

I went into Ray's office and brought him up to date on my findings at the morgue and the Lab. He said that Ted Nowicki had briefed him on Marty's interview. The intercom buzzed and Ray picked up. "It's for you," he said. "Doc Maguire."

"Hi, Doc," I said. "What do you have for me?"

"The level of toluene in Laura's system was a lethal dose and ten times the level in Marty's system."

"Thanks. Did Vince Jordan get down to see you?"

"Yes. Both Pomerantz and I agree, that coupled with the choking, Laura would have been dead in no more than three minutes."

"And Marty?"

"The dose he inhaled based on the concentrations we found in his blood and urine would have kept him out one to two hours at most."

"That correlates pretty well with your estimated time of death, right?"

"Of course," he said. "Did you expect otherwise?"

"From the greatest, albeit twisted, pathologist in the country? Of course not. Thanks again."

"Bye, Danny. See you on the table."

I related Maguire's information to Ray and he asked, "Who do you want to help you on this?"

"I'd like to keep Ted Nowicki from the Nine-Four and pair him up with one of our guys to handle all the interviews in the neighborhood. And I'd like one of our guys to pair up with me to do the interviews at Laura's school and Marty's law firm."

He picked up the duty chart and said, "Let's see who's available—how about Manny Perez to go with Nowicki and Tara Brown with you?"

"Perfect, I couldn't have picked them better myself."

"Then let's go fill in the troops."

When we were assembled in the main squad room Ray announced, "This meeting will cover only one topic—Danny's murder case this morning of Laura Samuels in Woodmere. You're on, Danny."

I filled the squad in on the entire case from the moment the phone rang at 3:38 a.m. right up to the call from Doc Maguire. Several of them took notes. There were no interruptions and no wise remarks, just concentrated attentiveness. When the subject was a bizarre whodunit, they were all business.

When I finished, Ray asked me to give my opinion and conclusions thus far. I said, "This was no burglary. Marty is involved in this as the killer himself, the killer with an accomplice, or he used one or two contract killers. The motive could be money—the one million in life insurance plus Laura's pension benefits and insurance at school."

There were no disagreements and Nancy Andrews then said, "I don't feel that the money is the only motive. They were pretty well off. I think you should find the girlfriend."

"Marty denies having an affair very strongly," I said.

"Then, in my humble opinion, it's certain," said Tara. "There's a honey out there somewhere and I'd venture to say she is several years younger and several degrees prettier than Laura Samuels."

"Well, Detective First Grade Brown," said Ray, "you'll have your chance to find her. You're out of the duty chart and partnered with Danny as of now. Manny, you're with Ted Nowicki as the assisting team. The case supervisor is Francis Finn. Let's get started."

The four of us met in Finn's office and we sorted out some of the other suggestions that were volunteered at the meeting such as getting hair samples from Marty and the kids to compare with those found in the ski mask, verifying the amount of insurance money and finding if other policies existed. However, the main, almost unanimous, recommendation remained—find the honey. I remembered my first few months in the squad with Willy Edwards hammering his knowledge into me—"Find the motive. If you can't find a motive, find the reason. And always look for the money or the honey. But, most importantly, remember this—there are no coincidences." I told Tara I'd meet her at Glickman's at 7:00 and that we'd hit Laura's school first thing in the morning.

I pulled into the driveway at 5:40 to the odor of meatloaf wafting from the screen door. I had been gone 14 hours. It was good to be home.

Jeanie greeted me with a big hug and said, "Tell me all about it, but first, do you want a drink?"

"No drink," I said. "I'd fall asleep. When will dinner be ready?"

"In about 20 minutes."

"Then I have time to grab a quick shower and change of clothes. I feel real grubby."

"I don't doubt it, but I can't wait to hear what really happened compared to what the news reports are saying."

"You know, I haven't had time to hear or see anything. What are they saying?"

"Oh, they're hyping it up pretty good—'strange murder in suburbia,' 'police mystified,' 'neighborhood in fear.'"

"Did they give any details about what they meant by strange?"

"Well, they said something about tape being over her mouth and her husband's mouth," said Jean.

"Oh crap, that wasn't supposed to get out. Anything about toluene?"

"No, what's with toluene? What is it?"

"Let me shower now," I said. "Then I'll fill you in."

The meatloaf, as usual, was excellent and between bites I told Jean the whole story. With her interspersed questions I didn't finish until dinner was over and I had to get going. "So," she said, "you definitely think that Marty did it?"

"Yeah, now all I have to do is prove it."

When I pulled into the crowded parking lot at Glickman's Tara was already there. We walked in together toward the viewing room and were impressed by the huge crowd of mourners already assembled. Marty spotted me and gave me a weak smile. I nodded back at him and Tara and I stayed near the back of the room. I saw Tammy and Jason scrubbed and dressed and pointed them out to Tara.

"Those poor kids," she said. "How could that scumbag do that to them?"

"I almost wish a burglar had done it," I said. "But it was him all right, the heartless bastard."

"See any possible girlfriends around?"

"Tara, there are dozens of women here, so how would we know?"

"I'll keep an eye on Marty and try to see if any woman shows excess affection as she pays her respects."

"Fine," I said, "and I'll watch for any likely looking burglars."

We stayed until the end of the allotted time and observed the departing mourners. Finally, only Marty, the kids and Joe and Debbie remained. I introduced Tara to all and we gave our condolences and prepared to leave.

"Anything turn up yet?" asked Marty.

"No," I replied. "No unidentified prints. The ones we lifted belonged to you or Laura. Your urine was positive for toluene, and your level of it indicated you were probably unconscious a couple of hours."

"My God," he said. "I could have been dead, too."

"That's the way we're going to investigate this. As I said before, I still believe the burglary was a pretext."

I slept in and got into the office around 11:00 a.m. Tara and I went to lunch then drove over to the Maple Lane Elementary School in Levittown and introduced ourselves to the principal, Mrs. Ruth Horton. Ruth had known Laura for as long as she had been principal at Maple Lane, over ten years. She was dressed in black and her eyes were rimmed in red.

"Did you just come back from the cemetery?" I asked.

"Yes, this whole thing is so dreadful. Laura was such a wonderful person and a superb teacher."

I explained that we would like to interview her and several teachers for any assistance they could give us.

"I don't have a problem with that, Detective Boyland, but how could I possibly help? I mean it was a burglar, wasn't it?"

"That's what it appears, but we have to cover all angles and rule out an intentional murder."

"That's absurd. Who in the world would want to kill Laura Samuels? And for what possible reason?"

"I don't know, but that's what I have to find out or eliminate. May we ask you a few questions?"

After fifteen minutes we were finished with Mrs. Horton. She had provided no helpful information. Since many of Laura's closest teaching associates had taken off and the school was virtually empty, we agreed with Horton to return on Monday and we called it a day. We headed back into the office to await Ted and Manny's return from the five towns.

We gathered in the coffee room at four o'clock with Sergeant Finn. Ted and Manny had interviewed a few neighbors and local businessmen and re-canvassed the residences in the area. Their results were negative, but they agreed with Principal Horton's assessment of Laura—devoted wife, mother, friend, teacher, no enemies, no vices and no bad habits. We began to despise her 'grieving' husband even more.

Monday at the Maple Lane elementary school was, as we had suspected, a total waste of time. We spoke to ten teachers and the interviews were repeats of the one we had Friday with the principal. Several of the teachers also knew Marty from social gatherings and they were almost as effusive in their praise for him as they were for Laura.

We went back to the office for our afternoon meeting. Ted and Manny told us they had stopped off to see Marty for a few minutes and obtained a list of neighborhood people and associates of both of them. They spoke with Rabbi Horwitz, Laura's beautician and her manicurist. And, before they told me, I knew what they heard—nothing. We were getting nowhere fast.

"What are we doing tomorrow, folks?" asked Finn.

"Tara and I are going to Queens to spend the day at Marty's firm. Maybe we'll get some answers there," I said.

"Ted and I figure to do a night tour and re-canvass again," said Manny. "We'll talk to those people we missed during the day."

"Sounds good. Let's meet again on Wednesday afternoon at five o'clock."

Chapter 3

The law firm of Keenan, Rosen, and Vario was located on Queens Boulevard in the neighborhood of Kew Gardens, about a half mile from the Queens County Courthouse. We found a parking spot two blocks away and were ushered into the senior partner's office at 9:30 a.m. I immediately recognized Mr. Philip Rosen from the funeral services. He was a big man with a florid face, and he welcomed us warmly into his luxurious office.

"Awful, awful thing," he said. "A lovely woman, and poor Marty, how he must feel."

"We agree with you, Mr. Rosen," I said. "It was a terrible family tragedy."

"How can I help you, Detectives? I've seen the news reports—it was a burglary, right? Why in God's name did he have to kill her?"

"An excellent question," said Tara. "That's why we're here."

"I don't understand," he said.

"Mr. Rosen," I said, "we feel that Laura may have been intentionally killed, and perhaps Marty, luckily, escaped the same fate."

Rosen gasped and his face turned even redder.

"Let me explain, but first let me set some ground rules for this interview. We will hold all information you give to us in the strictest confidence and we expect you to do the same. The only people with whom we will share what you tell us will be those in an official capacity such as fellow investigators and prosecutors. Can you agree with those terms?"

"Certainly, but I don't know how I can help you."

"What we are looking for," said Tara, "and I know this may sound distasteful and disrespectful, is the reason that they were attacked. Situations such as gambling debts, drug habits, and love affairs gone awry, maybe blackmail. You get the point."

"Shocking to think about," he said, "and I know you qualified your remarks as possibly being distasteful. In Marty's case they most certainly are. Marty Samuels is the head of our corporate tax department and a fine attorney. He performs his duties admirably. I have never seen him drink more than one beer or one glass of wine at any social function I've been to with him. The only gambling I've seen him engage in is the one dollar bi-weekly check pool. He drives a modest car and seems to live within his means."

"Any inkling of substance abuse?" I asked.

"None. He's always on time and performs his duties energetically."

"Any extra-marital affairs?" asked Tara.

"Uh, no, uh—none that I personally know of."

I zeroed in on that response and said, "What about an affair that you don't personally know about, Mr. Rosen? What about an affair that may be just a rumor you heard?"

"Well, I…you know, I wouldn't want to spread gossip that might be untrue…"

"Mr. Rosen, this is a homicide investigation. Rumors must be verified or dispelled. Now, please continue."

"Well, being the senior partner, I don't hear that much gossip, but I understand that Marty and Miss Wells may have had a little romance going."

"Miss Wells?" asked Tara.

"Nicole Wells is one of our paralegals and the only thing I can say, factually, is that I have seen them holding hands on occasion and they do go out to lunch together."

"How often?" I asked.

"Maybe twice, three times a week."

"Just the two of them? No others?"

"Usually just the two of them."

"Can you tell me how long this relationship has been going on?" asked Tara.

"Several months that I'm aware of, but now that you have me thinking about it, I don't recall seeing them together for the past several weeks."

"The in-house romance may be over?" I asked.

"I don't know," he said.

"Mr. Rosen," I said, "I'm assuming Marty is on bereavement leave?"
"Yes."

"We want to finish our interviews this week before he returns to work, for obvious reasons, and we would like to speak with as many of your attorneys and office personnel as possible. Can you provide us with office space and a telephone?"

"Of course, but I'm afraid you won't discover much more than I've already told you."

"Let us be the judge of that," said Tara.

"You've met Laura Samuels?" I asked.

"Yes, on numerous occasions. Lovely woman."

"Lovely, yes," I said, "but how about attractive?"

"Attractive?"

"Yes. Specifically, how does she compare to Miss Nicole Wells?"

"Nicole is much younger…"

"How old is she?" asked Tara.

"Twenty-eight or twenty-nine, I believe."

"And her looks?" persisted Tara. "Compared to Laura?"

Rosen was clearly embarrassed and fidgeted around in his chair. He said, "You know, physical beauty is not the only thing in a woman, there's inner beauty and…"

Tara stopped him short and said, "Forget Laura's inner beauty, her intelligence and her personality. I want to know, from a man's point of view, when he's looking at a woman in a sexual manner, what's the comparison?"

Rosen looked as if he wanted to crawl under his desk, but he answered quietly, "From that perspective, and only that perspective, Miss Wells is a knockout compared to Laura Samuels."

"Thank you," I said. "Now keeping that comparison in your mind, please answer this question. Would Marty Samuels murder his wife for the love of Nicole Wells?"

Rosen grabbed the edge of his desk to steady himself and started to speak several times before he could get out the words. He looked apoplectic, and I truly believed he was on the verge of a collapse from a stroke or heart attack. Finally he blurted out, "How dare you suggest something like that! How dare you!"

"Relax, Mr. Rosen," said Tara. "Sit down and calm down. We told you some of these questions would be tough to deal with, but we do have to ask them."

"And your response," I said, "told us a lot. It told us that although Marty Samuels may have flirted around a bit he is not, in your opinion, a murderer."

"He most certainly is not," he said, finally calming down.

"Good," I said. "Thank you very much for your cooperation, and please remember our confidentiality agreement."

"Yes, I will respect that," he said, standing again, obviously very relieved to see us leave.

"Can you show us that office space now?" I asked.

"It's right down the hall. Please follow me."

Rosen showed us into a small lavender-carpeted office with a window facing the street. It had a standard wooden desk with a swivel wooden chair and three wooden straight-backed chairs lined up along the wall.

"This will be fine," I said as Rosen started to leave, "but I need something else."

"What now, Detective?" he asked, slightly annoyed.

"We need a roster of all your attorneys, your paralegals, and your administrative staff."

"I have that in my office."

"What specific information does it contain?" asked Tara.

"Name, address, phone number and position here at the firm."

"Could you please jot down their date of birth, date of employment, length of time employed in the firm, and social security number in the margin next to their names?" I asked.

"I could do that, but I'm not sure I should provide the social security number—privacy concerns you know."

He was starting to piss me off, so I raised my voice a bit and said, "Mr. Rosen, this is a homicide investigation. Do you remember that?"

"Yes."

"If you force me to waste my time getting a subpoena and having you personally deliver the information to a Nassau County Court Judge, I will be forever upset with you."

"I'll note the numbers in the margin," he said quietly.

"Thank you," said Tara. "Please, just one more question—where do your employees usually go for lunch?"

"There are a number of places on Queens Boulevard, but the most popular is Vito's Luncheonette on the corner of 76th Road."

"Is that where Marty and Miss Wells go to lunch?" I asked.

"I saw them there occasionally, but there are other places, as I said."

"Mr. Rosen," said Tara, "thank you for everything. Your cooperation has been wonderful and we know the interview had its unpleasant moments, but murder, especially the murder of a beloved wife and mother, is not pleasant either."

"I understand, and I apologize for my outburst. This is very difficult for me. I'll get that roster to you right away."

I closed the door and walked over to the window. Tara sat in a chair and stretched her legs out. She said, "Well, well, Danny, I do believe we have found our honey."

"Yup," I said, "now we have the honey and the money. Let's call Finn."

We briefed Francis and he agreed with our interview scheme. We'd leave Nicole Wells for last and talk to as many attorneys and staff as we could to confirm the affair between her and Marty and to obtain whatever other information we could learn. Then we'd go at Wells on Friday. I didn't know about Tara, but I couldn't wait to meet Marty's squeeze. I remembered his answer to one of my questions: 'No, no affairs, past or present.'

Tara looked at her watch and said, "It's noon, and I'm hungry. Let's get some lunch."

"Any idea where we should go?"

"I heard about this place on Queens Boulevard—Vito's. Wanna try it?"

"Is that the place conducive to cheaters and illicit love affairs?"

"So I've heard," she said.

"Then by all means, let us go!"

We ordered pastrami sandwiches and a side of potato latkes with diet colas and our discussion turned to cheating spouses. "I was married twice," said Tara, "and both of my ex-husbands cheated on me—more than one time."

"I don't understand how anyone could cheat on a beautiful Halle Berry clone such as you."

"Halle Berry? Now I'm really liking you. But even if that were true, it doesn't matter to you guys—you all cheat."

"Uh-uh, not me—it's work, church and home—a straight arrow all the way."

"What crap," she laughed. "Maybe you don't cheat yet, but you will. All men will, given the right circumstances."

"Such as?"

"Just as we look at criminals—motive, opportunity and means. And don't tell me you haven't been tempted. You must have been hit on pretty heavy in your years on the job, especially when you were in uniform."

"Why do you say that?"

"Come on Danny, look in the mirror! Those classic good looking Irish features you have—thick black hair, gorgeous brown eyes, a square chin with that little cleft in it…oh, yeah, you were hit on all right."

"Are you hitting on me, Miss Berry?" I laughed.

"No way. I have enough troubles with single, brown men. I don't need to complicate my life by getting involved with white, married ones."

"See, I told you I don't cheat. I'm a happily married man with a beautiful wife and two magnificent children."

When we returned from Vito's, where the lunch had been very good at a reasonable price, Mr. Rosen handed us the promised roster and a set of keys to the office. He said, "I've informed my administrative assistant, Ms. Scott, of your interview plans. If you coordinate with her, she will choose those attorneys and staff that are between interviews and court times. I'd like to minimize the loss of billable… er, down time."

"We understand," I said.

"Then I'll let you two get on with your interviews. If there is anything you need—coffee, food, anything—let me, or Ms. Scott, know immediately."

We sat down at the desk, happy at the helpful attitude displayed by Mr. Rosen, and looked over the roster. There were 47 lawyers, 12 paralegals, and an administrative staff of 11.

"Where do you think we should start," I asked?"

"The lawyers and paralegals in Marty's department, then the paralegals in the other departments, and then the office staff."

"Sounds fine to me," I said, "but I can't see us getting through 70 people in three and a half days."

"I don't think we'll have to speak with everyone depending on the quality of the information we get from his closest associates," she said.

And what we got that afternoon and Wednesday was certainly what we were looking for—definite corroboration of a lengthy love affair between Marty and Nicole. The consensus was that it had begun in October and that Marty had been the initiator. Nicole had transferred to Marty's department from the matrimonial division in early September and his pursuit began. There was also general agreement that the relationship had cooled off sometime in mid to late April. None of those interviewed recalled seeing Nicole at the funeral services or the cemetery. At the conclusion of each interview, after reinforcing the mutual promise of confidentiality, we hit them with the big question—"Would Marty and Nicole murder Laura Samuels so they could live together happily ever after?"

The answers ranged from incredulous "No's!" to calmly spoken "Maybe's." When we added the money into the mix and asked our follow-up question—"What if living happily ever after in love was sweetened by a substantial life insurance settlement, say a million dollars?" Then most of the responses changed to, "Yeah, that could do it."

We pressed them for their reasons for the change of opinion once the money factor was added, and again the responses provided some very interesting information. Marty, it seemed, did like to gamble. He was known to study the sports pages of the Daily News religiously and place his bets with the local bookie on Queens Boulevard. Ah, Marty, lie number two! We wondered how deep in he was for we knew the deeper in debt, the stronger the motive.

Nicole was not a gambler, but she liked the good life. She often complained about her paralegal's salary and her modest lifestyle in Queens. One fellow paralegal, who felt she was Nicole's closest associate at the firm, told us that she would often point toward the Queensboro Bridge and say, "That's where I want to be, where I should be—on the other side of the bridge in Manhattan—in a beautiful apartment, eating in fancy restaurants, taking taxis and going to Broadway shows."

We wrapped up at 4:00 p.m. and fought the rush hour traffic back to Mineola where we briefed Finn and the other team. Tara checked her messages and she had a subpoena for court the next day to testify at an evidence suppression hearing. That jogged my memory and I asked her to make sure to spend some time with Jake Ellison in order bring him up to speed on what we had uncovered so far. Manny and Ted were still pursuing the Samuels's acquaintances and friends in the neighborhood, but still with no results. Finn said to them, "Contact the Vice Squad tomorrow and find out who the bookies are in the five towns; then squeeze them a bit to see if Marty bets out here as well as in Queens."

"I'll do a few more interviews alone tomorrow," I said, "and I think we should move up our timetable on the Wells interview."

"Why?" asked Finn.

"When Marty gets back to work on Monday, the cat will be out of the bag. He'll certainly go right to Nicole to find out what's been going on and then he'll start pressing the other lawyers for information."

"What makes you think they're not talking right now?" asked Finn.

"I would think they would feel it would be too dangerous. They might figure that their phones are tapped."

"Maybe we should consider doing that," said Manny.

"We don't have enough yet," said Finn. "Then there's the problem of cell phones which we can't tap. Tara, tomorrow when you brief Ellison on the case, ask him for a subpoena for Marty's and Nicole's phone records for all their home and cell numbers back to September. We better check anyway."

"I'll take care of it," she said

"So, after you and Tara talk to Wells on Friday morning, I assume you want to go at Marty in the afternoon?" asked Finn.

"Yes," I said, "before he suspects too much and lawyers up."

"Is he still sitting shiva?" asked Ted.

I mentally counted seven days and said, "Thursday night should be the last night, so Friday will be the day. I'll get him in here after lunch. Tara, tell Jake I'd like him here to observe the interview."

"And take down his confession?" she smiled.

"Wouldn't that be nice," I said, "but I'm not holding my breath."

I started early Thursday morning and by 12:30 I had completed interviewing the few remaining staff in Marty's department. The information was similar to what Tara and I had already obtained and served as further corroboration. I stopped by Ms. Scott's desk, and after reviewing the roster with her, decided to have her set up interviews with the attorneys and staff in Nicole's former department for the afternoon.

It was one o'clock and I was hungry. The June sun was out in full force and there was not a cloud in the clear, blue sky. I decided to go to Vito's, and I ambled down Queens Boulevard deeply breathing in the warm, dry air and dreading the humidity of July and August which would arrive all too soon. I loosened my tie a bit, undid the collar button of my shirt, and took off my suit jacket and slung it over my right shoulder. What a day for golf, or a ball game or fishing instead of sitting in a stuffy office conducting interviews. But they would be over soon, and maybe this whole case would crack open just as fast.

As I was about a half a block from the restaurant, a woman came out of the door and began walking toward me. As she got closer, I decided that walk was not the correct term for how she was approaching me. Sashay would be more appropriate. She moved sensuously, swaying her hips. She had shoulder length dark brown hair, deep blue eyes and was modestly dressed in a knee-length blue skirt, white long-sleeved blouse and black low-heeled shoes. She stopped, smiled, extended her hand and said, "You must be Detective Boyland."

I returned the smile and briefly shook her hand. I said, "What makes you think that, Miss...?"

"Wells. Nicole Wells. The gun on your hip is a clue, assuming you're not a mugger or a gangster."

"Do I look like a mugger? Or a gangster?"

"No, you look like a cop."

"And just what is a cop supposed to look like?"

"Why a dashing hero, of course—like James Bond."

"I remind you of James Bond?"

"Oh, yes. A young Sean Connery, for sure," she said.

"I'm very flattered, Miss Wells."

"Well, Detective tall, dark and handsome, how come you haven't interviewed me yet?"

"Uh, we'll get to you soon, Miss Wells. There are a lot of attorneys and staff at the firm and scheduling is a bit difficult. Are you concerned?"

"No, should I be?"

"Well, this is a homicide investigation..."

"And you've been hearing some tales about me and Marty Samuels, I presume?"

"Miss Wells, we'll talk about all that at the interview. I'll try to get to you tomorrow."

She smiled and looked directly in my eyes with her sparkling blue ones and said, "I'm looking forward to clearing up any questions you may have. I have to go now, my lawyers are calling."

She started to leave then stopped. "Call me Niki—and you are?"

"Danny."

"Danny," she said. "I like that."

She strolled down the boulevard and I continued toward Vito's. I stopped and turned and watched those swaying hips from a different view. She suddenly wheeled around and caught me staring. She gave me a big smile and a slight wave with her fingertips. I turned and walked away, not looking back a second time. Shit! I hated getting caught staring at a woman. It let's them know you're interested and they will use that to their advantage. But I was not interested in Niki, except in a professional sense. Then why did I turn around? There was something about her, some attraction I could feel, and I wondered if that was what Marty felt when he first set eyes upon her. Was that attraction sufficient for him to murder his wife and leave his children motherless?

I completed the rest of my interviews by 3:30 and obtained no new information. Only one of the attorneys knew Nicole well enough to realize she had something going on with Marty, and the paralegal had seen them leave for lunch together only once or twice. I stopped in to see Mr. Rosen to let him know that we would be back for our final interview the following morning and that we did not anticipate returning after that. He seemed relieved and offered to extend whatever further help he could.

"I do need one more thing," I said. "Do you have photo ID's of all your attorneys and staff on file?"

"Yes, I have them in my office."

"I'd like a copy of Miss Wells's and Mr. Samuels's photos when we leave tomorrow."

"I'll have them for you at that time, Detective Boyland."

When I reached my car I called the office and asked for Tara. She had gotten in to brief Jake Ellison and started to tell me about it, but I interrupted her. "Tara, tell me when I get back. I have a lot to fill you in on, too, and we have to plan our interview of Nicole Wells. How about we grab something to eat when I get there? Or I can pick something up on the way in."

"Let's go out," she said. "I'd like a drink or a glass of wine. I had a lousy day on the stand."

"Okay," I said. "With this traffic, I'll be there around 5:30, maybe 6:00."

I hung up and called Jeanie to let her know I wouldn't be home for dinner.

"Still going strong on your whodunit?" she asked.

"Yes, things are getting a bit clearer. Tomorrow may be the make or break day and we have to prepare our strategy."

"What's going to happen tomorrow?"

"The interview of the honey in the morning, and then we go at Marty Samuels in the afternoon."

"And if they both demand lawyers?"

"S-s-h, bite your tongue, woman. They are not officially suspects, so no Miranda warnings yet. Maybe if Tara and I are good enough we'll get our evidence before we have to read them their precious rights."

"Now, now," she chided, "this is America darling, and even murderers have rights."

"And where are Tammy's and Jason's rights to have a live, caring mother? And Laura? Where are Laura's rights? They're buried in the fucking ground with her body, that's where."

"Calm down, Danny, I was only teasing. I agree with you 100 percent. Nail that lousy bastard tomorrow."

"Spoken like a real cop," I said. "You've been hanging around me too long."

"I love hanging around you, and with you, and on you, lover boy. Hurry home."

"I'll be there by nine. Love you."

"Love you, too," she said. "See you then."

Tara had briefed Ellison on the case and also the bosses and our other team. We decided to get something to eat at Mulvaney's, our local squad hangout, where it should be relatively quiet and uncrowded. We got a booth near the rear and ordered drinks, red wine for her and a tap beer for me.

"What was so rough in court today?" I asked.

"Would you believe I was on the stand for over two hours on a lousy suppression hearing? Goddamn lawyer kept asking me the same questions over and over."

"So, I gather you lost the hearing?"

"No, we won."

"Then what the hell are you bitchin' about?"

"Danny, two hours on a minor, insignificant piece of evidence? Can you imagine what I'm going to have to go through at trial?"

"Drink your merlot," I said. "He'll probably cop a plea."

"I sure as hell hope so," she said, taking a long swallow from her glass. "Now fill me in on your day."

"I met Nicole today, by chance."

"You have my full attention."

When I finished relating the details of the encounter she said, "So, she actually admitted that she and Marty were an item."

"Sort of—I believe her words were that she knew we had been 'hearing some tales about her and Marty.'"

"How do you want to go at her?"

"I'll take the lead, and I'll be the good guy."

"Really? I figured being a woman I would be the good guy who she could derive some support from."

"I would have agreed with you until I met her, but I feel the opposite now. However, I want to reverse roles when we talk with Marty. I want to go at that son-of-a-bitch hard, very hard."

"I know what you mean, but it's not going to be easy for me being sympathetic to him. You sure we can't do a two bad guy routine on him?"

"Sounds tempting, but no. You play nice with him and be sure to flash him that sexy smile of yours as much as you can."

"Are you hittin' on me, Danny Boy?"

"No way, Miss Berry. I told you I'm a straight arrow."

Chapter 4

Nicole Wells arrived promptly at our office door at 9:15. I introduced her to Tara and directed her to sit in one of the chairs. Tara and I sat next to each other directly across from her with about four feet of space between us. This arrangement was deliberate, and designed so that we could have an unobstructed view of Nicole's body movements during the interview.

During our preparation the night before, Tara and I listed the possibilities surrounding Nicole's involvement in Laura's murder: no involvement at all; no involvement, but knowledge; active involvement alone, or with Marty; or the hiring of a third party contract killer.

I began the interview with the standard confidentiality agreement and then got right to the point. "Miss Wells, are you romantically involved with Marty Samuels?"

"No, not anymore."

She looked directly at me when she answered, but crossed her left leg over her right knee. I involuntarily glanced at those long, shapely legs a second too long, and she smiled. Goddamn it! Caught again. I looked back up to her face, trying not to stop my eyes at chest level, which was not easy as her full breasts were prominently outlined under her tight yellow sweater.

"Can you be more specific on the dates of your involvement?"

"Sure. We started seeing each other in October and broke it off in mid-April."

"Miss Wells, do you think Marty Samuels murdered his wife?"

"Heavens, no! Why would he do that?"

"For you."

"No way. We broke up two months ago. We had a fling, that's all. Marty Samuels would never give up his wife and kids for me, or any other woman."

"During your fling," said Tara, "did you ever push Marty to divorce his wife and marry you?"

"No, I'm not looking for marriage at this point in my life," she replied.

"Did Marty ever say that he was contemplating divorcing Laura so that he could marry you?" I asked.

"Never. Listen, we had an affair. He came after me and I figured why not? He's a department head and I was up for my review soon. We were hot and heavy for a few months then things cooled down, and we broke it off by mutual agreement."

"Did you get a good review from Marty?" asked Tara.

"Yes, and a nice raise, too."

"Niki," I said, "can you think of any other reason that Marty might have to murder Laura?"

"First of all, I don't think Marty Samuels is capable of murdering anyone."

"Why not?"

"Because he's basically a wimp—a real Casper Milquetoast."

"Suppose he hired someone to do it? Could that be a possibility?"

"I guess so," she said. "But why?"

"How about money?" asked Tara. "Suppose Marty stood to inherit a large insurance payout on Laura's death?"

"I can't see that. From what I know of Marty he's a well-off middle class family man with no extravagant tastes. He drives an older car and I never heard him express any desires for the fancy things in life."

"Unlike you, Miss Wells?" asked Tara.

"What's that supposed to mean?"

"We heard you like the good life—the Manhattan scene, not dull old Queens."

She smiled and said, "Ah, someone's been telling tales, but that's basically true. Just my dreams and fantasies, that's all."

"To realize your dreams and fantasies," I said, "did you and Marty kill Laura Samuels on the evening of June 10 in order to obtain her life insurance proceeds?"

She re-crossed her legs and folded her arms across her chest. Anger flashed in her blue eyes and she said, "That's absurd! I don't like your question and your tone. If you're accusing me of murder, perhaps I should call a lawyer."

"Miss Wells," said Tara, "you are not a suspect at this time. When we do consider you one we will advise you of your rights at which time you may certainly call a lawyer."

"Please bear with us," I said. "We warned you that some of these questions may be provocative, but we need your help and cooperation."

"Fine," she said. "Continue."

"You said that Marty seemed in no financial difficulty yet we have information that he gambled a lot."

"I never observed that."

"How about at the luncheonettes or diners you ate at with him?" asked Tara. "Ever see him study the sports pages or place a bet or two with the local bookie?"

Nicole seemed uncomfortable and took several seconds to answer. "Yes, on a couple of occasions. He liked football and basketball."

"Do you think he was in over his head? You know, deep into debt with the bookies?" I asked.

"I don't think so. As I said, I only saw him bet a few times."

"Why do you think Marty would lie to me?"

"About what?"

"About gambling—he denied he bets on anything. And about you—he told me he never had an affair."

"I have no idea, Danny. Are we almost through?"

"Just a few more questions, but these are the real tough ones. Don't take them personally, but this is a murder investigation, and we have to ask them."

"Fire away,"

"Niki, did you drive out to the Samuels residence in the early morning hours of June 10?"

"No."

"Did you enter the side door of the residence wearing a ski mask?"

"No," she said, once more folding her arms tightly across her chest.

"Did you bring with you a plastic bag, duct tape and toluene?"

"Of course not! I don't even know what toluene is, or where to get it."

"At a pharmacy or chemical supply house."

"Ridiculous!"

"Did you and Marty Samuels murder Laura Samuels by means of

toluene poisoning, suffocation and strangulation?"

"No!" she yelled. "That's it! I'm leaving!"

She stood up and I said, "Calm down, that's all I have for now."

"You two are just awful."

"Be that as it may," said Tara, "as Detective Boyland said before—this is a murder investigation. Now, before you leave, we want you to consider one last question, really a request."

"I'm listening," she said.

"Would you take a polygraph test and answer those questions, particularly those last few questions that were posed to you in this interview?"

"Polygraph? I…uh, I'm not sure."

"What's your objection?" I asked. "You told us you had no involvement in this crime or any knowledge of it. Why not get it on the record so we can move on?"

"I don't trust those machines; I'd have to first talk to someone about that."

"You do that," I said, "and when you're ready to take the test give me a call. Here's my card."

She took the card, and visibly shaken, left the room. I closed the door after her and said to Tara, "Well Detective First Grade Brown, what do you think?"

"Lying bitch."

"My conclusion exactly."

"Something else disturbed me though. Just what the hell was going on between you and Wells?"

"Huh? What are you talking about?"

"What was with the Niki and Danny stuff?"

"I told you I met her yesterday and she told me to call her Niki."

"And you told her to call you Danny?"

"Er…I guess I did. What's the big deal?"

"The big deal, Danny Boy, is that the lovely Niki Wells is a prime suspect in your murder case, that's what. But that's not all that concerns me."

"What do you mean?"

"I wish I had a videotape of that interview to show to you. You two were devouring each other with your eyes. I was watching her body language and yours, too. I swear it could have been the intro footage to a porno flick before the actors take off their clothes."

"You're crazy, Tara," I said.

"I saw what I saw. I've been a cop for fifteen years, but I've been a woman for almost forty and…"

"You're almost forty? Why you don't look…"

"Don't you change the subject on me. You are treading on dangerous ground here. Remember—she's a suspect. That's all I'm gonna say."

"I don't know what you saw, or thought you saw, ax-lady, but don't you worry. You know me—straight arrow—work, church and home."

"Hah!" she said. "Straight arrow, my butt. You're a man, that says it all. Come on, let's get back to the office."

We stopped in to Mr. Rosen's office and he had the photo ID's ready for us. We thanked him for all he had done, left the building and walked to our car. Tara drove while I dialed Marty at home and got a busy signal. I made a note of the time and said, "Busy. I wonder who he could be talking to?"

"Ten to one it's the luscious Niki Wells," she said. "Jealous?"

"Oh, stuff it with that crap, will you?"

"I saw what I saw."

I got through to Marty a few minutes later and I asked him if he could meet me in my office in Mineola for an update.

"Er, couldn't you come to the house?" he asked.

"I'm heading away from your area now and all my notes on the case are in my office. I want to give you a complete briefing on what we have so far, and I have someone else on another case coming in right after you. So, if it's not too much trouble…."

"Then what time do you want me?"

"1:30 would be fine."

"I'll be there. Should I bring my lawyer?"

"What ever for?"

"Just kidding."

"So, he's coming in?" asked Tara.

"Yeah, but he's edgy. Imagine if I'd told him that I wanted him in Mineola because it's a police dominated area and we're going to grill him until his balls sizzle?"

We stopped at Burger King and fortified ourselves with cheese whoppers, fries and thick shakes. We both needed that good junk food fix once in a while. I thought of what Tara had said and I then immediately pictured Niki. If she had looked good yesterday, she had looked better today—tight yellow sweater, short black skirt, black high heels that accentuated those great legs—and those eyes! Those deep blue eyes! I had to admit that Tara was right. I felt it yesterday and I felt it stronger today and it wasn't just mere attraction—it was something stronger than that—maybe allure would be a better word, or magnetism, or enchantment. Was Niki casting a spell over me? And was I falling under it willingly?

"Earth to Danny," said Tara. "Come in, Danny."

"Huh? What? I…"

"You looked as if you were in a trance. What the hell were you daydreaming about? I hope it wasn't Niki."

"Oh, no, no…the case, the interview with Marty. That's all. That's what I was thinking about."

"Sure you were," she said sarcastically. "Finish your burger and let's go."

I placed a call to the district attorney's office and told Jake Ellison of our scheduled interview with Marty.

"I'll grab a sandwich and meet you in your office," he said. "How did it go with Wells?"

"She didn't confess, but we both think she's lying. She's involved all right."

"Give me the details later. We should have some time before Marty gets there. Let me get a move on."

"See you then, Jake."

We got back to the office at 12:45 and Jake was already there and halfway through his turkey sandwich. We filled him, Ray and Finn in on what we got, and didn't get, from Nicole.

"Do you think she called him after the interview?" asked Jake.

"We're pretty sure of it," said Tara.

"So, we assume he knows what we're going to hit him with," said Finn. "That may work to our advantage."

"It just might," I said. "Wells claims he's a wimp, so if he's real scared maybe he'll crack."

"Or refuse to talk at all," said Ray.

I had a plan of questioning that I laid out to the group. They all approved it and threw in a couple of good suggestions in areas I had overlooked. I made a fresh pot of coffee and was on my second cup when

Marty arrived ten minutes late. I had begun to worry when he hadn't showed on time, but he apologized and blamed his delay on traffic construction, an excuse that any Long Islander will tell you is probably valid. He appeared nervous and there was little color in his face. I offered him a cup of coffee and he accepted. I escorted him into the interview room where Tara was already waiting. We set the chairs up as we had done with Nicole, and I began, "How are you and the kids coping?"

"Not too good. It's difficult to believe she's gone."

"Could be that things will get better when you get back to work and they get back to school," said Tara.

"Yes, maybe. Uh… any leads on the burglar?"

"Unfortunately, no. Let me tell you where we are in the investigation."

"What's to tell if you have no leads?"

I decided to hit him right away with my best shot. "Marty, remember the ski mask found in the bedroom?"

"Yes," he said, folding his arms across his chest.

"The Lab found two long, dark brown hairs inside that mask. Any idea whose hair that might be?"

"I assume it would be the burglar's."

"The length of that hair, and the characteristics of it, indicate it came from a woman," said Tara, as she watched Marty cross his legs.

"A woman?"

"Yeah, Marty. Any idea who that woman could possibly be?"

"How could I know that?"

"How about Nicole Wells? She has long, dark brown hair."

Marty re-crossed his legs and glanced over my head. "Is that the one way mirror behind you, Danny? Is everyone watching as on *Law and Order*?"

"Forget the mirror. I asked you a question about Nicole Wells, your paralegal who you had a six month affair with—the affair that you told me you never had. Remember? No, Danny, no affairs?"

"I'm not answering that. I think I want to speak with a lawyer."

"You have a bunch to choose from at your firm," I said. "Does Mr. Rosen or the other partners know about your affair with your subordinate? Isn't that a big no-no in the business world?"

Just then the intercom on the telephone buzzed. Tara picked up and listened for a few moments, making some notes on a piece of paper. I stared at Marty for a full 30 seconds and then said, "You don't have to answer that question. I understand why you probably didn't want to admit to any affairs at the time I asked you. I'm just a little upset that you lied to me."

"I'd still like to speak with a lawyer," he said, as Tara slid the paper in front of me.

She had written, "Nassau Vice says that Marty is into the local bookies for about 50K." I tapped on the paper and said, "And here's another lie, Marty. Didn't you tell me that you had no gambling debts? My information tells me you're up to your eyeballs with the bookies. Is my information wrong? Do the partners know you owe out fifty large?"

"I want to speak with a lawyer."

"Let me officially read you your rights, then you can tell me what you want to do," I said.

I took out the card with the printed Miranda warnings on it and read it slowly and deliberately to him. He responded, "I do not wish to answer your questions and I wish to exercise my right to a lawyer."

"Fine," I said. "I have no more questions for you, but you'll listen to me anyway. You're a lying, murdering scumbag and I'm coming after you with all I have. Tell that to your lawyer."

He tried to remain calm in the face of my verbal onslaught, but his face was deathly white and beads of sweat appeared on his forehead and chin.

"May I leave now?" he asked through clenched teeth.

"There's the door," I said, "but remember this—the next time we meet you'll be leaving for jail with these on." I reached to my belt and removed my handcuffs and slapped them down hard on the desk. Marty jumped from his chair and literally ran out of the room, down the aisle and out the office door.

Jake, Ray, and Finn joined us in the interview room. Ray said, "You took a good shot, Danny. I don't think any of us expected him to confess, but one thing is certain—he's your man."

"Yeah, Boss," I said, "now I just have to prove it."

"No you don't," said Jake. "That's my job. You just have to get probable cause to make the arrest and I'll do the rest."

"That'll be a first," said Ray. "Since when does the DA not want an iron-clad, beyond a reasonable doubt, case?"

"We still do," laughed Jake, "but I thought I sounded pretty noble with my offer."

"How about a search warrant for a sample of Nicole's hair?" asked Tara.

"Whoa, now," Jake replied. "There's nowhere near enough evidence against her for me to go to a judge with."

"How about for just the items used in the crime?" I asked. "The roll of duct tape and toluene container."

"Assuming Marty and/or Nicole haven't disposed of them by now, which any normal murderer would have done, you don't have enough there, either."

"Well, Mr. Prosecutor," said Finn, "just what do you suggest now?"

"You have to place Nicole at the crime scene. Get a witness who saw her, or her vehicle, in the area. Get somebody who can identify that ski mask as her property, maybe find out where she bought it. Get somebody that they discussed the murder with before, or after, it occurred. Preferably before."

"All easy things," I said. "We should have them by 4:00 p.m."

"And by tomorrow," said Tara, "we'll find the videotape they made of the murder. Will that satisfy you, Mr. Ellison?"

"Now, now, Tara, you know what I'm saying."

We sure did—all of us. We knew that the hard work was about to begin—the drudgery, the legwork, reviewing phone records, talking to a lot more people all the while hoping for a break, the big break that would eventually bring Martin Samuels to his knees.

After Jake Ellison left and Ray went back to his office I met with Tara, Ted, Manny and Finn for a further brainstorm session. We came up with a plan for the next couple of weeks for follow-up interviews and locating new information. The most promising suggestion was to find, and squeeze, every bookie in Queens and Nassau who Marty ever placed a bet with. Maybe he had opened up to one of them in some fashion. We would canvass the neighborhood again and also interview Nicole's neighbors to see if she was observed leaving her apartment on the night of the murder, and we would retrieve the ski mask from the Lab to attempt to find out where it was purchased, and by whom.

"Don't forget to review their phone records," said Finn. "They should all be here early next week."

We broke for coffee. I got back to my desk at 4:30 and was mulling things over when the phone rang. "Detective Boyland?" said a smooth male voice.

"Speaking."

"Detective Boyland, my name is Willard Ashton. I'm an attorney in the firm of Keenan, Rosen, and Vario, in the Criminal Law department, and I have been retained to represent Mr. Martin Samuels. I understand you consider him a suspect in the murder of Laura Samuels."

"Yes, I do, Mr. Ashton. He has been informed of his rights."

"So I understand, and I trust that you know you are not to attempt to question him further. All future dealings with him must now go through me. I'll follow up this call with a letter and my business card."

"I understand Mr. Ashton, and I assure you, I will play by the rules."

"Thank you, Detective Boyland. Good-bye."

I had expected this of course, but I was sure that the attorney was going to say, "I represent Martin Samuels and Nicole Wells." But it was only Marty. I wondered why.

I was one week into a real big case. I was tired, but glad that the week was over. I was also concerned. I knew that if I hadn't made the arrest during that first week after the murder the odds were that I would be in for a long, drawn out investigation. On the plus side, I was almost 100 percent certain who committed the crime, or contracted to have it committed. But how in hell would I ever prove it in court much less scrounge up enough probable cause to make an arrest?

The kids jumped on me at the door. I realized I hadn't seen much of them at all this week, so I promised myself to spend time with them this weekend; maybe take them to the beach. Jeanie greeted me with a hug and a kiss.

"How's the ace homicide detective?" she asked. "As they say on TV, have you collared up yet? Have you snapped the silver bracelets on the perp's wrists?"

"Not yet," I said, "but I will eventually, because I know who done it."

"The husband, right?"

"Of course. Make me a drink and I'll tell you all about it."

After dinner the kids disappeared to continue playing outside in the still bright, early June evening, and Jeanie and I relaxed on the sofa. I put the weather channel on and saw that the weekend promised to be sunny with a high in the low eighties both days.

"What do we have planned this weekend?" I asked. "Any barbecues?"

"Not until the fourth of July."

"How about we take the kids for a day at the beach and some surfcasting?"

"Great idea. Let's do it Sunday. We have to trim the lawns and the shrubs tomorrow."

"Then how about dinner out and a movie tomorrow night? Something funny or a musical?"

"I like that idea too, but don't you want to work on your case at all?"

"No. I've done all I can so far. I'm not going to neglect Pat and Kelly, and especially, you. Monday morning will be here soon enough."

"I'm pleasantly surprised, but I think I've got you figured out."

"Oh?"

She put her arm around me, snuggled close and said, "You're thinking about those two poor motherless children, aren't you?"

"Yes, Jeanie, them and their dead mother. I couldn't bear to lose you and the thought of Pat and Kelly without you is too terrible to consider."

"That awful man," she said. "Killing his wife for a tramp and money. Those poor, poor children."

"And you know what, Jean? When I arrest him, and put him away for life, those kids will suffer another blow."

"Yes, but maybe down the road they'll get over it and find some happiness in their lives."

"I hope so," I said. "Life can truly be a bitch."

On Wednesday the telephone records arrived with the morning's messenger service. It took us several hours to put a pattern together. There were no calls from Nicole's home phone or cell phone to Marty's home phone, but very many from her cell phone to his and vice-versa. They started in October and slowed down in mid-April, but didn't stop completely.

"How many calls did they make to each other after they claimed to break off their affair?" asked Tara.

"Not too many. Let's count them."

There were only six—two in late April, three in May and one in June. Tara asked, "Do you think they really broke it off or is this decrease in calls a planned deception?"

"It could very well be a ruse," I said. "After all they worked in the same department. They could always talk face-to-face there. It's hard to say, but we'll know better when the money shows up."

"The insurance settlement?"

"Yes, but that may not be forthcoming right away. I'm sure the insurance company is going to play hard ball with Marty when they find out he's a suspect. If they eventually do pay, it will be interesting to see if half of the million finds its way into Nicole's bank account."

"I'm glad you're saying Nicole now instead of Niki," she said.

"Are you still on that nonsense," I laughed. "As you reminded me, she is a murder suspect."

"And I saw what I saw," she said, but she smiled a little this time instead of scowling.

"Speaking of Miss Wells," I said, "I am very surprised that I have not heard from her lawyer."

"And I'm surprised Marty's lawyer is only representing Marty."

"I wondered about that, too. Maybe they really are through with each other and maybe she'll open up if she feels the heat. I'm sure she knows something about this case even if she didn't do it herself."

"You want to talk to her again?"

"Yes, but not until we get something to hammer her with. It would be a waste of breath now and might be the push she needs to really run to a lawyer. We have to wait."

"I agree," she said. "What's next?"

"I'm going to get that ski mask tomorrow and start to make some inquiries in her neighborhood."

"Do you need me to tag along?"

"No, but maybe you can contact the insurance company and see what's up with the settlement."

"Sure, and I'll also sit down with Manny and Ted and see how they're doing with the bookies."

"Okay, Tara, I'll see you tomorrow."

Chapter 5

I retrieved the ski mask from Detective Riggins on Tuesday morning and we chatted a bit about the case.

"No hair for me to compare yet, Danny?"

"Unfortunately no, but maybe I'll get lucky and find a guy who remembers selling this particular mask to one particular woman whose name and address is…"

Mary laughed and said, "Are you watching those crime scene shows, too?"

"Dammit," I said, "if they can solve their cases in an hour why can't I solve mine in a day?"

"Dream on," she said. "Hit the street and let me get back to my piles of evidence."

"I will see you soon, bearing a fistful of hair from my number one suspect."

"Assuming you find out where she bought this mask and that Jake comes across with a search warrant," she said.

"No problem, Mary. I'm on my way."

I got to Queens about 10:00 a.m. and located Nicole's apartment building. I figured to use that as my starting point and canvass about a mile in each direction. She lived three subway stops away from her office which was about a mile and a half down Queens Boulevard in Forest Hills. The well-maintained six-story brick building was a block north of the boulevard on 64th Road in a nice middle-class community where most of the residents commuted to work in Manhattan. I parked my car on a side street, walked to the boulevard and turned west. The first store I located that looked as if they sold clothing items was three blocks from my starting point. I showed the clerk the ski mask and she said they didn't carry them, but she knew that a local sporting goods store two blocks further down, called the Sportshop, probably did.

At the Sportshop I showed the ski mask to a bored salesman and he said, "You want a ski mask in June?"

"No, I want to know if you sell any similar to this one."

"Not now. Come back in the fall when the winter items come in."

"Let me put this differently," I said, pulling out my shield. "I'm investigating a serious case, and I'm trying to find the person who wore this mask. Understand?"

"Oh, sure, Detective," he said, finally showing some interest. "This one doesn't look like the ones we carry here. It's cheaply made and not one hundred percent wool."

"I noticed it has no label," I said. "Can you tell if it had one? Or should have had one?"

He examined the mask carefully and said, "It never had a label. No need for one. This item is a one size fits all type that they throw in a large pile on a table in a bargain store. One size, one price, probably $2.99. Ours sell for at least $14.99."

"Any of those bargain stores in the area?"

"Yeah, probably three or four, but you won't find any of these in stock yet, as I said."

He wasn't really a bad guy once I had gotten his attention and I thanked him for his help and then asked him one final question. "If you were a clerk in one of those stores and I showed you this item and showed you a picture of a person, could you remember if you sold this mask to him?"

"Not unless he was a regular customer. A one time purchaser I wouldn't remember."

I found three bargain stores, one in the same direction I was heading and two within a mile of 64th Road in the opposite direction. All three carried ski masks at the appropriate season, but none could recall ever seeing Nicole in their stores for any reason even when I showed them her photo ID. My communication skills were sorely tested as I attempted to get my questions answered. A recent newspaper article claimed that Queens residents now spoke over 100 languages other than English, and it was obvious that the article had been correct. I encountered three different ones in three different shops—Farsi, Korean and Chinese, but I was pretty sure I had gotten my message across.

I looked at my watch and it was getting near 2:00 p.m. I had grabbed a couple of hot dogs and a coke from a pushcart during my wanderings on Queens Boulevard and decided to call it a day and head back to Mineola. It was meeting day and a couple of beers would hit the spot later at Mulvaney's. Maybe they would wash away the day's discouragement.

When I got back to the office Tara filled me in on her day. Before she had a chance to reach out to the insurance company, an investigator had called and asked to meet with us. She set the meeting for Thursday at 10:00 a.m.

"He's a retired Suffolk County detective now doing claims and fraud investigations for the Island Insurance Group, and he is very curious about Marty Samuels," she said.

"That makes two of us. What's his name?"

"George Stanton."

"I'm sure we will give former Detective Stanton an earful, won't we Tara?"

"Oh, yes, we will."

It was about 3:45 and we were starting to gather for the 4:00 p.m. meeting when Gallagher yelled over to me, "Danny! Line two for you."

I found an empty desk and sat down. I picked up the receiver, and pushed the blinking button on the phone. "Homicide Squad, Detective Boyland speaking," I said.

"Hello, Danny," said a sultry female voice. "It's Niki."

"Uh, hello."

"I saw you today."

"You did?"

"On Queens Boulevard, walking with a bag."

I started to regain my composure and said, "Weren't you working today?"

"Yes, but I went home for lunch. I wanted to tape a TV program that's on tonight. I had forgotten to do it in the morning rush to get to work."

"Why not just watch it when you get home?" I asked, for no apparent reason other than to continue this curious conversation.

"Because I won't be home tonight, Danny. I have a date—with you."

That statement froze my brain momentarily and I said, "Wh-a-a-t?"

"Well, not a date exactly," she said. "A meeting. I have to talk with you some more. I may have misled you last week and I want to clarify some things."

"What things?"

"I don't want to talk about that on the phone, but I'm sure you'll be interested. Will you meet me later?"

There was no way I could refuse. Could this be the break I was looking for? I said, "Sure. Where?"

"There's a lounge on Queens Boulevard in Kew Gardens, about a block from Boro Hall, on the opposite side of the street. It's called Victor's. It has a big, green neon sign with flashing martini glasses. You can't miss it."

"What time?"

"How's 7:30?"

"Fine."

"Uh… Danny, this is just you and me. Please don't bring that woman."

"Tara? My partner?"

"Yes, I don't…she makes me feel uncomfortable."

"No problem. I'll see you later."

I hung up the phone and sat quietly mulling over this development. What the hell was going on here? Should I tell Tara? Or Finn? Should I bring a micro-recorder? My thoughts were interrupted by Sergeant Perski calling the meeting to order, and when my turn came I filled the squad in on all we had developed on the case thus far. All of it except the mysterious phone call I had just received from Nicole Wells.

I had two beers and a pastrami sandwich on rye at Mulvaney's and went over some of the case with Manny and Ted. Their follow-up with the bookies brought the total up to about $65,000 that Marty owed out, and that was just in Nassau County. The bookies were getting angry with him and were putting the pressure on to come up with some substantial payback real soon.

"Did they threaten him?" I asked.

Manny grinned and said, "Not that they would admit to, but one guy said to me, 'you know detective, when a guy owes me a lot, you gotta try to persuade him to pay off. Like, you know, tell him he would have difficulty walking with two broken knees—not that I'd ever do anything like that…'"

"But the important thing we found out," said Ted, "was that Marty promised to pay off all his debts, in full, very soon."

"Did he tell any of the bookies how he planned to raise the money?" I asked.

"No," said Manny, "but he assured them they needn't worry. He would repay every last nickel."

"Any luck with them saying Marty tried to hire a hit man?"

"No," said Ted, "and I believed them. They read the papers and know his wife was murdered, and they figure he did it himself."

I glanced at my watch and saw it was time to head to Queens. As I got up, Tara walked over and said, "What's up, guys?"

"Manny and Ted brought me up-to-date on Marty's debts. He owes out about 65K."

"Keeps going up," she said. "Are you leaving now, Danny?"

"Yeah, I'm bushed. I'm calling it an early night."

She looked at me suspiciously, or maybe I just imagined that she did, and said she'd see me in the morning. She took my place at the table with Ted and Manny and I swear I felt her eyes following me as I headed for the door.

I had no trouble locating Victor's Lounge and found a parking spot on a side street. I arrived at the front door at 7:25 and walked in. A man in the garb of a maitre d' greeted me with a smile and asked, "Will you be having dinner, sir?"

"No," I replied. "I'm meeting someone in the lounge, but I don't know if she's here yet."

"Are you Mr. Boyland?"

"Yes."

"Miss Wells is here. Let me escort you to her table."

"Thank you," I said, following him into a dimly lit, but spacious lounge area. We walked across a small dance floor to a row of red leather booths along the far wall, and when he gestured toward Nicole sitting in one of them, he turned away allowing me to walk the remaining distance alone. She arose and greeted me with a smile. I involuntarily drew in my breath as she walked toward me. If she was attractive the first day I met her on the street and very attractive during the interview, she now was absolutely stunning. Breathtaking would be a better word, I concluded, as I exhaled. She was wearing a short, cream-colored, silk summer dress with matching high heels. The dress was cut low enough to reveal the tops of her breasts and, as she approached me at eye level, I realized that her heels brought her height up to my five-eleven.

"Hi, Danny," she said, extending her hand.

"Hi, Niki," I said, taking her hand and allowing her to lead me back to the booth. There was a cosmopolitan cocktail almost untouched in front of her, and as we sat down, a waitress appeared. I ordered a Dewar's on the rocks.

"Come here often?" I asked.

"Occasionally. It's a nice, quiet place. Older crowd, no teeny-boppers, and the food is pretty good."

"Was that Victor at the door?"

"Yes, he's the owner. Victor Reggio keeps the place running smoothly."

"Did you ever come here with Marty?"

"Occasionally."

When my scotch came we raised our glasses and sipped, her eyes never leaving mine. "Well, Miss Wells," I said. "What is it you would like to clarify for me?"

"Boy, you jump right in, don't you?"

"I want the facts ma'am, just the facts."

"Detective Boyland, the facts have changed. What I believed last Friday and what I believe now, on Thursday, are two different things."

"How so?"

"I now believe that Marty was responsible for his wife's death."

"Really? Didn't you say he was too wimpy to commit murder?"

"Yes, and I still say so, but I believe he hired someone to assist him."

"What made you change your mind?"

"He called me Friday at work after my interview with you and he told me he was going in to speak with you that afternoon. He was nervous as hell and he called me again on his way home after the interview. His nervousness had now escalated to sheer terror."

"I went at him pretty hard. Did he tell you he lawyered up?"

"Yes. I think he knows if he talked to you again, you'd probably crack him wide open."

"What about you? Why haven't you gotten a lawyer?"

"Because, contrary to what you and Miss Brown think—what you accused me of—I had absolutely nothing at all to do with the murder of Laura Samuels."

"I'm listening," I said, taking a swallow of scotch.

"I had an affair with Marty, but he wanted more than an affair. He wanted to divorce Laura and marry me to the point of obsession. He became unbearable, so I finally had to break it off."

"Did he ever say to you that he would kill Laura so that he could have you?"

"Yes—to have me, and the money."

"Did he need money badly?"

"Very badly. I wasn't truthful about his betting. He was as compulsive with that as he was obsessed with me. I'm sure he owes a lot, but I don't know exactly how much."

"How did he react when you broke up with him?"

"Enraged at first, then the tears, and then the promise."

"Promise?"

"He promised that he would win me back and straighten out his life once and for all."

"How did you interpret that?"

"I took it that he would quit gambling. He knew it annoyed the hell out of me. Whenever we were together he'd be on his cell phone with his bookies, or checking the betting lines on TV or the newspapers."

"But you didn't take it that he meant to kill Laura?"

"No, not then. But as I just told you I changed my mind, especially when you mentioned insurance money."

"Did Marty ever tell you the amount of life insurance he had on Laura's life?"

"No," she replied.

"One million dollars," I said.

"Wow! I need another drink."

We ordered a second round and Niki excused herself to go to the ladies room. While she was away and I was mulling over her information, a light appeared on the small stage at the back of the dance floor. A disc jockey appeared, introduced himself, and asked the patrons not to hesitate to request their favorite songs. He started off playing an old 50's Platters' tune, and a few couples got up to dance. Niki returned and said, "Victor has live music on the weekends and the DJ on the other nights."

"This is a nice place," I said. "I can't stand those joints with the blasting music where you can't even think straight, much less carry on a conversation."

"When will Marty collect that insurance money?"

"Maybe never. He's the main suspect in his wife's murder. The insurance company will try to withhold the proceeds until the case is solved, and if he is convicted, he'll never get it."

"By the way, I know what you had in that bag today."

"And how do you know that?"

"It was the ski mask you mentioned in the interview," she said, and then added casually, "It's mine."

I took a long sip of my scotch trying to digest this unexpected admission. I said, "Yours? The one I found at the crime scene?"

"Yes."

"And how did it get there? Didn't you start this conversation with the intent of convincing me that you had absolutely nothing to do with the murder?"

"Yes, and that's what I still intend to do. I gave that ski mask to Marty back in November. He was at my apartment and I was cleaning out my closets of old items to give to Goodwill and he spotted the mask and a couple of pairs of gloves. He asked if he could take them for his kids."

"Where did you originally get the mask?"

"At a discount store in downtown Brooklyn, not on Queens Boulevard, as I'm sure you found out earlier today."

I smiled and said, "Yeah, no one recognized your picture."

"You have my picture? How sweet!"

"So, tell me, why is a ski mask that you say you gave to Marty for his kids lying on the floor in his bedroom, and he denies any knowledge of it?"

"I have an idea."

"Go ahead."

"Maybe he soaked it with the toluene and used it to kill Laura, or used it for the dose he gave himself. Or maybe he wore it in case Laura woke up while he and his hired man did the deed."

"The Lab didn't find any of his hair on the mask, but they did find two long, dark brown ones very similar to these," I said, as I reached across the table and touched her hair.

"Are you taking a sample, Detective Boyland? I'll give you some if you want, without a search warrant, but why bother? I told you it was my mask. Those two hairs are probably mine."

"Thanks for the offer, but I don't want a sample now."

"Speaking of offers," she said, "would you care to dance?"

"Uh...Niki...I don't think that would be...uh...you know."

"Appropriate? Come on, it's one of my favorites."

I did not want to dance with someone who had yet to convince me she wasn't a murder suspect, and I did not want to dance with a woman who was not my wife, but I got up anyway and we danced, closely and sensuously, to Rod Stewart's *Have I Told You Lately That I Love You.* All through that dance I kept telling myself that I shouldn't be doing this, to sit down now, but I couldn't let her go. Her body fit perfectly in my arms and the aroma of her perfume and the feel of her embrace willingly trapped me. I felt myself becoming aroused and tried to back away from her swaying body, but she gripped me tighter. Thank God the song was just about over.

"That was nice," she smiled as we walked back to the table. "Are you hungry?"

For what? I wondered, but I said, "No, I had a sandwich before I came here."

"So did I," she said, "but I could use some munchies. How about a plate of nachos and cheese? They make them great here."

"Sure," I said, and ordered a beer with the nachos. Niki ordered a diet coke.

"Diet coke?" I asked. "Watching your figure?"

"No. Are you?"

"Am I what?"

"Watching my figure?"

"I'm a married man Miss Wells, but I think Mr. Victor Reggio was watching your figure."

"Vic?" she laughed. "He's not my type."

"But Marty Samuels was?"

"God no, that was just a fling."

"So, who is your type?"

"You, Danny," she said. "You are definitely my type."

"But I'm unavailable, and if you are not a suspect in my case, you most certainly are a witness."

"Pity," she said. "A damned pity, but maybe those circumstances will change. I will convince you that I had nothing to do with Laura's murder, and I will help you arrest Marty."

"And how do you plan to do that?"

"I'll stay close to him and try to get him to tell me how he did it."

"You're going to resume the affair?"

"No way. I'll convince him that we are being watched very closely by the police and that a continued love affair would really draw the attention of you and your partners."

"Why do you think he'll admit to you that he killed Laura?"

"I don't know if he will, but if he doesn't get the insurance money soon he'll get desperate. Maybe I can work that angle to my advantage somehow."

"You sound like a homicide detective."

"Why, thank you. What do you think?"

"I think I want to eat some of these nachos."

We munched and sipped our drinks and I took the time to assess the conversation. What did I think? Isn't that the $64,000 question? Is she playing me like a fiddle? Is she sincere about getting Marty? Is she just trying to get herself off the hook? Is she trying to seduce me for real?

"Niki," I said, "I believe you've been truthful with me and I sincerely want to believe you had no part in the murder of Laura Samuels. I cannot picture you driving out to Woodmere with a roll of duct tape and a bottle of toluene and wearing your ski mask as you and Marty kill Laura and fake a burglary scene, and I have no evidence whatsoever that you did so."

"There is no evidence because I was not there. So will you take me up on my offer?"

"Yes. Buy a small voice-activated tape recorder. It's important to get his admission on tape, otherwise it's just your word against his."

"Okay," she said. "Care to dance again?"

"No. I have to get going, but I'd like you to do something for me, something I asked during the interview."

"What's that?"

"Take a polygraph exam."

"But...why?"

"Niki, I believe you, but I have to confirm it."

"If you believe me why do you need to confirm it?"

"It's not me. I have to show your credibility to my bosses. Then we can confidently proceed according to plan."

"I don't understand what your bosses have to do with this."

"Be reasonable. I have to convince them that you're no longer a suspect or they'll be on me to lock you up as an accomplice. That's our consensus right now of what happened until you told me different this evening."

"I can't take a polygraph."

"Why not?"

"I don't do well on them. I believe they are not infallible and wrong as often as they are correct."

"You don't do well on them?"

"No, I failed a polygraph test when I applied for a sales job in a jewelry store while I was going to college. Although I passed the written honesty test, they told me that the polygraph indicated I lied on some of the theft questions, and I knew that was untrue."

"Maybe it was the operator," I said. "If he wasn't trained properly he could have interpreted the results incorrectly. We have a real pro with twenty years experience in the department."

"I just don't trust those machines and I won't subject myself to that humiliation again despite your seeming faith in them. I do believe they are still not admissible as evidence in any court in the country."

"Seems we're at an impasse."

"I guess we are, so we'll leave it just where it was at the beginning of this meeting. Consider me a suspect, or an accomplice, or whatever, and spin your wheels while Marty remains silent. I assure you I will never bother you again. In fact don't even call me. If I'm a suspect, I'll have a lawyer call you in the morning."

Her eyes were flashing electric blue in anger and filling with tears. She got up to leave and I reached over and stopped her. "Sit down Niki. I need you. You're all I have right now. We'll work something out."

She dabbed at her eyes with her cocktail napkin and said, "When can I see you again?"

"You have my card. When you get something, call my cell phone. Do you have a cell phone?"

"Yes, let me write the number down for you."

I got another business card from my shield case and she wrote her number on it and handed the card back to me smiling. "Put this in your wallet right next to my picture."

We walked out together past the staring eyes of Victor and I asked Niki where she was parked. She was on a side street opposite from where my car was so we headed her way. The trees were in full leaf and rustled slightly in the night breeze. She stopped at a dark blue Toyota Corolla and unlocked the driver's door.

"Goodnight," she said. "I hope to see you soon."

"Goodnight, Niki. I hope so too."

She stepped close to me and kissed me lightly on the lips. "Thanks for a wonderful first date," she said, and then she kissed me harder wrapping her arms around my neck and pulling me tightly into her. I did not resist.

As she drove away I took out the card with her cell phone number on it and jotted down her license plate number below it. I walked back toward Queens Boulevard wondering what the hell I was doing and where it would lead.

Chapter 6

On Friday morning Tara and I met with former detective George Stanton. He was out of the Job three years and now investigated suspicious claims for his company. We filled him in briefly on what we had so far and he said, "Based on what you've told me, this settlement is not going to be paid to Mr. Samuels anytime soon."

"How long can you withhold it?" asked Tara.

"Until the case is solved assuming someone other than he gets convicted. However, if this drags on with no arrest for a few months, he'll probably have his lawyer sue us for the proceeds."

"What are his chances?" I asked.

"They get better as the time goes by without a collar, but even so, we can drag it out a couple of years before a court orders payment. Then we'll appeal."

"Maybe the bookies will close the case on Marty sooner than that," said Tara.

"The bookies?" asked George. "Is he also into the loan sharks?"

"He will be soon if he doesn't pay off the bookies and he's into them big time," I said.

"Then it seems not getting this settlement is going to put your guy into sorry shape. I'm glad to be of assistance."

"Thanks, George," I said, "I'll let you know if anything pops—and we'd appreciate your thoughts from any conversations you have with Marty."

"You got it," he said. "Talk to you soon."

We all met with Sergeant Finn in his office. The case was two weeks old and we had done all we could. We had no new information. I could not tell them about my dealings with Niki because I didn't know where that was going, if anywhere. Finn said, "Ted, I'm afraid I can't justify keeping you here any longer so you're going back to the Nine-Four Squad as of Monday. Manny, you're back in the duty chart, also on Monday. Tara, you can have another week out of the rotation with Danny, but if something doesn't pop next week you're back in the chart the following Monday."

The anticipated breakup of our team after two intense weeks together was depressing, but predictable, and Friday passed quietly. Our thoughts were similar—we had failed to solve the murder of Laura Samuels, but what was worse was the fact that we knew who did it, and right now there was not a goddamned thing we could do about it.

I found myself thinking of Niki more and more, especially that good-night kiss, but I justified my thoughts with the fact that I needed her to solve my case. I wondered if she had she gotten anything from Marty. Why hadn't she called?

The weekend dragged by. The beautiful June weather we were enjoying had taken a turn for the worse and a cold steady rain fell on Saturday. I puttered around the house and garage and finally lost myself in a novel. The kids went to a movie matinee and Jeanie and I decided to call the baby-sitter and catch a movie ourselves that evening. When we returned, the kids were sound asleep and Jeanie and I made love.

"Boy," she said, "that was great! Must be letting out all your pent up feelings over that murder case."

Or it could be that I was thinking you were Niki for the whole time. I felt ashamed, almost as if I had actually betrayed my wife with another woman. I said, "Yeah, it's been a helluva week, a lot of stored up emotions for sure."

On Sunday the rain finally stopped, but the weather remained overcast and chilly. All the home baseball games had been rained out so we watched some old movies on the TV and read some more. I went to the bathroom and then stopped in our bedroom to check my cell phone. I picked it up as I had at least a dozen times this weekend and this time the message icon was flashing. I checked the number. It was Niki's and the accompanying text simply said, "Call me."

That afternoon we had all decided to have pizza for dinner. Jeanie called in the order and I volunteered to go pick it up.

"You don't want them to deliver?" she asked.

"No, let me go get it. I'm stir crazy from being in the house. I need some air now that the rain has finally stopped."

"Okay," she said. "It will be ready in 20 minutes."

I drove up to Hempstead Turnpike and pulled into the pizzeria's parking lot. I dialed Niki's number and she answered after the second ring.

"It's Danny," I responded to her hello.

"I have some information for you. When can we meet?"

"How about Tuesday night?"

"That would be fine."

"Same place?"

"Sure, unless you'd like to come up to my apartment. I could make a light dinner."

As tempting as that offer sounded I knew that whatever was for dinner, the recipe could be for disaster, so I said, "No, Victor's will be fine."

"Can I get another dance or two from you?" she asked.

I felt a stirring in my groin and said, "Depends on your information. See you at 7:30."

We sat in the same booth and ordered the same drinks.

"It's good to see you again," she said.

"Likewise," I said.

Our drinks arrived. We touched glasses and sipped our cocktails. "To Marty," I said. "May he rot in jail."

"You have to arrest him first, but that may not be so easy."

"Oh? I thought you had good news for me."

"I said information—didn't say if it was good or bad."

"So, tell me."

"I got this from him over the phone," she said. "We had a few conversations on our cell phones this past week. He desperately wanted to see me, but I told him you could be watching us. By the way, do you have him under surveillance?"

"No, there's no good reason to do so. Tara and I are the only two working the case now, and after this week, it'll just be me."

"So, maybe I should meet him face to face?" she asked.

"I think you'd have a better chance at getting an admission from him that way, but I wouldn't advise you to resume the fling, as you call it."

"Why not?"

"Because I don't want you to."

"I understand," she smiled. "Let me tell you about my information. Marty told me he got a call from some investigator for the insurance company and the guy said he wasn't getting the settlement for the foreseeable future. He checked with his lawyer and was told he would have to wait months before they could file a lawsuit."

"Did he sound worried? Is the pressure building up?"

"He found another way out."

"How?"

"He refinanced the house and was able to pull out $75,000. Then he tapped his children's college savings accounts for $15,000 apiece and paid off all his debts."

"Damn!" I said. "Has he stopped betting?"

"No, he's got a new line of credit and he knows he's going to win this time."

"Sure he is. He's got a cushion now for quite a while. Any leverage we had is gone. What the hell do I do now to catch this guy? He has no reason at all to make an admission to me, you, or anyone else."

"Sorry for the bad news," she said. "Let's dance."

We danced to a couple of slow oldies by the Penguins and the Five Satins and a couple of up-tempo ones including one of my favorites, *Give Me That Old Time Rock and Roll*. I was working up a sweat and relieving some of my frustrations. We went back to the booth and ordered beers and nachos. Niki looked great again tonight—white slacks, red silk blouse and matching red spike-heeled shoes. I was enjoying her company despite the depressing news. We danced some more and had another beer, and then I told her I had to leave.

"So early? Want to come up to my place for a nightcap?"

"I'd love to, but I really have to get going."

The DJ started a Johnny Mathis medley and Niki said, "How about just one more dance?"

We danced to *Chances Are* and *Misty*, and when *The Twelfth of Never* played, she whispered in my ear, "Oh, Danny, this is my all-time favorite golden oldie. As Johnny says, hold me close."

"And never let you go?"

"No, never let me go—not until the twelfth of never."

When the set was over I said, "Niki, I really have to go now."

"When am I going to see you again? When am I going to get to spend more time with you? When are you going to stop running away from me?"

"I'll call you."

We walked to her car and briefly kissed goodnight.

"Are you mad at me?" I asked as she got behind the wheel. She reached over and opened the passenger's door.

"Sit with me a minute," she said.

I got in and shut the door. She slid over toward me and gave me a long, slow, delicious kiss and said, "I just wanted to give you something to remember me by, a reminder for you to call me—soon."

I grabbed her and kissed her back and then we were all over each other as if we were two teenagers at an old drive-in movie, groping and squeezing. When we came up for air she said, "I don't think we can finish this in a Corolla. Are you sure you don't want to come back to my apartment?"

I sure as hell did, but I answered, "Not tonight, Niki. I'll call you."

"I'll be waiting," she said. "Don't disappoint me."

I left her and walked toward my car which was parked a half block from hers, wondering to myself just what the hell I was doing. I had to stop this now. Niki was no value to the case anymore. There was no need to ever see her again. If by some miracle Marty admitted the murder to her, and she got lucky enough to get it on tape, she would call me. Sorry to disappoint you Niki, but you will have to wait a long time for me to call you again.

I called her the next morning. I had gotten home about 10:00 p.m. that night and watched the news with Jeanie who fell asleep on the sofa before it was over. When we went to bed I couldn't sleep and Niki was the reason why. I wanted to be with her to the point that I felt a deep sickness in the pit of my stomach, an ache that refused to lessen as I tossed and turned in bed. Yet I also knew if I saw her again I might enter down a path from which it would be difficult to return. I finally drifted off to sleep at 4:30 with a firm resolve to not go down that path. The resolve had lasted six hours.

"Hi, Niki," I said.

"Danny, I missed you terribly, and it's only been since last night. I'm so happy you called."

"I switched a tour on Friday night to a four-to-twelve. I'll technically be working, but we can spend a few hours together."

"Can you be at my place for dinner, say 6:30?"

"I'll be there," I said, and flipped my cell phone closed.

As I walked toward the coffee room Tara fell in step with me and joined me at the table. She stared at me for a long minute then finally said, "Danny, what the hell is going on?"

"What are you talking about?"

"You know damn well what I'm talking about—Niki."

"Niki? You mean Nicole Wells?"

"Don't you jive me. You know exactly who I mean, and what I mean."

"Tara, I…"

"Be still! I see what I see. You're walking around as if you were a moonstruck teenager. Just what the hell do you think you're doing?"

"Tara, I was going to fill you in today anyway, so let me do it now."

"Fill me in on what—your sexual escapades with nympho Niki?"

"Would you stop for Pete's sake, and listen."

She crossed her arms over her chest and glared at me. I explained the developments in the case with Niki, omitting the dancing and kissing.

"Why didn't you tell me sooner? I am your partner on this case. And why wasn't I with you during these meetings with her?"

"I told you I was going to tell you today. After last night it became clear that this line of investigation has fizzled out. It's over. I struck out, and unless Marty trips himself up, this case is going to remain open for a long time."

"And I wasn't invited to these meetings because?"

"Because Miss Wells doesn't like you, Detective Brown, and she would only confide in me alone."

"Bullshit," she said. "She wanted you alone so she could get her hooks into you, Danny Boy."

"Come on, Tara, give it up."

"Did you fill Finn in yet?"

"No, let's do it now."

We went to Finn's office and brought him up to date. Tara asked for a couple days off since she was going back into the rotation on Monday concluding that nothing was going to happen on my case for a while. Finn agreed and then said, "Danny, if nothing new pops next week that'll be it for you too. You go back into the duty chart the following Monday."

Tara and I spent the rest of the day catching up on our paperwork and when it came time to go home I said, "Enjoy your time off Tara and thanks for all your help on this case. You're a real pro and a great interviewer."

"My pleasure," she smiled. Then her smile turned into a frown and she said, "But Danny, please, please, please stay away from her."

"Tara!"

"I saw what I saw," she said, walking out the door.

Friday morning I got up with Jeanie and we had breakfast together and saw Patrick and Kelly off to school.

"First four-to-twelve in a while," she said.

"Yeah, the case is winding down. I've got a couple of people left to interview who are never around during the day. I'll wrap that up tonight."

"And what are you going to do on this beautiful summer day?"

"I am going to hit the little white ball over at Eisenhower Park, that's what. I haven't swung a club since this case began."

"I'm jealous," she said. "Hit 'em good."

"I don't know if I'll hit them good, but I'm going to hit them hard. Every time I tee up I'm going to picture Marty Samuels's face on the ball."

"So your big case is at a dead end?"

"For now it is."

"What are you going to do next?"

"I don't know, Jeanie. I just don't know."

That question floated around my mind as I stumbled my way through a lousy round of golf not even breaking 100. What was I going to do next? I would find out shortly. This would be it with Niki—break it off now or probably go beyond the point of no return. I got back home around 2:00 p.m., had a sandwich, showered and shaved, and got dressed for work. I left a few minutes early and stopped in a liquor store for a bottle of merlot which I had them gift wrap.

At 5:45 I grabbed a set of keys and told Nancy, who was catching cases this tour, to page me if she needed help. "I'll be out a few hours doing some final interviews in the five towns area and Queens," I told her.

"No problem," she said. "This has the makings of a quiet night so far, so I hope I can leave you alone."

I transferred the wine from my car to the unmarked police car and headed west on the Long Island Expressway. The sun was still high in the sky on this second day of July and it was still hot enough outside to keep the car's air conditioning going strong. I found a parking place not too far from where I parked when I did my ski mask interviews and I buzzed her apartment, 2E, right at 6:30. She immediately buzzed back and announced, "Come on up, the first course is about to be served."

I handed her the wine and she kissed me lightly on the lips. She said,

"Why don't you open that and let it breathe and I'll make us a cocktail. What would you like?"

"Scotch on the rocks will be fine," I said, admiring her and feeling very relaxed and happy to be there.

"I'm going to splurge and make myself a very dry vodka martini, shaken, not stirred, as James Bond would say."

"You know that sounds good. Scratch the scotch and make two of those."

We sipped the ice cold martinis and she said, "Ready for the first course now?"

"Sure," I said.

She brought out a bowl of salad from the refrigerator and two chilled salad plates and set them on the kitchen table. We put our drinks down and I took her in my arms and said, "Niki, I'm glad I came."

"Me too," she said putting her arms around me and kissing me on the lips. I returned the kiss hugging her tightly. Things rapidly escalated and we began to pull our clothes off. As we rushed into her bedroom she said, "I guess the salad will be the second course tonight."

We made love fast and furiously devouring each other with our arms and mouths. "Oh, Danny," she said, "I've been waiting for this moment ever since I first laid eyes on you on the street that day."

"It was definitely worth waiting for," I said.

"This is only the beginning, the first fast session. Wait'll you see what I have in store for you later, my dear."

"I'm looking forward to that."

"But right now let's have our salad. Good love making always gives me an appetite."

We put most of our clothes back on and sat down to dinner. She put two thick pork chops in the broiler and they sizzled as we ate our salad and finished our martinis. I poured the wine and she served the chops with green beans, mushrooms and risotto.

"You're beautiful and you can cook," I said. "What other talents do you possess?"

"You'll find out very soon if you think you have it in you to have our dessert in the bedroom."

"I love having dessert in bed, but let us digest this meal first and finish the wine."

And so began my love affair with Nicole Wells. I never dreamed I would ever have an affair, or that I would ever cheat on Jeanie, or that I would ever say the things I said and do the things I did with Niki. But I did, willingly and eagerly and lustfully, and after an evening of lovemaking two weeks later she said to me, "Oh, Danny Boy, I love you so."

"I love you too, Niki. I love you as I never loved anyone before." And I meant every word.

I had never understood my fellow cops who carried on with other women. I was the first to criticize their cheating ways, especially when I knew their wives. Oh, once in a while a guy was married to a real nagging bitch, or a drunk, or a drug addict and at least there was some justification for chasing after other women. But most of the guys who cheated had decent wives who were usually better looking than the ones they were partying with. Of course, as Tara would have said, "It's a man thing. All men are pigs and will stick their thing in any warm hole that's available." That was probably a good assessment, but weren't we supposed to overcome that animal behavior when we said, "I do?" And I had. For eleven years I remained faithful to Jeanie despite numerous opportunities that were not initiated by me, but with Niki I fell head over heels off the cliff and wondered why. Why her and not any others? Why?

The intense romance took its toll on me both physically and mentally. I couldn't eat and sleep properly and was deathly afraid Jeanie would find out. Whenever I looked at her I imagined she saw the word "cheater" flash on my forehead in bright red letters.

As July turned into August and the affair became one month old, Niki said to me one night, "Where do we go from here, Danny?"

"What do you mean?"

"Are we going to sneak around like this forever? Or are we going to make a break for an island in the Caribbean?"

"You mean quit our jobs? And I divorce Jean? And then we run off to paradise and live happily ever after?"

"Something like that."

"Well, with our combined savings we could probably do that for a couple of months. Then what?"

"We come back and go to California, or someplace else, and go back to work."

"You're serious."

"I'm deadly serious. The fact is, I love you and I want to be with you and you alone—forever."

"And I love you too, but let's not rush this. Let me check out my pension plan and I'll check with a lawyer to see what a divorce would cost me and what alimony and support payments would be."

"And I'll check my 401(k) account at the firm."

I couldn't believe I had actually said those words out loud—divorce, alimony, child support, quitting my job—all the things in my life that meant everything to me. Here I was ready to discard them for the love of a woman and an uncertain, if not disastrous, future. And I didn't care. She had captured me completely, heart and soul and body, and I just didn't care about anything else in the world.

"When do you think we can make the break?" I asked.

"Right after Labor Day," she said. "That will give us a good month to cut the ties that bind."

A month. Thirty days to a new life with Niki, but I couldn't shake the feeling that I would be making a colossal mistake, a mistake from which there would be no recovery and no return.

Before we had a chance to put our plans into action—I was in the office and about to call a divorce attorney—Sergeant Finn came up to my desk and said, "Get your jacket and let's go take a walk over to the DA's office."

"Sure," I said. "What's up?"

"Barry Walsh called and said he may have something on the Samuels case. He's getting Jake Ellison to join us."

"Did he say what the something is?"

"Nope, I'm as curious as you."

We assembled in Barry's office and had coffee.

"Anything new on the Samuels case?" he asked.

"Not from my end, but it sounds as if you have something," I said.

"I'm not sure. I got a call about an hour ago from a Queens ADA in their Organized Crime Unit, name of John Malone. Malone tells me he got a call from the attorney who represents a low-level street bookie named Anthony Messina. He says Messina has some information on the Samuels case."

"What's in it for him?" asked Finn.

"He just got out of Riker's a couple of weeks ago after serving 30 days on a misdemeanor gambling charge and he doesn't want to go back. While he was on the inside, Queens Vice raided a big gambling operation and got records showing felony level bookmaking on him, and others."

"Do we know what he's got?" I asked.

"No, but they're willing to talk if we're willing to listen," said Barry.

"I'm all ears," I said. "I have nothing else to go on."

"I'll call him back and set up the interview for tomorrow. Jake, I'd like you to go along with Danny on this."

"Sure," he said, "Maybe this is the proverbial big break we've been praying for."

Barry made the call while we were all still there and we heard him say, "Hold on, I'll check. He turned to us and said, "They want to do it this afternoon at 2:00 p.m. Is that okay with you two?"

Jake and I looked at each other and nodded and Barry said into the phone, "They'll be there."

I went back to Jake's office with him to review the case, especially the gambling connection to Marty. He said, "Danny, are you okay?"

"Yeah, why?"

"You look like hell. You're not sick are you?"

Yeah, sick in love. "No, just not eating and sleeping right. Got a lot on my mind, not the least of which is this case, and how Samuels has gotten away with murder and I can't lock him up for it."

"Hey, maybe we'll get lucky this afternoon. Let's get some lunch and head over to Queens."

Chapter 7

We met in a conference room on the third floor of Boro Hall overlooking Queens Boulevard. As we awaited the arrival of Messina, I stood looking out the window and spotted Victor's Lounge across the street, which immediately brought Niki to mind, not that she was ever that far out of it. In about three weeks I was contemplating the biggest life change in my 35 years. I wouldn't be Detective Daniel Boyland anymore, nor husband to Jeanie, but I'd still be Pat and Kelly's father. How would they take this? Would they hate me? Why couldn't I be like the other cheaters and keep Niki on the side without having to give up my wife and kids and job? I love her, I want to be with her, but…

My thoughts were interrupted by the entrance of Messina and his attorney. Introductions were made all around and the attorney, Sam Green, began, "Gentlemen, my client, Mr. Messina, believes he has some valuable information on the Laura Samuels murder. He is willing to freely and voluntarily share it with you, in writing, as well as verbally. He will do this in return for your consideration in a reduction of charges, from felony to misdemeanor, in the current case being prosecuted against him here in Queens."

"Thank you for your directness, Mr. Green," said Malone. "If my associates from Nassau County assure me that Mr. Messina's information is of substantial value to their murder case, I would most certainly consider such a reduction."

"Mr. Green," said Jake, "after we listen to Mr. Messina's story, and if we find value in it, would he consent to taking a polygraph examination to verify his veracity?"

Messina looked at Green with a puzzled expression.

"He wants to know if you'll go on the box to verify you told them the truth," said Green.

"Oh, sure," he said. "No problem. I'm a bookmaker, not a liar."

"Good," said Jake. "You're on, Mr. Messina."

"Call me Whitey," he said, pointing to his pure white, full head of hair, which was combed straight back. He had a pleasant mannerism and appeared to be one of those Goodfellas characters—a likable criminal who really wasn't such a bad guy after all. I guessed he was about 56 or 57 years old and, from his speech, a native Brooklynite.

"Shoot, Whitey," I said. "We're all ears."

Malone clicked on a tape recorder which was in plain view on the table. There were no objections.

"As you know, I'm a bookie. I take bets, er…used to take bets, along a stretch of Queens Boulevard—numbers and ponies. I don't do other sports."

"Why not?" I asked.

"Those are mostly done over the phone, not in person. My territory goes from here in Boro Hall down to Junction Boulevard. I take, uh…took action from the barber shops, bars, mom and pop stores and the luncheonettes. About two weeks before the Samuels woman was murdered I was approached by a young lady in Vito's Luncheonette. You know it?"

"Yes," I said. "Near 76th Road."

"That's it," he said. "Nice place, good food. So this young broad comes up to me. She was sitting at a table with Marty Samuels."

"You know Marty Samuels?"

"Sure, he threw down a few bets with me, but only once in awhile. Marty's thing is football, baseball, basketball, and like I say, that's not my action."

"How much does he bet?"

"Nothing heavy, a sawbuck on the daily number if he got a hunch and a twenty or so on a horse if someone gave him a tip. Like I say, it's not his thing."

"How about the young lady?" asked Jake. "Does she bet with you?"

"No, never. I don't know her as long as Marty."

"Go on."

"So she sits her cute little ass at my table and gives me a big smile and asks me a question that surprises the hell out of me. She says, 'Whitey, you must be in the mob. I need some advice. How much is it to hire a hit man?' I nearly choke on my pastrami sandwich and I tell her, 'Hey, lady, I'm a bookie. I ain't in the mob, and I don't know any hit men.' She says, 'Sure you do. Come on, I'll make it worth your while.' So, I decide to play along with her."

"Did you think she was serious?"

"I didn't know, but like I said, I figured I'd string her along a bit and then I got convinced that maybe she was serious."

"How come?" asked Jake.

"I told her that I might know somebody who could do the job, but it was going to cost a bundle. She asks me how much, and I tell her twenty G's plus a two percent vig for me."

"How did she react to that?" I asked.

"She seemed surprised. Said she had to talk it over, and she would get back to me."

"Did she say talk it over, or think it over?" I asked. "Take your time, Whitey."

He thought for a moment and said, "She definitely said, talk it over. I'm sure of it."

"What happened then?" asked Jake.

"She goes back to Marty and they huddle up and talk for a while."

"Could you hear the conversation?" I asked.

"No, they were whispering. Then when I'm getting up to leave, she comes over again and says she'd like to meet me later after work to discuss the issue further. 'Maybe arrange a down payment,' she says. She tells me she'll pick me up right there in front of Vito's about a quarter after five, and I say sure."

"Whitey," I said, "if you don't know any hit men why were you stringing this out? Did you plan to take some money and rip her off?"

"Nah, I was going to tell her to forget it, but the way she said down payment made me definitely feel that she had something other than money in mind."

"You mean sex?" asked Jake.

"Yeah, and boy was I right about that."

I started to get a sinking feeling and I asked Whitey if she had told him her name.

"Yeah, Niki."

I took out my wallet and showed Niki's photo ID to him. "Is this her?"

He reached into his shirt pocket and withdrew a pair of glasses. He put them on and picked up the ID card. "Yeah, that's her all right. That's Niki."

"So, did you meet her later as planned?" asked Jake.

"Yeah, she showed up right on time driving this blue Corolla and I got in and she drove a few blocks to an industrial area and parked behind a vacant building. She tells me that twenty grand is kinda steep and maybe we could negotiate the price down a bit. I say I don't know about that and she reaches down and grabs my crotch and says, 'Maybe when I'm done with you you'll change your mind.' And then she proceeds to give me one of the best blow jobs I ever had in my life. I mean that sweetie could really suck a cock."

I wanted to reach across the table and punch this lying son-of-a-bitch right in the mouth, but of course I couldn't do that, so I just tried to breathe deeper and slower.

"Well," said Jake, "they say your best blow job is always the last one."

"Not in this case, pal," he said. "Hey, I'm 55 years old and I'm getting piped by a twenty something beauty—for free! It don't get any better than that."

"For free?" I asked. "I thought you were negotiating price."

"That's the kicker," he said. "I told her, 'you were right, honey, that was a $5,000 blow job if there ever was one. I'll see if my guy'll do the job for $15,000.' So I guess it wasn't a freebie. I paid $5,000 in imaginary bucks for it."

The urge to smash Whitey's laughing face in was becoming overwhelming. I reached for a glass of water and sipped it, eyeing him.

"Then what happened?" asked Jake.

"I don't see her at Vito's until over a week later. She comes over to me and says, 'Whitey, what we talked about last week? Forget it. Forget the whole conversation.' And I say, 'Gee, Niki, how come? Maybe I can get my guy down to $10,000.' She laughs and says, 'Don't you wish, you dirty old man, but we found another solution to our problem, so let's just forget it.' I tell her, 'no problem,' and that was the end of it."

"Again," said Jake, "are you certain she said we found another solution, not I found another solution."

"We," he said. "She definitely said we."

"Why did you take so long to come forward," I asked, still trying to control my anger.

"I went up for sentencing two days after that last conversation and got 30 days in Riker's. The murder happened when I was in there and I didn't connect the dots until I got out. Then I get hit with this indictment and figured that Niki and Marty knocked off his old lady, so here I am."

"Anything else?" asked Jake.

"No, that's it,"

"Mr. Green," said Jake, "could you and Mr. Messina excuse us and wait outside a few minutes while we discuss this?"

"Sure," he said. "Take your time."

After they left, Malone said, "Some story. Does it make any sense with the facts in your case?"

"If it's true," said Jake, "then I think we may have a shot at a conspiracy charge against Niki and Marty."

"If it's true?" I said. "Jake, don't tell me you believe that lying old bastard? Can you picture Niki Wells giving him a pipe job?"

"I see your point," he said. "It is a bizarre story, but let's see how he stands up to the polygraph."

"Jake, how do you want me to deal with Green?" asked Malone.

"Tell him if Messina's story proves out with the polygraph that you'll keep his case on hold until we can get some prosecution going, if that's okay with you. It's your gambling case."

"That's fine. I'll be happy to help you out. And if you can make an arrest for conspiracy based on his information, I'll drop the felony down as he asked."

"That's great. I really appreciate it," said Jake. "Let's get them in here and give them the good news."

Green and Messina were indeed pleased and waited while I phoned the Lab to set up the polygraph exam.

"How's eleven o'clock tomorrow morning?" I asked, looking at the lying old bastard.

"Fine with me," said Whitey.

"I really don't have to be there," said Sam Green.

I got back on the phone and finalized the appointment. "It's in Nassau County, Mr. Messina. Do you need transportation?"

"Nah, I got wheels. Give me directions and I'll be there."

We got up and the attorneys began a round of hand shakes. I walked out to avoid that scene. I'd be damned if I would shake that liar's hand. What the hell was he trying to do? He had to know the polygraph would blow him out of the water, didn't he?

On the ride back Jake said, "It seems we finally may be getting some-where. This could be our break."

"Let's not hold our breath. Let's see what the box has to say about Whitey Messina."

"He sounded believable to me."

"He's lying. You'll see."

The next morning I helped the polygraph examiner, Detective Lloyd Jamison, frame the questions and I watched through the one-way mirror as he administered the test to Messina. When it was over Lloyd unhooked him and stepped into the viewing room.

"Lying?" I asked.

"No, one hundred percent truthful. On everything."

"Lloyd, are you sure? I can't believe it."

"Shouldn't you be happy that he tested truthful? He is helping your case, isn't he? Or am I missing something here?"

"No, you're right. There's just something about him that gives me the creeps. I appreciate your work. I'm sorry if I sounded as if I didn't trust your judgment."

"No offense taken. You want to give him the good news?"

"Would you do that for me? And then send him on his way? I just don't want to deal with him now. Tell him I'll contact him when the written transcripts of his story are ready for his signature. Do that for me?"

"Sure, go ahead. I'll handle it."

"Thanks, I owe you one. I'm going back to the office."

I had a lot to think about. It was Friday, August 13, and I wouldn't get to see Niki until late Monday when I was working four to twelve. Despite the volunteered information and the polygraph results I couldn't believe the story. I was so upset with the blow job allegation that I failed to grasp the greater crime—Marty and Niki conspired to kill Laura by actively soliciting a hit man to do the job. When they found it was too expensive, they did the murder themselves.

I explored every angle to find a way out for Niki and I couldn't find one. I had to confront her with this right away, and I prayed and hoped and prayed some more, that the woman I had fallen for could explain her way out of this situation credibly and believably. She was not involved in

Laura's murder. She swore to me that she wasn't. She loves me. She'd never give that old bookmaker a blow job. Not my Niki. No way.

The weekend passed in a fog and I averaged no more than two or three troubled hours of sleep a night. Jeanie became more concerned over my appearance and lack of appetite for food and for her. I explained it away with the Samuels case telling her the Messina story, not all of it of course, and how we now might be ready to make an arrest for conspiracy. I said I had to work on getting all my ducks in a row, so we would do it right, with no mistakes. She seemed sympathetic and left me alone with my thoughts.

On Monday I drove down to Jones beach and lay on a blanket in the hot sand trying to collect my thoughts. I was able to nap for four hours and had time for a twenty minute swim in the cool surf before heading home. Although I was refreshed, I still had no answers. It would be up to Niki to provide them.

When I got into the office I ordered up the latest photo of Anthony "Whitey" Messina and put it in my shirt pocket after it rolled off the printer. At 6:30 I headed out the door telling Manny Perez to call me if he needed me.

Niki buzzed me up and greeted me with her usual big hug and kiss. She stepped back, looked at me and said, "What's the matter?"

"Nothing, why?"

"You feel all tensed up and you don't look good. You're not having second thoughts about our escape are you?"

"No, of course not. I need a drink."

"Tough day?"

"Tough week."

"What happened? Wait, let me fix you a drink first. Scotch?"

"Yes, on the rocks."

She brought me the drink and sat next to me on the couch. "You look awful, but at least you have some color back in your face."

"I went down to the beach for a few hours today. I finally got some sleep there."

"Pretty soon that's exactly what we'll have until we decide we had enough—the beautiful, warm beach. Now tell me about your tough week."

"Some guy comes in with his lawyer trying to cut a deal on a gambling charge and he tells a real unbelievable tale. His name's Anthony Messina. Goes by the nickname of Whitey. Ever hear of him?"

"No. Should I know him?"

"He claims to know you. Here's his picture," I said, pulling the mug shot out of my pocket and handing it to Niki.

"Oh, yeah, I know this guy, but I didn't know his name."

"How do you know him?"

"He's the local bookie. He comes into Vito's a lot. Marty used to bet with him once in a while."

"When was the last time you saw him? Can you remember?"

"Let me think—somewhere around early June. I don't recall seeing him after that."

"Did you have a couple of conversations with him around that time?"

"You know I don't gamble."

"Did you speak with him at all, on any topic?"

"No, Danny. Where is this going? I feel you're interrogating me."

"I'm sorry, that's just the detective in me. Please, bear with me. You never had a private conversation with him?"

"Never."

"He says you did. He says that you asked him to find, and hire, a hit man."

"You've got to be kidding! That's absurd!"

"There's more. He says you balked at the high price so you gave him a blow job to knock it down $5,000."

Niki opened her mouth and stared at me. She took a large swallow from my scotch. "My God! Who did he tell these lies to?"

"To me, and two assistant district attorneys."

"How could anyone believe that? Danny, you don't...."

"Of course not. He's making it up to get himself a lesser sentence, but I'm not so sure the district attorneys believe he's lying."

"Then they're awfully stupid," she said. "How can they not see through this sham? It's obvious to me."

"What's obvious?"

"Come on, it's Marty. He's the one behind this lie. Whitey is Marty's guy. Marty took some of the house money and bought him off. He's trying to blame the murder on me. Why can't they see that?"

I wanted to believe her and she had given a plausible explanation, but after a minute of acceptance I realized it was full of holes—huge holes. If Marty were trying to fix the blame on Niki, why did Whitey implicate him all the way with *we* and *talk it over*? And the biggest hole—the polygraph test. I chose not to mention that to her. She would only pooh-pooh the results anyway based on her past experiences. Yeah, it was porous all right, but there was that one thread of hope that she just might be telling the truth. At least, that's what I chose to believe then.

"I'll talk to them, Niki. I'll pull this lying bastard in and sweat the truth out of him for sure."

"Good, but I'm really getting worried now. What will Marty do next to try to frame me? He wants that insurance money so desperately I'm afraid he'll stop at nothing."

"Screw Marty," I said. "He can't frame you because you didn't do it. He did. Besides, we'll be outta here in a couple of weeks."

She smiled and said, "Yes, we will. How are things progressing?"

"Fine. I have an appointment with the divorce lawyer on Wednesday and my pension statements are on the way."

"Mine too," she said. "Oh, Danny, I'm so excited. I can't wait."

"Neither can I."

Despite my lingering doubts we made love slowly and with relaxing satisfaction. We lay next to each other afterwards and made plans for our great escape to paradise. I was happier than I had been in weeks—Niki could work that magic with me every time. It was difficult leaving, but I had to get back to the office before the tour was over. We said good-night with a long, passionate kiss.

"Good-bye, Danny," she said. "I love you more than I've ever loved anyone. I want you to know that, and remember it always."

"And I love you, too."

"Tell me that you really mean it, Danny. Tell me"

"Of course I mean it, you know that."

"Yes, I do, and I really mean it, too. It's important that you know that."

"I know that."

"No, really. You must know that I love you, and that I will always love you. Remember that, Danny. No matter what happens, I will always love you."

"Until the twelfth of never?"

"Beyond the twelfth of never," she said.

With that she kissed me again even more passionately than before, almost desperately. There had been tears in her eyes as she spoke. Her words had been almost a farewell speech, as if she were not going to see me for a long time.

"Gee, Niki," I said, "you sound like we'll never see each other again."

"Don't be silly, but I am going away for a few days."

"Oh, where?"

"Out to Montauk for a vacation with a couple of the paralegals I work with. We got a good mid-week deal and we all need some beach time before the summer ends."

"When will you be back?"

"Friday afternoon."

I checked my schedule book and saw I was doing a four-to-twelve that Friday. "Good," I said. "I'll be able to see you Friday night. How about we have dinner at Victor's?"

"I'd love that. I'll miss you so much."

"Friday will be here before we know it," I said

"Yes it will," she smiled, kissing me one more time.

I drove back to the office. I couldn't shake the feeling that something was not quite right. Her explanation of the Whitey incident still troubled me, but there was something else. Then it hit me. She had said, "We all need some beach time before summer ends." But wasn't she supposed to be shortly escaping with me to a beach paradise. Or was that just a slip of the tongue, and she only meant the others? Or am I being paranoid? Or was I looking for a reason—any reason—not to go through with this crazy plan after all.

Chapter 8

The next day I stayed in the office and tried to figure things out. My pension statement had arrived and it showed I had $22,382 that I could cash out right now based on my contributions and interest during my twelve years on the job. Since I had over ten years in, I also had a vested interest of about 30 percent of my final salary, but I couldn't begin to collect that until I was age 55.

As I reviewed the figures I looked up at Ray's office door and wondered if I was really going to walk in there in two weeks, put my gun and shield on his desk and say, "I quit." And then go home and say to Jeanie, "I quit my job and now I'm quitting the marriage." And then kiss the kids good-bye, grab my clothes and walk out of their lives forever. Could I really do that? Would I really do that?

That was the plan, wasn't it? All this was to be given up for Niki and given up willingly, but now things were not adding up. I could not shake the apparent truth of Whitey Messina's story, and it confirmed our theory of the murder. Niki had driven out to Woodmere that night and entered the house with the duct tape, toluene and plastic bag, wearing her ski mask to avoid recognition. They murdered Laura and then Marty took a small dose of the toluene after they staged a burglary. Niki left with the evidence, but forgot the ski mask. Now all they had to do was collect the insurance money and live happily ever after. But there was a fly in the ointment—the money was not forthcoming, so they turned on each other. Niki now claimed Marty was trying to frame her for the murder which made some sense. If Niki gets convicted, Marty gets the money. At the same time Niki was working with me to help arrest Marty. And just what does she get out of it? Why me of course, with my big 22 grand and a divorce settlement looming. There'll be no Manhattan high life for her on that—so why? Because she loves me, that's why. What were her words? I will always love you, Danny. No matter what happens, I will always love you. Beyond the twelfth of never.

I stayed late at Mulvaney's that night to avoid going home and I drank a bit too much. At the squad meeting Finn had asked if I'd heard from Jake Ellison yet and was surprised I hadn't, figuring we should be working on the conspiracy charge. I agreed and promised to touch base with Jake the next day.

I was a little hung over on Friday morning and needed an extra cup of coffee and a couple of aspirins to get my head straight. I called Jake, but he was in court so I left a message for him. The last thing I wanted was to work on a conspiracy case against Niki and Marty. I secretly hoped that the testimony of one underworld gambler with a long arrest record and a plea-bargain in the works would not be enough for a judge to issue an arrest warrant, or for a grand jury to hand up an indictment. I was certain we needed more, but maybe the ski mask might tilt the balance.

I walked to lunch and stopped at the lawyer's office which was near the court buildings. His name was Wilt Harkins and though I did not know him personally, he came highly recommended by Jeff Levy. We spent a half hour together and I walked out of his office in shock. Wilt was a no-nonsense tell-'em-like-it-is attorney who pulled no punches.

"Figure ten grand for me and fifteen grand for her lawyer, minimum," he said. "She gets custody of the kids and the use of the house until the kids are emancipated. That's 21 years old in New York, 22 if they go to college. Then the house gets sold and you split the proceeds. She gets minimal maintenance since she has a decent job—that's a lucky break for you, but your child support payments for two kids are 25 percent of your gross income, meaning before taxes."

"Suppose I have no job?"

"If you change jobs or voluntarily reduce your income you are still liable for the original 25 percent which was in effect when you filed the papers. If it amounted to $20,000 it stays at $20,000—unless you get an increase—then it goes up."

"Somehow this doesn't sound fair, Wilt."

He laughed out loud and said, "Fair? Who the hell told you that anything is fair? Life? The criminal justice system? You know they're not fair, and the civil justice system is the un-fairest of them all."

"I appreciate your straight forwardness," I said, "but I have to feel I'm getting the shaft."

"You are," he said. "You might want to re-think this. Maybe you and the wife just need a vacation or some counseling, and not a divorce."

"I'll do that. Thanks for the advice."

I lost my appetite after that informative session so I walked over to the county court building and went up to see Jake. The receptionist buzzed him and said, "I'm sorry Danny, he's in conference with Barry and a few other people."

"Please ask him to call me when he gets a chance."

"Sure thing," she said, reaching for her message pad.

Back at the office I called Niki on her cell phone, but got her voice mail so I left a message for her to give me a call when she got off the beach while I'm trapped in my stuffy office on this beautiful August day.

By lunch time neither Jake nor Niki had gotten back to me. I was going to try Niki again, but then I figured maybe she needed these three days to think things out. I certainly was thinking constantly, and now that I had not seen her for a couple of days, I was really questioning my decision for the future. Why couldn't we just keep going as we had been for a little while longer? Maybe wait until after Christmas to make sure we really want to take such a drastic plunge.

I spoke with Finn to let him know I was trying to get hold of Jake or Barry to no avail. "That's odd," he said. "I put a call into them this morning myself and didn't get a call back."

"Maybe they have a hot one going on."

"Like what? What could they have so hot that we wouldn't be in on?"

"Good point. Who knows?"

Finally, at two o'clock, Finn came out of his office and said, "Barry Walsh just called and he wants me, you and the boss over there now to discuss the conspiracy case against Marty and Nicole. They've all had their heads together the last few days exploring the legal angles and now it's decision time."

I thought of Niki enjoying her last afternoon in Montauk and hoped that the great legal minds in the Homicide Bureau had decided that there just wasn't enough to pursue a conspiracy case. I'd know soon enough, and tonight I'd be with her once again, hopefully bringing good news.

We assembled in the conference room and sat around the table—me, Ray, Finn, Jake and Barry. Barry who was at the head of the table arose and said, "Excuse me a minute there are two more joining us."

He opened a door and two men in suits entered. I noticed that Ray looked at the older of the two with a quizzical expression as if he might have recognized him. They did not take seats and the older one spoke. "I am Captain Michael Jenkins and this is Sergeant Gerard McHale. We are assigned to the Internal Affairs Division."

He looked directly at me and said, "Detective Daniel Boyland, I am placing you under arrest for the murder of Laura Samuels and the attempted murder of Martin Samuels. I am also suspending you from the Force without pay pending a resolution of these charges. Please give your gun, shield, and cell phone to Sergeant McHale."

For a moment I was stunned, but then it dawned on me. "Very funny, you guys—breaking my balls because I couldn't make an arrest. Pretty good scam. You had me going there for a few seconds, but this doesn't nearly measure up to the jokes played on me when I was a rookie in the squad."

"I'm serious, Boyland." said Jenkins, "Hand those items over now."

"Yeah, yeah, sure," I said. "Who are you anyway? Some defense attorney that Barry commandeered in the hall?"

Jenkins pulled out his shield and ID card and stuck them a few inches from my nose. I looked around the table. Barry and Jake sat quietly with their heads bowed so as not to look me in the eyes. Ray and Sergeant Finn looked perplexed, and they were not smiling. Ray said, "Captain, what the hell is going on here?"

"It's as I said. Now, will your man comply with a lawful order, or not?"

I didn't like the way this was going, so I said, "No problem, I'll play along. Here's my stuff. I gave McHale my gun, shield, ID and cell phone. "Want my cuffs, too?"

"Yes," said the captain, "and we'll also take your extra ammo clips."

I handed them over and said, "How long are you going to keep this up?"

"For the last time, Boyland, this is no joke. Now please empty your pockets out onto the table."

I complied, placing my wallet, handkerchief, pocket comb, a small pen knife and my loose change on the table in front of me. Ray stood up and said, "Captain, may I have a word with you outside? As Danny's commanding officer I believe I'm entitled to know what's going on."

The captain hesitated then nodded and they proceeded out into the hall. They returned after a few minutes and sat down. Ray looked as white as a ghost and I was starting to realize that something very bad was going down. Captain Jenkins said to Sergeant McHale, "Gerry, please inventory these items as we go through them."

The sergeant took out a pad and listed all the items both personal and department property and then opened up my wallet and began to list each item it contained separately—pictures of Jeanie and the kids, police association cards, registration, license, and then McHale said, "A driver's license in the name of Arthur Davis with Detective Boyland's picture on it."

"What?" I asked. "My picture? What's going on here? Let me see that."

McHale slid the license to Ray and said, "Please show that to Detective Boyland, but keep it in your possession, Lieutenant."

It was my picture all right, and the name was indeed an Arthur Davis with a Forest Hills address. I was mystified. "I have no idea how this license came to be in my wallet," I said.

"We didn't plant it there," said Captain Jenkins.

"I'm not suggesting you did. I saw it come out of the wallet, but somebody planted it in there."

The next item McHale noted was one of my business cards, the one I recorded Niki's phone number and license plate number on. "Before I ask you about these numbers," said Jenkins, "I am going to officially advise you of your rights."

He removed a card from his briefcase and read me the Miranda warnings and concluded, "Do you wish to answer my questions now, without an attorney present?" I detected a slight shake of Ray's head out of the corner of my eye and I said, "That depends. You have to give me some reason for arresting me for murder. I mean you have to know I got to the scene after the murder took place. Remember?"

"So you say Detective Boyland, but we have evidence to the contrary and very strong physical evidence to tie you to this crime."

"Such as?"

Jenkins looked at Barry Walsh. Barry said, "Danny, Nicole Wells, over the past few days, has given us a detailed affidavit relating your affair with her and your admissions to her concerning the death of Laura Samuels and the attempted murder of Martin Samuels. She provided us with information that enabled us to execute a search warrant at your home this morning. In your garage we found a tan plastic garbage bag containing a roll of duct tape, a bottle labeled 'toluene' with approximately a half inch of liquid remaining in it, and a quantity of absorbent cotton rolled in paper. Those items have been delivered to the Lab and we are now awaiting their preliminary findings."

"Search warrant? My garage? What the hell is happening here? Jeanie! Does she know about this?"

"She was home when we executed the warrant and she called her office to tell them she was not coming in today," said Jenkins.

The information was overwhelming me. I felt I was in a heavyweight match with Mike Tyson and he was pummeling me senseless with punch after punch to my head. I looked around the table. Ray was stone faced. Francis had his head leaning on one hand.

"I don't know what to say other than this is some huge mistake or I'm being set-up." Then thinking about Ray's head shake, I did the smartest thing that I'd done in the last month. I said, "No, I do not want to answer any questions until I can confer with my attorney."

Everyone except the two Internal Affairs officers seemed relieved with my decision.

"There's the phone," snapped Jenkins, pointing to the wall. "Make your call."

I thought for a moment and then asked Jake if he had Jeff Levy's number. Jake removed a card from his wallet and handed it to me with what I perceived was an affirmative nod and a slight smile, indicating to me that I had made a good choice. I got up on shaky legs and walked to the wall phone and dialed Jeff's number at Cartman and Zuckerman. Fortunately, he was in his office and the operator put me right through.

"Jeff," I said, "it's Danny Boyland. I need your help."

"Sure, what's up?"

"I...I..." That was all I could get out. I slumped into the wall and the receiver slipped from my hand and banged to the floor. Barry rushed over and picked up the phone and Ray came over and helped me to a chair.

"Jeff, this is Barry Walsh. Danny's very upset. We have just arrested him and he asked for you to represent him."

They spoke a few more minutes and when Barry hung up the phone he said, "Jeff's on his way from Garden City. He should be here in ten minutes. Captain, can we wait on the arraignment until he gets here?"

"Sure," said Jenkins, "we have to wait for the Lab results anyway."

"Captain?" asked Ray. "I'd like to ask a favor."

"What is it, Lieutenant?"

"I'd like for Danny to be processed here prior to the arraignment. I don't want him dragged over to headquarters to do it. I am very familiar with this case and I find these charges impossible to believe. And Captain, please remember, he is one of our own."

"We can do that," he said, softening a bit.

"Thank you, sir."

Barry called his secretary and asked her to bring in a pot of coffee as we waited for Jeff to arrive.

"Ray," I said, "would you please call Jeanie for me and fill her in?"

"I will, and then Francis and I will visit her personally this afternoon when we get more information."

"Thanks, Boss, I really appreciate it."

Barry's secretary brought the coffee in and handed him a note. When she left Barry said, "It's from Inspector Naylor in the Police Lab."

He walked over to the wall phone and dialed Naylor and they spoke for a few moments. After Barry hung up he said, "They have some answers, Captain."

"Well, you may as well divulge them; the defense is entitled to lab results on discovery down the road anyway."

"All right. The end of the piece of tape removed from the mouth of Marty matches the end left on the roll found in the garage. Chemical tests to confirm that are being done now. The liquid in the bottle is definitely toluene. The plastic bag has a tiny corner missing which matches the piece found on the piece of tape that came from Laura's mouth." Barry paused and glanced around the room seeming to hesitate before continuing. "A latent print found on the toluene bottle matches Detective Boyland's right index finger and a second latent found on the surface of the roll of duct tape matches his left thumb."

"Impossible!" I shouted, "I never saw those items! This is a set-up!"

"Calm down," said Ray. "We'll get to the bottom of this."

The wall phone buzzed and Jake picked it up and announced, "Jeff's here. I'll go get him."

Jake returned shortly and introduced Jeff to the IAD officers. Captain Jenkins summarized the charges and evidence for him and Jeff said, "I'd like some time with Danny alone and then we'll let you know if he'll give a statement or answer any of your questions."

"That will be fine, Mr. Levy. We'll be waiting."

Jake showed us into an unused office and closed the door as he left.

"Danny this is mind-boggling. What's going on here?"

"You're asking me? I certainly didn't murder anyone, but I know who did and now they are setting me up for the fall."

"Let's hear all about it."

I told him everything—only a fool withholds information from his lawyer. When I finished I said, "Jeff, I don't know how I'm going to pay you even if you give me a police discount. I've been suspended without pay."

"Don't concern yourself with that now. I want you to prepare a brief statement and that is all we are going to give them. We will answer no questions."

When we returned to the conference room Jeff said, "I have discussed these charges with my client and he vehemently denies them and intends to fight them vigorously. He has prepared a hand-written statement which he will now read to you. You may have this statement typed and he will sign it under oath and I will witness it. Danny?"

Jeff handed me the statement I had just written out and I read it to all in the room:

"I received a call at 3:38 a.m. on June 10. I was at home in bed with my wife at the time I received the call. I was informed by Central Detectives that a homicide had occurred in Woodmere and I proceeded to the scene arriving at about 4:40 a.m. Laura Samuels was dead prior to my arrival. My investigation concluded that Laura was murdered by her husband, Martin, acting in concert with Nicole Wells, a paralegal at his law firm with whom he was having an affair. The motives were a one million dollar insurance settlement and the continuance of their affair now that Laura was out of the way.

"I was unable to make an arrest as Martin Samuels refused to answer my questions and obtained a lawyer. Nicole answered my questions and denied her complicity in the murder. About ten days after the murder Nicole began a planned seduction which enticed me into having an affair with her. She told me she now believed Marty had murdered Laura and offered to help me arrest him by getting him to admit the murder on tape.

"Recently, information from a Whitey Messina, given to me and Jake Ellison, convinced us that Marty and Nicole had indeed conspired to murder Laura and we were supposed to be pursuing that conspiracy arrest today when my arrest occurred.

"I believe I have been set up by Nicole and Marty and that they planted the evidence consisting of the tape, toluene and plastic bag in my garage. I believe that Nicole planted a phony driver's license in my wallet for reasons I do not yet know. I believe Nicole felt I was getting close to arresting her and Marty and that they planned this elaborate frame-up to prevent that. I am innocent of these charges and demand the investigation of Marty and Nicole continue with all the resources of the police department and the district attorney's office. I will voluntarily submit to a polygraph examination to verify this statement."

I lowered the paper and looked around the room. It was difficult to tell if anyone there believed what I had just read.

"How do you explain your fingerprints on the roll of tape and toluene bottle?" asked Captain Jenkins.

"My client will answer no questions, Captain," said Jeff. "He stands by his statement and that is all we will say on the matter at this time. After he signs it you may proceed with the arraignment, but let me caution you. When Danny is exonerated of these charges, civil remedies will be instituted against anyone, and everyone, involved in this miscarriage of justice."

Barry called for a typist, and 20 minutes later I signed the statement. Jeff left for his office telling me to plead not guilty and to tell the judge that he was representing me. I was printed and mugged and placed in a holding pen until I was summoned for arraignment at four o'clock. I did as Jeff advised. I was held over without bail and my case was adjourned for two weeks for a hearing, but I figured I would be indicted before that. I was handcuffed and transported by the Department of Corrections to my new temporary home at the Nassau County Jail.

PART TWO

So now you know why I have so much time to write all this down. Not much else to do in my small jail cell, except to read and write. They don't want me near the general population, afraid somebody might not like cops and try to do me some harm. And I'm on a suicide watch, per my lawyer's request. A lot of ex-cops, and disgraced cops, take that route, but Jeff needn't have bothered. Suicide is the last thing I'm thinking about. What I'm thinking about is revenge—revenge on Marty and Niki for ruining my life.

Just as I predicted, I was indicted before my scheduled hearing and a trial date was set for November 1. So far I've been sitting here four weeks and have another six to go, and a lot has happened in that time. Jeanie had me served with divorce papers. She couldn't even wait until the trial was over. I don't believe she thinks I did it, but she knows I cheated on her. She refused to speak to me, so I confessed and begged her forgiveness, using Ray Roberts as the intermediary—to no avail. She wants the house, the kids and the car. And who can blame her? I haven't seen Patrick or Kelly since before my arrest and that's breaking my heart. When will I ever see them again? Read them a story? Take them to the beach? Tuck them in? Did I give all this up for a lying, manipulative bitch?

Jeff hired Lewis Investigations. My old mentor, Willy Edwards, and his partner, Sam Lewis, are digging around on my behalf in preparation for the trial. The department's attitude was 'case closed' by my arrest. The Homicide Squad was directed to not investigate Marty and Niki—after all, the culprit was already in custody. And that's another worry—how do I pay Sam and Willy? And Jeff? And the divorce lawyers? That's why I need money so desperately and why I'm writing so furiously.

Oh, there's another minor thing hanging over my head—the death penalty. The DA has 60 days after indictment to decide if he wants to request the death penalty in a murder case and so far he has not done so. Jeff tells me the chances are remote that he will, but when you're alone in your cell you think the worst as you sit and wait.

So, as I ponder my fate and try to figure out how they framed me so cleverly, my thoughts and dreams often turn to Niki. You are saying, how could he think of that bitch who put him where he is right now? What an idiot, you say - another stupid male who let his brains fall to his balls. And I agree. You're right, but…but when the nights are long and lonely and I lie on my bunk, I do think of Niki standing by her door the last time I ever saw her. I hear her words—the words so full of meaning that I believed them with all my heart and soul, and I still want to believe them. "I will always love you. Remember that, Danny. No matter what happens, I will always love you."

And I smile and say, "Until the twelfth of never?" And she smiles back and says, "Beyond the twelfth of never."

Chapter 9

Four more weeks passed and the DA finally decided that he would not request the death penalty in my case. He took 59 of the 60 days to make up his mind, the sadistic bastard. Ironic, isn't it? I'm breathing a sigh of relief knowing I'm not going to die for a crime I did not commit!

The death penalty is one of those situations I've always wrestled with, just as everyone else has. You would think being a cop, and especially being a homicide detective, that I would want to fry everyone convicted of murder. Not so, for a lot of reasons, the main one being that I know there really are innocent people on death row. I'm not really sure the existence of the death penalty statute is a deterrent to anyone who is bent on killing someone, but I do know this—if you execute someone he will never kill anyone else ever again. If you have no death penalty, what do you do with a guy who murders again and again? Kills a fellow inmate or a corrections officer? Or escapes and kills your wife and kids? What do you do then?

I have a lot of time to think about these big philosophical issues now. It's a mental diversion to take my mind off the upcoming trial. Jeff visits occasionally and brings me reading material and to prepare our defense. Willy Edwards and Sam Lewis stop by once in a while to say hello. They've been digging around, but so far have come up empty. They periodically tail Niki and Marty, but it appears they have had no contact with each other since my arrest. We figure they are staying apart until after the trial, hoping I get convicted. I said, "You watch Willy, within a month after they convict me at trial they'll get the insurance money and you'll see half of it go right to Niki Wells."

"Hey," he said, "don't talk like that. You didn't murder anyone and you're not going to get convicted of anything."

One thing that none of us could figure out was the meaning of the phony driver's license that found its way into my wallet and we still didn't know all the things the prosecution had in their arsenal to throw at me, but we'd sure find out soon enough.

About two weeks before the trial was to begin Jeff got the witness list from the prosecution. The prosecuting attorney would be Paul Valentine, a seasoned member of the Queens Homicide Bureau. Because of my relationships with the Nassau Homicide Bureau prosecutors, they felt it necessary to go to another county to avoid the appearance of favoritism. Jeff met with him and told me he appeared to be a decent guy, but focused on his job, which in this case was to convict me of murder. We looked over the witness list in the small conference room in the jail where they allowed prisoners to confer with their attorneys. The first name on the list was Nicole Wells, the second was Victor Reggio.

"What the hell is Victor going to say?" I asked

"I don't know him," said Jeff. "Apparently you do."

"He's the owner of Victor's Lounge on Queens Boulevard where Niki and I went several times."

"What can he say to damage us?"

"Nothing that I'm aware of other than to say that Niki and I were there, but I already admitted to the affair."

The next on the list was a man by the name of Ronald Millstein, owner of the Boulevard Pharmacy in Rego Park. Neither of us had ever heard of him or had any idea what he would say. I knew most of the rest of the names on the list. They were the expert witnesses from the Lab, the guys from IAD, Doc Maguire who performed the autopsy, and we figured we knew what they would testify to.

"Jeff, who do we have for our side?"

"I'm going to call Sergeant Finn, Detective Brown, maybe Lieutenant Roberts, Detective Perez and Detective Nowicki."

"All those who worked the case with me?"

"Yes, and I also plan to put Barry Walsh and Jake Ellison on the stand."

"Really? Your former fellow prosecutors?"

"They are crucial Danny. It sounds as if they were going to authorize an arrest of Niki and Marty for conspiracy, but switched gears when Niki showed up with her book of lies."

"Anyone else?"

"Marty Samuels, of course—and you—if necessary."

"If you think it's necessary, I'm willing."

"Let's see how things progress. How about Jean?"

"My soon to be ex-wife, who hates my guts?"

"She could be our savior."

"In what way?"

"The medical examiner states that the murder occurred around 1:00 a.m. give or take fifteen minutes, right?"

"Right"

"And where were you at 1:00 a.m.?"

"Sound asleep in bed."

"With Jean?"

"Yes."

"And the phone rang at 3:38 a.m.—we have that documented with the phone records—and you got up to go to the scene."

"Correct."

"So, if you were home in bed sleeping with your wife at the time of the murder, you could not possibly have done it. Will Jean testify to that on your behalf despite the uh…circumstances?"

"I don't know if she would, but your question is a moot one."

"Oh?"

"Jeanie is a very sound sleeper. She didn't hear the phone ring at 3:38 and had no idea that I left the house shortly after. For all she knows I could have left the house at midnight. I called her later in the day and I remember her telling me she hadn't known I was gone until the alarm rang at about 7:00 a.m."

"Dammit!" said Jeff. "I was really counting on that one fact to blow their whole case out of the water."

We sat in dejected silence for a few minutes and then Jeff got up to leave. He said, "Hang in there, Danny; we'll give them a helluva fight. I promise."

"Thanks, Jeff," I said. "I'm sure we will." But after he left I began to worry more and more about my fate. What was Reggio going to say? Who the hell was Ronald Millstein? And what the hell was he going to say?

The first of November finally arrived and I was transported very early in the morning to the Nassau County courthouse and placed in a holding cell. Jeff had Willy drop my clothes off the night before—a charcoal gray pin-striped suit, white shirt, red tie, black socks and shoes. On one of his visits, Willy had told me that he had taken all my clothes, at Jean's request, over to his house. Obviously she wanted no reminders of me around.

I dressed and waited. A correction officer asked if I wanted a buttered roll as he handed me a plastic container of coffee. I told him I was not hungry and he smiled and said, "I can understand that. Good luck today."

At 9:15 I was escorted through the door of the courtroom where the judge comes in and took my place at the defense table with Jeff. As I walked to the table I was shocked to see that the courtroom was full, but I didn't recognize anyone.

"Prospective jurors," said Jeff.

The team from the Queens DA's office arrived and Jeff introduced me to the lead prosecutor, Paul Valentine. At 9:30 the judge entered and we all rose until he took his place at the bench. I knew Judge Alexander Delaney well. He was fair and moved things along, but allowed the attorneys a lot of leeway, providing they didn't go off on irrelevant tangents just to hear themselves talk.

The judge got the preliminaries out of the way in a hurry and told the jury pool to be prepared for a trial of about two weeks based on the current witness list and possibly three weeks if rebuttal witnesses were called.

"Any particular types you're looking for?" I asked Jeff.

"Yeah, twelve males, race and ethnicity do not matter. Preferably all twelve cheated on their wives on at least one occasion."

"Ouch," I said.

"You asked."

The jury was picked and seated by 3:00 p.m. and the judge set opening arguments for the next morning at ten. Jeff had used all his preemptory challenges to eliminate as many women as possible, but we ended up with five anyway.

"At least they're all in the right age group," he said.

"What do you mean?"

"From 25 to 47. I figure they'll be sympathetic because you're such a handsome, Irish devil."

"Or maybe they'll be sympathetic to my wife."

"Could be. You never really know, but I went on the O.J. Simpson comment I had heard as his trial began. A radio show took a call from a black woman who said O.J. would be found innocent whether he did it or not because, 'those black women on the jury ain't never gonna convict a good-looking black man like O.J.—no way.'"

"I hope some of them believe me," I said. "Male, female, black, white. I don't really care."

"We don't need some of them, Danny. We only need one of them."

Paul Valentine started his opening argument at 10:05 the next morning. He was brief, professional and devastating as he explained to the jury what I had been arrested, indicted and was now on trial for, and how he would prove the charges well beyond the shadow of a reasonable doubt. "Ladies and gentlemen of the jury," he said. "The prosecution will show that at or about one o'clock in the morning of June 10, the defendant entered the home of Martin and Laura Samuels with the intent of killing one or both of them. We will show the motive for these crimes and provide testimony and physical evidence linking him with these crimes. At the conclusion of the testimony I'm certain you will all agree that Mr. Daniel Boyland committed these acts and that you will convict him as charged.

"And what are the motives for committing these heinous crimes? Daniel Boyland's motives were obsession and jealousy—obsession with a young woman named Nicole Wells who will be my first witness. She will most definitely explain motive to you.

"Other witnesses will detail the bizarre, elaborate plot conceived by Mr. Boyland to carry out the murder of Laura Samuels and the attempted murder of Martin Samuels—when, where and how he purchased duct tape and toluene, when and where these items were discovered, and how these items are connected to the defendant by solid, scientific evidence. Let me reiterate, ladies and gentlemen, there will be absolutely no doubt in your minds at the conclusion of this trial of the guilt of Daniel Boyland. Thank you."

"Mr. Levy," said Judge Delaney, "you may proceed."

I wondered what Jeff would say to take the edge off of Valentine's presentation. The jury had been paying close attention as he spoke and a couple actually nodded their heads in agreement. He was good all right.

Misinformed, but very good. Jeff walked over to the jury and said, "Not guilty, ladies and gentlemen. Daniel Boyland is not guilty of murder, or attempted murder, despite Mr. Valentine's assertions to the contrary. But Danny is guilty of several other things. Poor judgment—no, make that extremely bad judgment—leading to infidelity and malfeasance in the performance of his sworn duties. That's what Daniel Boyland is guilty of, by his own admission, and he is now paying dearly for those acts.

"Sitting in this courtroom is Danny's wife of eleven years, Jean. His two children, Patrick and Kelly, age nine and six are not here. Jean has filed for divorce and Danny has not seen his children since the day before his arrest some two and a half months ago. Regardless of the outcome of this trial, Danny's family is gone from him forever.

"Also sitting in this courtroom are several of Danny's fellow detectives from the Nassau Homicide Squad, the elite unit to which he will never return. Again, regardless of the outcome of this trial, Danny will never be a member of the New York Metropolitan Police Department in any capacity. He will be fired from the Force.

"No family that he loves, no job that he loves. How did Daniel Boyland get to this point in his life? Mr. Valentine already told you the answer. It is in the person of his first witness, Nicole Wells. Daniel Boyland was deliberately entrapped into an affair with Miss Wells. When Mr. Valentine referred to a 'bizarre, elaborate plot,' he was correct. But the plot was spun by Nicole Wells and Martin Samuels, and carried out with deadly consequences to Laura Samuels and Daniel Boyland.

"Martin Samuels and Nicole Wells were about to be arrested for conspiracy to murder Laura Samuels. Daniel Boyland was the lead investigator on the case. A few weeks prior, Nicole realized that Danny was developing information that would eventually lead him to the truth in this case, the truth that she and Martin Samuels murdered Laura Samuels. And they did that heinous murder for two reasons—to continue their love affair and to collect the life insurance money on Laura—a sum of one million dollars."

Jeff definitely had the jury's attention. They hung on his every word. I think they realized that this trial was going to be a real-life soap opera. Jeff continued, "My client is not guilty of murder. Daniel Boyland is the victim, the patsy if you will, in a carefully conceived, well-executed frame-up. I will show you the real murderers, ladies and gentlemen, one of whom is Nicole Wells, Mr. Valentine's star witness."

He turned to Valentine and said, "Please Mr. Valentine, feel free to call your first witness."

There was dead silence in the courtroom for a moment as I admired Jeff Levy for his magnificent presentation. Judge Delaney called a ten minute recess and asked both attorneys to approach the bench. Jeff was smiling when he returned.

"What's up?" I asked.

"Delaney asked me if I was going to try to pull a Perry Mason exposé of the real murderer and I said, 'I'm going to do my best, your honor.' Then he admonished me to remember who was on trial here and to cross-examine the prosecution witness accordingly."

"Is that going to hamper you, Jeff?"

"I don't think so, but I have to be careful since I've already been warned. But now we're ready to rock and roll. Take this yellow pad and note any and all discrepancies and lies in her testimony. Pass the pad to me so I can read them as they occur. Don't say anything—no outbursts of denial, no facial expressions, no throwing up your hands in horror."

"I got it."

"Your honor," said Valentine, "the prosecution calls Nicole Wells."

All eyes turned as the courtroom doors were opened by a uniformed court officer and Niki began the walk down the center aisle toward the witness stand. I remembered making that walk countless times in my career. The courtrooms in this building were imposing and intimidating—high ceilings, tall windows and a long distance from back to front. It was as if you were walking a gauntlet or the proverbial "last mile" to the execution chamber. I used to fix my eyes on the objective—the witness chair—and breathe deeply, controlling my pace, resisting the urge to run. And no matter how many times I did it, no matter if I knew the judge, the bailiff, the stenographer and all the attorneys, I would always get butterflies in my stomach and a slight feeling of panic, both of which did not go away until well after I was sworn in and into the first few questions.

I wondered what Niki was feeling as she walked in controlled, measured steps down the aisle. Her clicking heels were the only sound in the cavernous courtroom. I tried to avoid turning around with the rest of the spectators, but couldn't avoid it. When I did, I spotted Jeanie staring at me with pure hatred in her eyes. She watched me watch Niki, who did not glance my way as she went by. She was sworn in and took her seat. She then looked directly at me and, if I were able to read her mind I would have believed she was saying, "Danny, I will always love you." But that couldn't be true for she was here to destroy me, not to love me. She was dressed conservatively in a dark blue suit. The skirt fell to just below her knees and she wore plain medium-heeled shoes. Her hair was pulled back and her makeup was limited. She had on a white blouse buttoned at the neck. With no cleavage and minimal leg showing, she was quite the prim and proper legal assistant and, God help me, I fell in love with her all over again. I smiled as I had a vision of one of those *Twilight Zone* episodes where time and motion stop, except for the two main characters. Niki gets up from the stand, walks down to me, takes my hand and we walk out of the courtroom past the frozen crowd. "Let's go Danny," she smiles. "The plane is waiting to take us to paradise."

My fantasy was broken by the sound of Paul Valentine beginning his first question. He asked her the standard preliminaries—name, address, age, occupation. Then he asked the first question of any consequence—and her first answer was a lie.

"When did you first meet Mr. Boyland?"

"Sometime around the middle of March. Probably on March 16, but I can't be certain."

"Where did you meet him?"

"Victor's Lounge on Queens Boulevard."

"Can you describe the circumstances of that meeting?"

"I was having a drink at the bar. It was about 6:30, 6:45 and I was going to have dinner there."

"Were you alone?"

"Yes, just sitting at the bar, and then Danny came in and sat next to me."

"Danny?"

"Yes. Detective Daniel Boyland."

"Is he in this courtroom?"

"Yes."

"Please point him out, Miss Wells."

"Right there," she said, pointing at me and looking me directly in the eyes.

"What happened then?" asked Valentine.

"He asked if he could buy me a drink and I said okay. We had a couple and we danced a few dances—they have a DJ there. Then he had to leave. I think he said he was working on a case and had to get back to the office for an interview."

"Did you have dinner with him?"

"No. He left and I dined alone."

"When did you see him again, Miss Wells?"

"A week later. We had exchanged cell phone numbers and he called me a few days after we met to set up the date."

"Were you seeing anyone else at the time?"

"Martin Samuels, but that relationship was winding down. At least I thought it was."

"Can you explain that, Miss Wells?"

"I wanted the affair to end, but he didn't."

"Did Detective Boyland become aware of your affair with Marty?"

"Yes, I had to tell him because Marty was becoming obsessive and wouldn't leave me alone."

"What did Detective Boyland say when you told him that?"

"He said, 'Don't worry Niki, if he doesn't back off I'll take care of him.'"

"Did he explain what he meant by 'take care of him?'"

"No, not then."

I began to write on the pad again. My first entry had been about her response to the first question. I had written, "March 16? A lie! First met her a week after the murder, on June 17." Now I wrote, "A lie! I never said that!"

"What happened then, Miss Wells?"

"We got into a serious relationship."

"Were you in love with Daniel Boyland?"

"Yes."

"Did he say he was in love with you?"

"Yes," she said, looking at me. I could feel Jeanie's eyes drilling into the back of my head at warp speed.

"How long did this affair last?"

"Right up to the time I voluntarily went to see Mr. Walsh in the DA's office," she said.

"Why did you do that?"

"Because I finally became convinced that Danny had tried to kill Marty and actually did kill Laura."

"How did you become convinced?"

"By a lot of things that finally added up. When Marty kept refusing to leave me alone, Danny asked me on several occasions if I wanted him to make Marty back off. He got extremely angry when I told him that Marty threatened to blackball me at work by giving me a bad review. He said, 'I'll kill that son-of-a-bitch.'"

"Another lie—she got a good review and a raise," I wrote on the pad as Valentine followed up and asked, "Detective Boyland actually used the word, 'kill'?"

"Yes, he did."

"Did Marty ever stop trying to get you back into the relationship?"

"No, and Danny was really getting angry. I was afraid of losing him. I was afraid he might have thought I didn't want to really break it off with Marty, so one night I said to him, 'Danny, why not talk to him. Get him to leave me alone,' and that's when he said it."

"Said what, Miss Wells?"

"He said, 'I've got this guy figured out. Pretty soon he won't bother you or anyone else anymore.'"

"Did he elaborate on that statement?"

"No. I told him don't you dare do anything drastic, just talk to him. He just smiled and told me not to worry. He said he would take care of Marty once and for all. All he would tell me was that he knew about these things and that he read a lot of books."

"Any idea what he meant by that?"

"Not at that time, but later I did."

"When was that?"

"The night before I went to see the DA, the night he was at my apartment and confessed to me."

"What did he confess to you?"

Nicole lowered her head and said, "The murders of Laura Samuels and Marty Samuels."

Everyone in the courtroom sat in stunned silence as Nicole uttered these words.

"Miss Wells, may I remind you that Marty Samuels is alive. I don't understand your response."

"I'm sorry, Mr. Valentine. You're correct of course, but Danny made a huge mistake. He told me he was supposed to murder only Marty and give a small dose of the toluene to Laura so she wouldn't awaken, but the result was the opposite."

"Daniel Boyland actually described the murder to you?"

"Not in all the details, but he did tell me that Laura woke up and began to struggle as he was putting the toluene-soaked cotton on her face. Then Marty began to stir so he switched the toluene to him, but Laura was not out, so he switched back to her, and put his hands around her neck to hasten her into unconsciousness. Then he went back to Marty and thought he gave him a large enough dose to kill him, but obviously a lot of the liquid had evaporated from the cotton. The result was Laura's death and not Marty's."

"Did he tell you that he faked a burglary?"

"No, I read about that in the papers, but he said not to ask him any questions about the case. In fact, he said we were not to talk about it ever again."

"So why did he confess to you?"

"I made it a condition of our continuing the relationship. I told him I could deal with the truth, but I couldn't live with a liar. I was hoping, desperately hoping, that he didn't do it and that he would convince me of that. However, he told me he did it and did it for me. He said he couldn't bear the thought of me being with another man, past or present."

"Did he tell you what he did with the tape and toluene?"

"He admitted that he was shaken with the turn of events, the struggles that he hadn't expected. He got out of there fast and sped home. After all, he was the on-call homicide detective that night and knew that his phone would ring when the murder was discovered, so he hid the tape and toluene in his garage and got back into bed."

Paul Valentine thought a moment and said, "Thank you, Miss Wells. I have no further questions."

I wrote on the pad, "The whole story is one big fucking lie," and passed it over to Jeff. He glanced at it, nodded his head, rose from his chair and stood about ten feet from Niki. He took a long time before he asked his first question.

"Miss Wells, before today when was the last time you saw Daniel Boyland?"

"It was on August 16, I believe."

"Was that the night you told him you were going to Montauk for the next few days with two of your co-workers from your office?"

"Yes."

"But you didn't go to Montauk at all, did you?"

"No."

"So you lied to him. Is that correct?"

"Yes."

"You lied to him because you knew you were going to see the district attorney the very next day. Is that correct?"

"Yes."

"When you went to see Mr. Walsh did you bring an attorney with you?"

"Yes."

"What is his name and affiliation?"

"Bradley Steiner. He's in the criminal law department at the firm where I work."

"And when did you first retain the services of Mr. Steiner?"

"About two weeks prior to the meeting, I believe it was on August 1."

"Why did you feel you needed the services of an attorney?"

"I...uh...started to feel that Marty was going to try to blame Laura's murder on me."

"On you? But didn't you testify that Detective Boyland confessed to committing the murder himself?"

"Yes, but that was later. After I hired Mr. Steiner."

"Wasn't the real reason you hired Mr. Steiner the fact that you thought Danny was getting close to discovering the real killers—you and Martin Samuels..."

"Objection!" shouted Valentine, "Miss Wells is not on trial your honor."

"I'll allow it, Mr. Valentine. Answer the question Miss Wells."

"I did not kill Laura Samuels. Danny had nothing to discover," she replied.

"What else did you tell Danny on the evening of August 16?"

"I don't recall."

"Did you tell him that you loved him?"

"Yes."

"Did you tell him that no matter what happened you would always love him?"

"Yes."

"Another lie. Isn't that correct, Miss Wells?"

"Uh...no...not really," she said.

"Not really? You were going to betray him the very next day—a man who you say is a murderer—a man who confessed murder to you. And now you are telling this court that you still love him?"

"I don't know, Mr. Levy. Sometimes you can't turn off your feelings. I did love him very much and then he told me he killed Laura Samuels, and I became...confused."

"Are you still confused over your feelings about Danny Boyland?"

"Yes."

"Then is it possible that you're confused about who really murdered Laura Samuels?"

"No. Danny confessed to me that he did it."

"Do you have his confession on tape?"

"No."

"To your knowledge has he confessed to anyone else?"

"No."

"So basically, it's your word against his. Correct Miss Wells?"

"I guess so."

"Miss Wells, I am going to excuse you for now, but I may recall you after I've put my witnesses on. Please don't leave the jurisdiction of the court."

The judge broke for lunch and I told Jeff that he was doing a great job. "We'll see how great I am when you walk out the door," he said. "If I do call her back I'll try to discredit her further—catch her in more lies."

"How can you be certain?"

"I believe Nicole Wells is torn very strongly between her self-preservation and her feelings for you. She is, in my opinion, still very much in love with you, but in order to save her own ass, she has to fry yours."

"Maybe Marty killed Laura by himself," I said.

"Really? You're still in love with her, aren't you?"

"I...uh...yeah. I suppose I am."

"How tragic, Danny. How very tragic," he said, shaking his head.

Chapter 10

It didn't take long to find out Victor Reggio's part in this case. He testified that I first started coming into his place on or about the same date that Niki had mentioned in her testimony. How convenient! Jeff couldn't shake him, but it was obvious to me he was lying his ass off. I hoped the jury got the same impression. Jeff asked if Niki paid him to testify on her behalf or promised him any other consideration.

"No."

"Did you and Nicole Wells ever date? Ever have an affair?"

"No."

"Ever have a drink with her at your bar?"

"Yes."

"Ever have a few dances with her?"

"Yes, once in a while."

"Ever kiss her?"

"No."

"Are you aware of the penalties for perjury? For lying on the witness stand, Mr. Reggio?" Jeff asked, raising his voice.

Reggio shifted in his seat and quietly answered, "Yes."

"You're excused, subject to recall. You might use that time to re-read the perjury statutes."

"Your honor," said Valentine getting to his feet, "Mr. Levy is impugning and badgering my witness. I ask…"

"I agree, Mr. Valentine," said Delaney, "Mr. Levy, please refrain from such behavior in the future."

"Yes, your honor. I apologize."

"Accepted. Call your next witness, Mr. Valentine."

He called Ronald Millstein. Finally we would find out what he was all about. Victor Reggio had looked as I remembered him—a tall, handsome guy in his early 40s. He had curly black hair with a hint of gray beginning at the temples and projected confidence and strength, but Jeff had shaken him. Millstein, on the other hand, was anything but confident. He was also tall, about six feet, but lean with thinning brown hair. He wore steel rimmed glasses and had the bearing of a college professor. He stuttered and stumbled over Valentine's first few questions and looked as if he'd rather be on a bed of hot coals than in this courtroom. I certainly agreed with him on that feeling.

"Now, Mr. Millstein, have you ever sold toluene in your pharmacy?"

"Yes, I have," he replied.

"Why would people use this substance?"

"Experimenters use it for various processes."

"Amateur chemists?"

"Yes, and also by those who build model airplanes and ships. It's used as a solvent for the glue employed in the assembly of the parts."

"Any other reasons for someone to purchase toluene?"

"Unfortunately, it's occasionally abused for the purpose of getting a 'high' by inhaling it or sniffing it."

"Do you need a license or permit to purchase it?"

"No. It's not an illegal item, nor is it a controlled substance, but I am required to keep records of the purchase by the DEA."

"The Drug Enforcement Administration? Why, Mr. Millstein?"

"Solvents such as toluene, acetone, chloroform, methylethylketone and others can be employed in the manufacture of illegal drugs."

"Do you report all such sales to the DEA?"

"Only if the amounts are excessive, but I keep a record book subject to their inspection."

Valentine walked over to the prosecution table and picked up a bound black ledger. He handed it to Millstein and asked, "Is this your record book for the current year wherein you record the sales of these sub-stances?"

"Yes, it is."

"I wish to draw the court's and jury's attention to the fact that this is a bound ledger containing 100 numbered pages. None of the pages is miss-ing. Mr. Millstein, I ask you to please turn to page 12 of the ledger."

Millstein adjusted his glasses and opened the book. "I have page 12."

"About one-third of the way down the page there is an entry for the sale of toluene on May 26. Do you see it?"

"Yes."

"Please read the entry."

"May 26—one pint toluene, USP Grade—sold to Arthur Davis, Forest Hills, NY—Driver's license #945839796 NY."

"Thank you. Now Mr. Millstein do you recognize Mr. Davis in this courtroom?"

"Yes," he said pointing at me. "That's him."

Valentine feigned surprise and said, "Are you sure, Mr. Millstein? That man you're pointing at is the defendant in this case, Detective Daniel Boyland."

"I don't know what he calls himself, but he's the guy I sold the toluene to on May 26. No doubt at all."

"How can you be positive?"

"First, I recognize him, and second, his picture was on the driver's license he showed me for identification."

Valentine returned to his table and came back with a small object in his hand which he handed to Millstein. "Does this look familiar?" he asked.

"That's the license he produced. That's his picture and the number matches what I recorded in my ledger."

"Thank you, Mr. Millstein. Your honor, I would like to offer this ledger into evidence at this time as Exhibit A. I will offer the license after further testimony."

The judge inspected the ledger and had it brought over to our table where Jeff and I looked it over. "I have no objection," said Jeff.

Valentine passed the ledger around to the members of the jury who studied it carefully and then Judge Delaney had it marked into evidence.

"Did Mr. Davis—strike that—did Detective Boyland, the man you identified as Mr. Davis, purchase any other items in addition to the pint of toluene?"

"A roll of duct tape and two large boxes of absorbent cotton."

"Do you place labels on the products you sell identifying your store Mr. Millstein?"

"Sometimes. There should be a label on the toluene bottle just underneath the manufacturer's label, but not on the tape or cotton."

Again Valentine went back to the table and reached into a plastic bag withdrawing a brown bottle which he held by the cap with the bottom resting on the palm of his other hand. "Your honor, I will lay the foundation for this exhibit with another witness, but I ask permission to show the bottle to Mr. Millstein for identification purposes only at this time."

"Objection," said Jeff.

"Overruled," said Delaney. "Proceed, Mr. Valentine."

Millstein identified the bottle of toluene as a brand he carried and pointed out the Boulevard Pharmacy sticker at the place he said it would be. He also identified the duct tape and cotton that Valentine produced from the bag as being similar to the types that he carried in his store.

"I have no further questions your honor," said Valentine.

As Jeff rose to begin his cross-examination he slid his legal pad over to me. He had written, "I think Millstein translates from German or Yiddish to Millstone. I'm afraid he has hung a big one around our necks."

"Mr. Millstein, how long did it take you to duplicate this ledger adding Arthur Davis's name to page 12?"

"What? Duplicate? I did no such thing!"

Boy, Jeff had gone right to the throat with that one—and it definitely had an effect on the pharmacist.

"Do you know Nicole Wells, a paralegal employed at the law firm of Keenan, Rosen, and Vario on Queens Boulevard?"

"Uh…yes…a lot of the employees of that firm shop in my store."

"She was the one you sold the toluene and tape and cotton to, wasn't she, Mr. Millstein?—not Detective Boyland."

"No, I sold it to him," he said, again pointing at me.

"Did you ever date Miss Wells?"

"No."

"Never went out with her, say to the movies or dinner?"

"No, never."

"Are you aware of the penalties for perjury?"

"Yes," he said, his voice quivering.

"Are you married?"

"Yes."

"Children?"

"Three, I have three children."

"Is Nicole Wells blackmailing you? Did she threaten to expose your affair with her?"

"No, no. I had no affair with her," he shouted.

"I have no further questions at this time, your honor, subject to recall at a later time."

The judge looked at his watch and said, "We'll adjourn for the day. I'm pleased with the progress we made so far and the good conduct of the attorneys. Let's strive to continue in the same manner throughout the trial. If we do we may wrap the testimony up in a week."

I sat with Jeff in the emptying courtroom discussing the day's events. The correction officers who were going to transport me back to the county jail stood at a respectful distance out of earshot. One mouthed to me, "Take your time." I nodded and smiled. At least someone, besides Jeff, was sympathetic to me.

"So," I said, "what do you think so far?"

"I think we're barely hanging in there, but we know what's coming next, that's for sure. The two IAD guys will testify finding the Davis license in your wallet and the results of their search in your garage. The Lab will testify to your prints on the items, but I'll throw doubt on that."

"How, Jeff?"

"Transference. Prints can be lifted from one object and re-deposited on another."

I thought of all the glasses I drank from in Niki's apartment and my stomach began to churn. "Jeff," I said, "you were making some not so subtle insinuations about Niki and Victor and Niki and Millstein. Do you really think she had affairs with both of them?"

"I really don't know, but what other explanation can there be? It was obvious to me they were lying when I brought Niki up."

"Me, too," I said. "You had them sweating and squirming all right. But what could she possibly be holding over their heads to convince them to come in here and perjure themselves for her?"

"Pictures." said Jeff. "I didn't ask Reggio if he was married with children, but I'll have Willy find that out. And Millstein was extremely nervous when his wife and kids were brought up."

"Are you going to recall them?"

"Depends on what I turn up. If nothing new appears that can tie them to Niki, it would be useless to put them back on the stand. They've made the commitment and it will be nearly impossible to get them to recant now."

"So now what?"

"We prepare our witnesses. Please start jotting down any thoughts and ideas you may have so that I can prepare your testimony."

"Things look that bad?"

"They ain't looking too good."

Later that night after I had scribbled some stuff down for Jeff, I finally was able to fall asleep. I dreamed of Niki. We were dancing somewhere and the band was playing the *Twelfth of Never* and when the song was over she took my hand and led me into a huge hotel room and said, "Danny, I will always love you."

We resumed at 9:30 the next morning and Valentine put on an expert witness from the Department of Motor Vehicles. He testified that the Arthur Davis license was a phony and could have been made in any number of places in the city. His testimony was factual and brief. Jeff began his cross-examination which turned out to be equally as brief. "Mr. Welch, would it be necessary for a person, Detective Boyland in this case, to personally visit one of these forgery mills to have his photo re-taken?"

"No, it would not."

"If someone took Detective Boyland's real driver's license from his wallet, without his knowledge, and brought it to the forger, could the phony license be made from that?"

"Yes, it could."

"Then the real license and the phony license could both be slipped back into Detective Boyland's wallet at a later time."

"Objection," said Valentine. "That's hypothetical."

"Sustained," said Delaney. "The jury will disregard the question."

"Thank you, Mr. Welch," Jeff smiled. "No further questions."

Captain Jenkins testified next and described inventorying the contents of my wallet emphasizing the phony license and my business card with Niki's cell phone number written on it. He then described the search of my garage where he found the evidence and how the pharmacy label led them to Millstein's store. At the conclusion of his testimony, Valentine offered the phony license and my business card into evidence as Exhibits B and C. They were accepted by the judge and inspected by the jury. It was now Jeff's turn. "Captain Jenkins, would you explain how and when you became involved in this investigation?"

"Mr. Walsh called my office and requested our participation in the interview of Nicole Wells. That was on Tuesday, August 17."

"In essence, Captain, what did Nicole tell you?"

"She told us that she had an affair with Detective Boyland and that he confessed to her the murder of Laura Samuels and the attempted murder of Martin Samuels. She told us we would find the evidence of the crime in Boyland's garage."

"Do you normally inventory the contents of a person's wallet when you arrest them?"

"Yes, it's routine."

"Were you looking for that phony license? Did you know it was in there?"

"No, I did not."

"Had Nicole Wells told you to look very carefully for that license?"

"No, she did not."

"Captain, you're an experienced police officer and so is Detective Boyland. Were you surprised that such a piece of incriminating evidence as that license would still be in his wallet? Wouldn't an ordinary person, much less an experienced detective, dispose of that immediately after he used it for the intended purpose?"

"I suppose so, but criminals do stupid things. You know that, counselor."

"Please just answer my questions, Captain, and keep your commentary to yourself. But it's appropriate you brought that up. Do you believe Detective Boyland is a stupid person?"

"No, but…"

"The no answer is sufficient, Captain."

"When you officially arrested Detective Boyland did you advise him of his constitutional rights?"

"Yes, I did."

"Did he answer any of your questions?"

"Not really. He asked on what basis he had been arrested and we gave him the information on the results of the search warrant. Then he said he wouldn't answer any questions without his attorney, and then he called you."

"Did he say anything else?"

"Not that I recall."

"Do you have a good memory, Captain?"

"I believe so."

"Do you remember Detective Boyland saying that he believed this was some huge mistake or that he was being set up?"

"Something like that."

"Something like that? Didn't he give you a hand-written statement attesting to his version of the events?"

"Oh, yes."

"Why didn't you remember that? You said you have a good memory?"

"Well…uh…"

"Didn't Detective Boyland have that statement typed up and sworn to? Do you remember that?"

"Yes."

"And didn't Detective Boyland volunteer to take a departmental polygraph examination to verify the truthfulness of his statement?"

"Objection, your honor! Shouted Valentine

"Forget it," snapped Jeff. "I withdraw the question. I have no further questions for this witness at this time."

Paul Valentine told the judge that although Sergeant Gerard McHale was on his witness list he would not call him at this time as his testimony would be substantially the same as Jenkins's.

"I appreciate that Mr. Valentine," said Delaney. "Let's break for an early lunch. We'll resume at 12:30 sharp."

After lunch the parade of expert witnesses began with Doc Maguire up first. His testimony was factual and necessary, but not damaging to me. He gave the cause of death, time of death and the manner and mode of death of Laura Samuels. He also gave the results of the tests for toluene on Marty and the children. Jeff had a lot of good questions for him.

"Doctor Maguire, in your medical and professional opinion, how much excess toluene was in Laura's system above and beyond the amount required to kill her?"

"I would estimate at least three times as much, perhaps four."

"Can you estimate how long a toluene soaked rag or bunch of cotton would have to be held over her mouth and nose to yield that amount in her system?"

"I would estimate at least two minutes," he answered.

"Two minutes? So someone would have to hold her still for that long as she struggled?"

"Not necessarily, Mr. Levy. If the toluene had been administered very gradually, a little at a time while she was sleeping, she would have slowly drifted into unconsciousness. Then the continued administration of it would eventually have killed her."

Is there any way to tell which way her death occurred, either the way you just described, or involving a struggle?"

"I believe she died in a struggle due to the finger marks around her neck."

"That struggle being someone forcibly holding her down and choking her?"

"Yes."

"Can you determine if her death could have been accomplished by only one person?"

"I cannot say for certain, but my opinion leads me to believe that two people would be more likely in this case."

"Thank you, Doctor. Now what was the level of toluene in Martin Samuels's blood?"

"About ten times less than what I found in Mrs. Samuels."

"Ten times less. Would that be enough to kill him?"

"Obviously not, since he is still alive."

That got a chuckle from the spectators and some members of the jury, but Jeff was certainly making points. "What effect would that level have on a person."

"It would render them unconscious for about an hour, perhaps two."

"And Doctor, how long would a toluene soaked rag take, when placed over a person's mouth and nose, to accomplish that?"

"Approximately ten to twelve seconds."

"Ten to twelve seconds?" asked Jeff, in a surprised tone. "Is that consistent with attempted murder, Doctor Maguire? If someone really wanted to murder Martin Samuels would they have administered toluene for only ten to twelve seconds?"

"Not if they knew what they were trying to accomplish."

"No further questions your honor," said Jeff.

It was obvious to me that Jeff scored big time with Maguire's testimony and I hoped the jury thought so, too. It also must have been obvious to Valentine because he jumped up to ask some questions on re-direct to try to downplay the importance of Maguire's testimony, but the good old doc was unshakable and actually reinforced his testimony. Valentine shortly realized he was on a fruitless quest and excused Maguire with a weak, "Thank you."

•

It was nearly 3:00 p.m. by the time Doc Maguire finished up. He hadn't looked at me throughout his testimony, but as he walked past me he glanced over and gave me a little smile. That meant a lot to me. I knew he didn't think I committed these crimes and that little smile told me so and lifted up my spirits, at least for a while.

Detective John Dennison, the prosecution's latent finger print expert was called next and he testified, as expected, about discovering my prints, one on the toluene bottle and one on the roll of tape. He made the comparisons from my fingerprint records which were on file with the Department from the time I first applied for the job. Jeff knew better than to attack an expert's credentials, but he had to cast some doubt on this very damaging finding.

"Detective Dennison, was it possible for you to determine exactly when the fingerprints were left on those two items?"

"No."

"Then, in your opinion, they could have been left there on the day of the murder, or at a previous time, or at a subsequent time?"

"Yes, there is no scientific method available to determine time of placement."

Jeff walked back to our table and picked up a tumbler that was half-filled with water. He raised it to his lips, slowly drank it down, and then placed it on the ledge of the witness stand in front of Detective Dennison. "Detective, can you see my fingerprints on this glass?"

Dennison looked at it carefully, then picked it up and rotated it from side to side. "Yes," he said.

"All five of them?"

"I see your thumb on one side and your four fingers on the other."

"Now in order to lift one of my prints, you would place a sticky tape over it, press, and then lift it, or peel it away. Is that correct?"

"Basically, that's the way it's done," he said.

"Could a print be lifted with cellophane tape that you could purchase in any stationery store, or perhaps, a pharmacy?"

"I believe so."

Jeff reached into his pocket and brought out a roll of cellophane tape and handed it to Dennison. "Would you try to lift my thumbprint from that glass please?"

"Objection!" cried Valentine.

"On what grounds, counselor?" asked the judge.

"Uh…where is this going…uh…"

"Overruled, Mr. Valentine, I think it's obvious where Mr. Levy is going."

Dennison removed a piece of tape, placed it over the thumbprint, pressed it down, then carefully peeled it away from the surface of the glass. As he was doing so, Jeff retrieved another glass tumbler from our table and made a show of polishing the surface with his handkerchief. He handed the glass to Dennison and asked if he could see any fingerprints on it.

"No."

"Would you attempt to transfer the fingerprint you removed from the other glass to this glass?"

Dennison placed the tape on the glass and pressed it down firmly. He carefully peeled it away.

"Were you able to transfer the print, detective?"

"Yes, it's faint, but it's there."

"Is it readable? Are there enough ridges and loops and whorls for you to make an identification?"

"I believe so."

"Were the fingerprints on the toluene bottle and the surface of the roll of tape faint or strong prints?"

"Faint."

"Like the one you just transferred from glass to glass?"

"Yes."

"Thank you, Detective Dennison. No further questions."

Valentine got up and said, "I have some re-direct, your honor. Detective Dennison, despite this demonstration that Mr. Levy just subjected all of us to, is your testimony still the same?"

"Yes."

"And that testimony is that the prints you lifted belong to Detective Boyland?"

"Yes."

"And there is no way to determine for certain that they were placed there other than by Detective Boyland?"

"Correct."

"Thank you. You may step down."

"Not so fast," said Jeff, leaping to his feet. "I have a further question or two for Detective Dennison on re-cross examination."

"Go ahead, Mr. Levy," said the judge.

"In your opinion, Detective, those prints could most certainly have been transferred in the manner we demonstrated. Isn't that so?"

"Yes."

"And in fact, is it your opinion that the appearance of the prints, their faintness, is more consistent with prints that have been transferred as opposed to those which were deposited directly by a finger?"

"Yes, that is correct."

"Thank you, Detective. Now you may step down."

Delaney checked his watch and announced he would adjourn for the day until 10:00 a.m. on Thursday. I sat with Jeff at the table and congratulated him for his performance today.

"Thanks, Danny, I'm glad it worked. I practiced it enough times at home last night. Greasy hand lotion helps leave very good prints."

"About time we scored some points with the evidence," I said.

"You're right on with that observation. I think that's where the jury will look and how they will decide. The prosecution is making a good verbal case against you and I'm hoping I'm making a good verbal case against Nicole and Marty, but that leaves the jury in a quandary. Just who the hell do they believe?"

"Which leaves only the objective physical evidence."

"Right, and so far we've been taking a beating on that. They've seen a bound ledger book and they've seen a phony driver's license. They've seen tape, toluene, and a plastic bag and Valentine has connected them all to you. I'm trying to discredit these items one by one, but I don't know if I'm succeeding."

"You're doing great. I really wish I was paying you."

"Hey, if you were paying me," he laughed, "you would have been exonerated already."

"Seriously, Jeff, I can't thank you enough. I'll find a way to pay you, I…"

"Danny, stop," he said. "I don't want you to have to worry about money at all. Concentrate on your defense. Besides, my firm has already received three calls from prospective clients looking to retain my services after this trial is over. The newspapers have been kind to me."

"They should be. You're doing a bang-up job."

"I think Valentine will wrap up tomorrow. We may start our defense in the afternoon or Friday morning, and I'm thinking of jumping right in with you first. Are you ready?"

"I sure hope so, but I must admit I'm not looking forward to being cross-examined by Valentine."

"That's part of the game," he said. "You'll do fine. After all, you're innocent—now we must convince the jury of that fact."

Chapter 11

The first witness up the next morning was Detective Frank Mattio from the Lab's Trace Evidence Section. He put on a great presentation showing that the two pieces of tape from the crime scene had a matching end and that the opposite end of one of the pieces matched the end from the roll of tape found in my garage. Not only did he show the court the physical end matches, he also explained that he had contacted the tape's manufacturer and obtained their "differential dye-staining process" used to determine the penetration of the water repellant chemicals on the non-sticky surface of the tape. He pointed out the different colored bands that ran through the tape and even a dummy could see that the pieces were from the same roll and were, at one time, joined together.

Frank also testified to the fact that he jigsaw matched the small piece of tan plastic stuck to one corner of the tape from Laura's mouth with the plastic bag found in my garage which had a small piece missing. He did a masterful job and I could see that he impressed the jury. The physical evidence thing again. Tough to get around, but Jeff tried.

"Detective Mattio, do you know how these items—the roll of tape and the plastic bag in this instance—got into Detective Boyland's garage?"

"No."

"How long do you know Detective Boyland?"

"About a year, maybe 15 months."

"Does he spend a lot of time in the Lab in your unit, and other units?

"Yes, he does. We all like to work with Danny...uh...Detective Boyland, because he has a true respect for the value of physical evidence."

"So, he is well aware of the power that the scientific analysis of physical evidence can bring to a prosecution."

"Yes."

"Knowing that Detective Mattio, does it seem plausible to you that Detective Boyland would hide these items in his garage, items that if connected to him could lead to a murder charge against him?"

"Not at all, Mr. Levy."

"Furthermore, after allegedly hiding them in his garage on the night of the murder, he left them in there untouched, unmoved and not destroyed—left them there for two months and seven days—left them there until they were found by Internal Affairs on Friday, August 20. Does that seem plausible to you?"

"Objection!" shouted Valentine. "This is speculation, purely hypothetical, and outside the scope of this expert witness's opinion."

"Your honor," said Jeff, "I am asking this question in the context of Detective Mattio's personal and professional association with Detective Boyland, not his role as an expert witness."

"I'll allow it," said Delaney. "Objection overruled."

"The question, Detective Mattio was—does that seem plausible to you?"

"No, sir, not plausible—in fact, totally unbelievable."

"Your honor!" shouted Valentine. "The witness is volunteering information and opinion that is highly speculative. I demand that answer be stricken."

Delaney said, "Let the record reflect that the answer to the last question should read, 'No, sir, not plausible.' The jury will disregard the rest of the answer."

They would like hell, I hoped and prayed. Jeff excused Frank and Valentine called his final witness, Detective Vince Jordan from the Chemistry Section of the Lab. Vince's testimony proved that the remaining liquid in the bottle found in my garage was indeed toluene. Jeff excused him without asking him a question and Valentine announced that they had completed their case.

"Good," said Judge Delaney. "Are you prepared to present your defense after the lunch break, Mr. Levy?"

"Yes, your honor," he said, looking at his watch. "May I have a little extra time before we resume?"

"How's 2:30?"

"That would be fine. Thank you, your honor."

"Who will be your first witness, Mr. Levy?"

"Detective Daniel Boyland"

That statement caused a distinct rumbling among the spectators in the court room.

"Court is adjourned until 2:30," said Delaney, banging his gavel loudly on the desk. "Let's all be prompt."

Jeff asked that I not be put back in the holding cell as was usual, but that we be allowed to stay at the defense table during the lunch break. The correction officer in charge agreed and volunteered to send one of his guys out for sandwiches. Jeff thanked them and we took him up on his offer. Willy Edwards, who had attended every minute of the trial thus far, stopped at the table to touch base with us on his way out to lunch. "Sam Lewis found out that our lying friend Victor Reggio is indeed married with children—two to be exact."

"Willy," I said, "something's bothering me here. You're going on the assumption that Niki had affairs with Victor and Ronald Millstein, right?"

"Right."

"How could she fit them in? I mean Marty went after her in October. Then she started in with me in June."

"She may have only begun with Marty in October, but she's lived in that same apartment in the neighborhood for over four years. The pharmacy and Victor's Lounge are within a mile of her place and her office."

I didn't like that answer because it forced me to think of her with other men, but why those two? If she was looking for a gold mine, why them? Marty I could see, just for the fact of the million dollar policy. Had she been plotting the same scheme with Victor and Ronald, but it hadn't panned out?

"Danny?" Jeff said.

"Oh sorry, I was thinking there for a moment."

"Let's get moving and go over your testimony. You're the star of the show."

I got on the witness stand at 2:30 p.m. Jeff asked open-ended questions and I took the jury through the entire case from the first notification right up through my arrest. Every so often, at junctures he considered critical, he changed his method of questioning to have me pound home specific points: When had Marty become a suspect, how he lawyered up and refused to answer questions, how he refused to submit to a polygraph (that brought Valentine to his feet shouting objections) and how Marty claimed no knowledge of the ski mask found on the bedroom floor.

He also heavily probed the days before my arrest when we were preparing a conspiracy case against Niki and Marty and had me state emphatically that I believed the two of them actually committed the murder together. He then concluded with his intervention on my behalf and he had me read the statement that he helped me prepare wherein I denied the charges and claimed a frame-up by Niki and Marty. I concluded with the last sentence, "I will voluntarily submit to a polygraph examination to verify this statement."

"Did Mr. Walsh or Captain Jenkins afford you the opportunity to take a polygraph examination that you willingly volunteered to take with my approval?"

"No, they did not."

"But they did allow an informant, Mr. Anthony Messina, to take one, didn't they?"

"Objection, your honor," said Valentine. "The relevancy of the polygraph has never been established and no foundation has been laid concerning the identity, or relevancy, of an Anthony Messina."

"Sustained. Withdraw the question, Mr. Levy."

"Yes, your honor, but I assure the court that I will most certainly establish the relevance of Anthony Messina. He will be called as a witness. One last question, Detective Boyland. "Did you murder Laura Samuels and attempt to murder Marty Samuels in the early morning hours of June 10?"

"I did not, Mr. Levy."

"Thank you, Detective. Your witness, Mr. Valentine."

I had been on the stand for over two and a half hours when Judge Delaney adjourned until the next day. I was primed and ready to face Valentine right then and there, but I would now have 16 hours to wait and worry before he began his attack.

Friday morning arrived gray, rainy and chilly. The depressing November weather matched my mood as the corrections van transported me to the courthouse. I made a firm resolve to stick to the facts and the truth, although I really wanted to minimize my involvement with Niki. I knew, however, that if you told no lies you couldn't be caught in one in front of everybody later on, a fact that sadly every generation of politicians has failed to learn.

I returned to the stand at 9:45 prepared to face my accuser, the representative of the People of The State of New York, Assistant District Attorney Paul Valentine. He looked exceptionally well-dressed this dreary morning—a navy blue, pin-striped power suit, crisp linen white shirt, subdued dark red tie and highly polished black oxfords. As he approached me I tried to detect visible signs that he was salivating at this opportunity. It is rare for the defense to put the defendant on the stand. It was a huge gamble and usually reserved as a last desperate measure, one final stab to prove innocence when the evidence was all against him, and there was nothing left to lose. Paul Valentine knew that, and he also knew if he could shake me and show me to be a liar, all our other witness's testimony would be meaningless. In short, if he cracked me, they convict me. He wasted no time and went right for my jugular.

"Detective Boyland, isn't it a fact that you drove to Woodmere at or about 1:00 a.m. on June 10 and murdered Laura Samuels and attempted to murder Martin Samuels by the means of toluene overdose and strangulation?"

"No, Mr. Valentine, that is not a fact. That is untrue."

"Wasn't your real intention to murder Martin Samuels and only render Laura Samuels unconscious?"

"No."

"So you mean that you really intended the result that occurred?"

"I intended no result. I did not kill anyone, or attempt to kill anyone."

"Then what did you intend to do?"

"My job, which was to investigate the crimes you just mentioned."

"I see. So you are telling the jury that you were not at the scene until officially notified and you then proceeded there?"

"That's correct, Mr. Valentine."

"Where were you at 1:00 a.m.?"

"At home in bed, sleeping."

"Was anyone in bed with you?"

"My wife, Jean."

"I don't see her name on the witness list, Detective Boyland. Isn't she going to verify that statement?"

"No, she cannot verify my presence in bed at that time. She is a heavy sleeper and does not remember me leaving the bed and the house when I actually did, which was about 30 minutes after I received the telephone call at 3:38."

"That's too bad, Detective. However, even if your wife did testify on your behalf it would be up to the jury to decide the credibility of her story. But in this case that won't happen because you have no credibility at all on this issue, do you?"

"Yes, I do have credibility. I am telling the truth. I was not at that scene until approximately 4:40 a.m."

"But you can't substantiate that can you? You have no proof that you were in bed at 1:00 a.m., other than your word. Correct?"

"That's correct."

"But the state has testimony to the contrary. Did you hear Miss Nicole Wells state, under oath, that you confessed to her and part of that confession was that you were at the scene at or about 1:00 a.m.?"

"Miss Wells lied and she lied under oath."

I think you get the idea of how my day went, all day, six hours on the stand. He hammered and hammered at me trying to shake me and almost got me when he explored my affair with Nicole. I stuck to the truth, including the sex and the love we professed for each other, and then he hit me with the big one.

"Detective Daniel Boyland, do you still love Nicole Wells?"

"How can I love someone who is trying to frame me for a crime I did not commit?"

"You answered my question with a question, Detective Boyland. I ask you again, do you still love Nicole Wells?"

I hesitated, and then answered, "Under the circumstances how could I still love her?"

"Is that a yes, or a no?" he shouted at me.

Just as he finished asking this question there was a loud sob in the gallery and Jeanie got up and walked hurriedly out of the courtroom. It served me right for waffling. Obviously, Jeanie believed I still loved Niki, and probably so did everyone else in the courtroom. I tried to undo the damage. I responded in a loud clear voice, "No, Mr. Valentine, I do not love Nicole Wells anymore."

"Thank you," he said with a sardonic smile which said it all. I finally caught you in a lie Detective Boyland, didn't I?

But that was it, the low point of my testimony, the only time he came close to getting me. After that exchange I got into high gear. After all, I am an experienced witness. I know how to make my points and when to only answer "yes, sir" or "no, sir." When he sarcastically asked me if I was telling the court that I had absolutely no idea how that phony license got into my wallet, instead of just answering, "No, I do not," I said, "I have a strong idea that Nicole Wells put it in there."

The cross-examination was a contest of wills and stamina and endurance, and just when I thought he was beginning to wear me down, when I had to think a little too long on an answer, when I thought I might make a mistake—he threw in the towel. I heard the magic words, "No further questions of this witness, your honor." My relief was enhanced when Jeff said, "I have no re-direct, your honor."

It was 5:30 on Friday afternoon and I had survived the week. Contrary to Judge Delaney's high hopes that we might be able to wrap this up, we were heading into another Monday, but I was sure that it would not be necessary to go beyond a second week. The decision on my fate was drawing closer.

On Saturday morning Jeff and Willy Edwards came to visit me at the jail.

"You did a great job yesterday," said Jeff. "You held up terrifically most of the day."

I knew what he meant by that, but I didn't want to bring up Niki now. "Thanks," I said. "And thanks for not keeping me up there for re-direct. I was on the brink after Paul finished."

"I could see that. There were several questions I wanted to ask, but then Valentine would have had another opportunity to re-cross examine you and I didn't want that. I may have to recall you though, or maybe I can clear up those questions during my summation."

"What did you want to clarify?"

"Danny, let me be frank here."

"Sure."

"This whole thing with you and Nicole is very troubling and very damaging. I saw the reaction on the juror's faces when your wife stormed out of the courtroom in tears. Please tell me just what the fuck you are doing to yourself and this case?"

"Uh...Jeff...I don't know what you mean. I..."

"You know goddamn well what I mean—your constant indecision over Nicole. 'Do you love her? Well, uh...I don't know...uh...' Thank God you finally stated that you no longer loved her, but that may have been too late and, to be honest, I didn't believe it and I don't think the jurors did either."

"Jeff, I don't know what to say."

"Well, you better shape up. We've got to convince the jury that Nicole Wells is a scheming, conniving, poisonous bitch and that you despise her for setting you up for murder. If we can't do that, you're going to get convicted. And although the actual charges are the murder of Laura and attempted murder of Marty, the jury is really going to convict you for murdering your family. Do you get what I mean?"

"Yes," I said quietly. "I understand."

"Danny, you have to help me. I feel we have a good shot at beating this. It's becoming apparent that you were set up, but your continued feelings for Nicole are casting doubt on that. You've got to break free of her. You must."

"I'll try, Jeff, I'll try."

"Try? Willy, pound some sense into him, will you? I'll go for the coffee."

After Jeff left, Willy took over. "Danny," he said, "I'm not going to beat you up. Jeff did a good job of that already. He's right. I'm there everyday and you do have a chance of beating this. Jeff is doing a magnificent job. Don't let all his effort be wasted. That's all I'm going to say on the subject."

"Thanks, Willy. I got the message."

"Good, so how are you holding up? I agree with Jeff, you gave that Valentine a run for his money."

"I'm hanging in there."

Willy reached into his inside jacket pocket withdrawing a thick white envelope. The words "For Danny" were written on the front. I opened it and pulled out a stack of bills with a note folded over it. I opened it and read, "Danny, from your friends in the squad." It was signed by all of them, some with a little added notation—"Good luck." "We're with you all the way." "When you're found not guilty we'll get that bitch," and so on. I was on the verge of tears and Willy hugged me around the shoulders.

"We don't forget our own," he said. "Everyone contributed a minimum of $100 and I know the two sergeants threw in a lot more than that. The boss put in $500. There's over three grand there."

I was overwhelmed and had to wipe my eyes. I handed the money to Jeff and said, "Here's your down payment, counselor."

Jeff took it and said, "I'm going to set up an account entitled, 'The Daniel Boyland Defense Fund.' That will keep this out of the hands of your wife's divorce lawyer."

We discussed the upcoming week and the order that we would put our witnesses on the stand. "We're coming down the home stretch," said Jeff. "Let's push as hard as we can."

After they left I lay on my bed and thought over what Jeff had said. I tried to convince myself that Niki was truly trying to destroy me. All the evidence and her testimony certainly confirmed that, and my factual, investigative mind believed it, but I couldn't fully come to terms with my emotional attachment to her. There was something in the way she looked at me in court and her words to me on the last night I was with her would not leave my mind: *'Remember, Danny, I will always love you.'*

On Monday morning, Jeff called Martin Samuels to the stand. I had mentioned to Jeff, as we waited for the judge to appear, that the thought crossed my mind that Marty might plead the Fifth Amendment and refuse to testify.

"I thought the same thing," he said. "He could do that because he was a suspect in the case. He could argue that if you are found not guilty, he could be investigated again—but he won't do it. He can't do it."

"Why not?"

"Can you imagine the effect on the jury? Nicole willingly testifies, you willingly testify, and then he refuses? It's practically an admission of guilt and your ticket to exoneration. No, he'll testify, and I'll make it difficult for him—I promise you."

Jeff began calmly, allowing Marty to tell his story as he had told it to me at the crime scene, and then he got to the point. "So, Mr. Samuels, when Detective Boyland informed you of your rights against self-incrimination you decided to invoke those rights and not answer his questions. Is that correct?"

"Yes."

"Did Detective Boyland offer you a chance to take a polygraph test to confirm the story you told him at the scene?"

"Yes."

"And you refused to avail yourself of that opportunity?"

"Yes."

"Do you still consider yourself a suspect in this case?"

"No, of course not."

"Because Detective Boyland has been charged with these crimes?"

"Sure."

"Suppose Detective Boyland were acquitted. Would you then consider your status as a suspect might change?"

"Perhaps."

"Then why are you willing to answer my questions now? Aren't you concerned that your answers might incriminate you?"

"No, I discussed that with my attorney and he assured me I had nothing to worry about as long as I told the complete truth."

A perfectly coached answer. I wondered how long Marty and Willard Ashton spent on his preparation, and I bet Mr. Ashton was costing Marty a tidy sum despite their association at the same firm.

"Mr. Samuels, when you and Detective Boyland discovered the ski mask next to your bed you told him you had never seen it before and that it did not belong to anyone in the household. Is that correct?"

"Yes."

"That was a lie, wasn't it?"

"Not really. I had forgotten about it."

"What do you mean?"

"I did tell Detective Boyland what you said, but later on I remembered that Nicole had given that mask to me for use by my children."

"When did you remember that?"

"About two weeks later."

"And did you inform Detective Boyland of your improved memory?"

"No, because my attorney advised me to have no further conversation with Boyland or any other law enforcement person after I was told that I was a suspect."

"Didn't you think that your knowledge of that ski mask might have helped in the investigation of your wife's murder?"

"Uh…I don't know."

"You don't know?" asked Jeff, raising his voice. "You certainly do know, Mr. Samuels. You do know that that mask would have been tied directly to Nicole Wells's presence at the murder scene, don't you?"

"No, she gave it to me a long time before that."

"Did it ever occur to you that you could have informed your attorney of your new found recollection of the ski mask and that he could have passed the information on to Detective Boyland?"

"No, I didn't think about doing that."

"And I think I know why, Mr. Samuels. You were not concerned about catching the burglar who killed your wife and attempted to kill you because there was no burglar. The burglar was a phantom, wasn't he? The real killers are you and Nicole Wells. Isn't that right, Mr. Samuels?"

"No, no. I did not kill my wife," he shouted.

"Oh, yes you did, and I'll tell this court and jury exactly why you killed your wife—money and obsession."

"I didn't kill Laura!"

"Money, Mr. Samuels—one… million… dollars. And an overwhelming obsession with Nicole Wells. That's why you did it, didn't you? Didn't you?"

Valentine leaped to his feet objecting that Jeff was badgering the witness. Delaney said, "Tone it down, Mr. Levy."

"Yes, your honor. I apologize. Mr. Samuels, do you gamble? Do you bet with bookmakers?"

By the time this line of questioning was completed Jeff had obtained admissions from Marty of his betting habits, the amounts he had lost and the means he had gone to in order to pay off his debts. Then he went after the insurance money.

"How much life insurance did you have on Laura on October 1 of last year, Mr. Samuels?"

"One hundred thousand dollars."

"And when did you increase the coverage to one million dollars?"

"Around April 15."

"Ah…how convenient! Just seven weeks before Laura was killed. How very convenient! Have you collected the proceeds yet?"

"No."

"Why not?"

"The insurance company is delaying payment pending the outcome of this trial."

"So, if Detective Boyland is exonerated, the insurance company pays you nothing because in their eyes you would still be a suspect?"

"Yes."

"And if Detective Boyland gets convicted, you get the money and happily resume your affair with Nicole Wells?"

"No, I have nothing to do with Miss Wells anymore."

"Really? You're not going to give Nicole her share of the insurance money for helping you murder Laura? That's not fair."

"I did not murder Laura and neither did Nicole. Detective Boyland is on trial here, not me."

"So he is, Mr. Samuels, so he is. But maybe he shouldn't be. Maybe you should be, Mr. Samuels. No further questions."

Valentine asked only a couple of questions ending with one more denial by Marty that he had nothing to do with his wife's murder, nor any part in attempting to frame me for it. During Jeff's direct examination he had asked Marty if he knew Whitey Messina and Marty admitted he bet with him occasionally, but denied any knowledge of Nicole's solicitation of him for a contracted 'hit.' Messina was up next, but Marty's testimony took all morning, so Delaney recessed for lunch. I told Jeff that he had really scored points on Marty. "You're on a roll," I said. "Keep those killer instincts going."

Anthony "Whitey" Messina, with his jovial street-wise speech and mannerisms, added a little lightness to the proceedings. Jeff had him relate his encounters with Nicole prior to the murder of Laura and emphasized the fact she had gone back to her table and conferred with Marty. And of course, the spectators were shocked when Messina described the "$5,000 blow job."

"Mr. Messina, you told this story freely and voluntarily to Detective Boyland and Assistant District Attorneys Barry Walsh and Jake Ellison, correct?"

"Yes, I did, and my lawyer was with me."

"Did Mr. Walsh ask you to take a polygraph test to verify your story?"

"Yes, and I took it and passed it the next day."

"And what was supposed to be your reward for providing this information, Mr. Messina?"

"My lawyer told me that if my story held up on the polygraph, which as I said it did, they would keep my case in a pending status, and if my information was sufficient to make a conspiracy arrest, they would drop my rap down to a misdemeanor."

"A conspiracy arrest? Who were they planning to arrest?"

"The Wells broad and Marty."

"What was your reaction a few days later when they were not arrested, but Detective Boyland was?"

"I was like—holy mackerel—this is unbelievable! And then I realized I was screwed. My deal was going down the drain. But then I thought that poor Boyland was screwed a hell of a lot worse than me. Can you believe this frame job?"

"Objection! Objection!" shouted Valentine, leaping to his feet. "I demand that answer be stricken."

And then, before the judge could respond, Messina said in a highly perturbed voice, "Hey calm down, I'm only tellin' the truth here…"

"Mr. Messina," said Delaney, "be quiet and say no more. Do you understand me?"

"Oh, sure, your honor. I'll keep it zipped."

"Objection sustained," he said. "Strike Mr. Messina's response to that last question."

Jeff finished up and Valentine, still red and shaking, began his cross examination. "Mr. Messina, when Nicole made her request of you in Vito's, you said she went back and spoke with Marty. Did you overhear their conversation?"

"No, they had their heads close together."

"So you don't really know what they were speaking about, do you? It could have been about the weather, correct?"

"Yeah, it coulda been, but hey, I figured…"

"Stop!" shouted Valentine. "Stop right there, Mr. Messina. You may step down. No further questions."

"No problem," he said as he got up from the witness chair. "Glad to have been of service."

I didn't think that in Paul Valentine's lengthy legal career was he so glad to be rid of a witness. We took a 15 minute break and the courtroom was buzzing over the testimony of Whitey Messina.

Chapter 12

After the recess, Jeff called Barry Walsh to the stand. Barry was sworn in and then Jeff asked to approach the bench. Paul Valentine joined him in front of the judge.

"Your honor, I wish to state on the record that I did not call Mr. Walsh as a witness without due consideration, but I feel his testimony is crucial to my defense. He is my former boss and a personal friend and I consider him to be a man of utmost honor and integrity. I state this now to avoid any challenges to his testimony by Mr. Valentine."

"Mr. Valentine?" asked Delaney. "Any objections?"

"No your honor, I also know Barry and I agree with Mr. Levy's assessment. I trust though, that Mr. Levy is not exaggerating when he uses the word crucial."

"Well, let us find out, shall we? Proceed, Mr. Levy."

"Mr. Walsh, after Mr. Messina's information was validated by the polygraph examination, were you preparing to arrest Nicole Wells and Marty Samuels for conspiracy to commit murder?"

"We were going to consider it. Jake Ellison is the member of my staff assigned to this case. He and I had a discussion along those lines and we were planning to meet with the detectives on the case to finalize a decision."

"When were you going to meet with them?"

"In a day, two at the most."

"But you never had that meeting did you?"

"No. Nicole Wells walked into my office with her attorney and told us the story she told this court last week."

"What was your reaction to her story?"

"Total disbelief at first."

"And your mind changed when the information she provided led to the discovery of the items in Detective Boyland's garage?"

"Yes. I was stunned when the Internal Affairs officers found those items just where she said they would be."

"Then you brought Danny in and he admitted to the affair with Nicole which added more corroboration to her story, and then you found the phony driver's license in his wallet. Then the final piece—the Lab called and said they have found his prints on the tape and bottle. So, based on that, you had Detective Boyland arrested. Correct?"

"Yes."

"Did you ever consider that you might have made a mistake? Arrested the wrong person?"

"No. The evidence was overwhelming."

"Yes, it was, wasn't it? Very overwhelming. Did you ever consider that Detective Boyland might have been set up? That the entire story may have been fabricated? That the evidence may have been planted in his garage?"

"I considered that possibility."

"But you didn't pursue it, did you?"

"There was no reason to. As I said, there was just too much evidence."

"Before Nicole walked into your office, and let's assume for a moment that she had not come in that week, how certain were you that you had a viable conspiracy charge against her and Marty?"

"Jake and I were ready to have Danny, uh…Detective Boyland make that arrest, but as I said, we wanted to confer with him and the other members of his team and add up all our facts to substantiate the charge."

"Assuming all the facts were compiled, plus the ski mask which belonged to Nicole being found at the scene, plus Whitey Messina's information, you had pretty good probable cause to make those arrests, and you would have made them. Is that correct?"

"Yes."

"Then you would have arrested the wrong people, Mr. Walsh. Isn't that correct?"

"I…yes, I suppose so."

"But, based on the evidence in front of you at the time, it certainly seemed that it would have been a correct decision. However, it would have been a tragic mistake. Is it possible that you also made a tragic mistake when you arrested Detective Boyland?"

"No, not in light of the new evidence, which was much more compelling than what we had with the conspiracy charge."

"By the way Mr. Walsh, I agree with your decision here. As a former prosecutor, I might have proceeded exactly as you had, but I would have been somewhat troubled by the fact that everything seemed just too pat, just too perfect. Mr. Walsh, how long do you know Detective Boyland?"

"Ever since he came to the Homicide Squad, maybe 15 or 16 months."

"What is your opinion of him?"

"He's a sharp, bright, innovative detective and, for his experience, one of the best in the squad."

"Would a man as you just described—a sharp, bright, detective—would a man like that leave a phony license in his wallet? Would he store the evidence of his crime in his own garage for over two months?"

"I've pondered those questions myself, Mr. Levy, and my answer is no, he would not. But then he entered into an affair with his suspect, which was not only not bright and sharp, but very, very stupid."

"You know, Mr. Walsh," Jeff smiled, "I would have been perfectly satisfied with the first part of your answer, but now that you brought her up, let's talk about Nicole Wells. Is it possible she seduced you and your staff just like she seduced Danny Boyland?"

"No, her information proved correct."

"Did you ask her to confirm her veracity by taking a polygraph test?"

"Yes, I did, but her attorney refused to allow it."

"I see Mr. Walsh. Let me sum things up here. My client, Detective Daniel Boyland, volunteered to take a polygraph test, but you wouldn't allow him to do so. Is that correct?"

"Yes."

"And Martin Samuels and Nicole Wells refused to take a polygraph test to confirm their stories. Is that also correct?"

"Yes."

"So you go ahead and arrest Danny, but not Nicole and Marty. Correct?"

"Yes, but…"

"That's all, Mr. Walsh. No further questions."

Paul Valentine tried to undo the damage that Jeff had so skillfully caused by harping on court decisions concerning the admissibility of polygraph tests, the unreliability of its results and the training of the operator, but he soon realized he was impressing no one, so he excused Barry and another day was over.

On Tuesday morning Jeff decided to call only one more witness—Tara Brown. "I gave this a lot of thought last night, Danny. It may not be necessary to call Jake Ellison. His testimony will be the same as Barry's, but I need your input. What do you think?"

"I don't know. I'm sure Jake doesn't believe I did it. Is it worth having the jury hear what Barry said all over again? You tell me, you're the boss here."

"It might, but it might backfire. He may say something we don't want to hear. No, I won't call him."

"You said you were going to call the whole investigative team, how come now only Tara?"

"She was your partner and was with you when you first interviewed Nicole. The others are unimportant. I don't want to annoy the jury with repetitive witnesses."

"I see your point, and I agree. So, it's just Tara, and then what?"

"Paul and I give our closing statements and the case goes to the jury."

"Today?"

"Yes, today."

"Detective Brown, were you assigned to assist Detective Boyland in the investigation of the death of Laura Samuels?" asked Jeff.

"Yes, I was assigned as his primary partner."

"And when was that?"

"The day after the murder, Friday, June 11."

"Were any other detectives assigned to this case?"

"Yes, Detective Perez from our squad and Detective Nowicki from the Nine-Four Squad."

"So you went with Detective Boyland as one team and Perez and Nowicki went out as the second team?"

"That's correct."

"Could you please tell us, Detective Brown, how you and Detective Boyland proceeded with the investigation from the beginning of your involvement until you were re-assigned to regular duties?"

"Yes."

Tara took the court through our attendance at the wake, the funeral, the interviews at Laura's school and then to the interviews at the law firm.

"So, during the week immediately following the murder, you and Danny spoke with several attorneys and staff at the firm where Marty and Nicole were employed. What did you uncover?"

"We soon found out that it was common knowledge that Nicole Wells and Martin Samuels had an affair."

"Was this affair still going on? Were you able to determine that?"

"It appeared that the affair began during the past October and continued up to mid-April of this year. Those we interviewed didn't recall seeing them together after that very often."

"When did you interview Nicole Wells?"

"On Friday morning, June 18."

"Was that the first time you ever met Miss Wells?"

"Yes."

"To your knowledge, was that the first time Detective Boyland met her?"

"No, he met her the day before, Thursday. I had to be in court all day and Danny worked alone on the interviews. He told me that he met Nicole on the street as he was walking to lunch."

"Did he relate the conversation he had with Nicole at that time?"

"Objection! Your honor, that's hearsay."

"No, it's not, your honor," said Jeff. "Detective Boyland's testimony is on the record. This is corroboration."

"Overruled, Mr. Valentine. You may answer the question, Detective Brown."

"Yes, he did. He told me she asked him how come he hadn't interviewed her yet and Danny told her he would get to her soon. She then said that she presumed he had been hearing tales about her and Marty and she looked forward to clearing them up."

"Anything else that you remember Danny telling you about that chance encounter with Miss Wells?"

"He said she was very friendly and insisted that he call her Niki."

"So, on Friday, the next day, you were back with Danny conducting interviews at Keenan, Rosen and Vario?"

"Yes, and we only had one to go—Nicole Wells."

"Can you please tell us the results of that interview?"

"We began at 9:15. Nicole readily admitted to the affair with Marty, but insisted they broke it off in mid-April."

"Who initiated the affair?"

"She said it was Marty, but she initiated the break up because Marty was getting too serious—almost obsessive. She said that to her, the affair was only a brief fling, but Marty wanted much more."

"What more did he want?"

"He wanted to divorce Laura and marry her."

"And Nicole didn't want that?"

"Not at all. She treated the affair lightly, but she had an ulterior motive."

"Oh? What was that?"

Tara explained the favorable review and salary increase that Nicole was seeking and then continued to detail the rest of the interview in response to Jeff's questions covering Marty's gambling, Nicole's taste for the good life, her adamant denial of any involvement in Laura's murder and her refusal to take a polygraph exam. I knew what was coming next, but I also knew it had to be said.

"When did you finish the interview, Detective Brown?"

"About eleven o'clock."

"And what did you conclude?"

"We both concluded that she was lying."

"How did you conclude that?"

"Her response to our questions, her body language when critical questions were asked, and her refusal to take the polygraph exam."

"Did you notice anything else during the interview, Detective Brown?"

Tara glanced over at me and said, "Yes, sparks."

"Sparks? I'm not sure I understand."

"There was something going on between Danny and Nicole, some romantic interaction. It was obvious."

"Did you confront him with your observations?"

"Oh, yeah, right after the interview and on the ride back to Mineola."

"And what was his response?"

"He told me I was wrong, but I told him I saw what I saw."

"Are you convinced that prior to the chance encounter they had on Thursday, Danny had never met her before in his life? That the Thursday meeting was the first time he ever laid eyes on her?"

"Yes."

"Why?"

"Danny Boyland really was a straight arrow—work, church and home, as he used to say. I never saw him as much as look at another woman."

"Until he met Nicole Wells?"

"Yes, until he met that…er…Nicole."

"Were you aware that Danny entered into a full-blown affair with Nicole?"

"No, although I suspected something was going on. But then I concluded it couldn't possibly be happening."

"Why, Detective Brown? Affairs happen all the time."

"The stakes were too high. He had a lovely wife and family and he was a homicide detective. I figured he would never jeopardize all that for that…for her."

"I guess you figured wrong."

"I sure did. I still can't believe it, but now in retrospect there were indications."

"Such as?"

"The main one was Danny's focus on the investigation. He felt that Marty was the driving force behind the murder and that Nicole was not involved to any great extent, if at all."

"Was that contrary to your conclusions?"

"Yes. I and the other members of the team and the supervisors all felt they were in it together, with Nicole as the main driving force."

"And what was Danny's reaction to that?"

"He told me that I was wrong, we all were wrong. He said he had been working with Nicole to get a taped admission from Marty. Nicole had told Danny she was afraid Marty was going to frame her for the murder, so he could collect the insurance money."

"Did Danny really believe that?"

"He swallowed her story hook, line and sinker. That was obvious."

"Why was it obvious?"

"He's here on trial for murder, isn't he?"

"And you think he's innocent?"

"Of course he's innocent. He was set up. Nicole Wells and Marty Samuels killed Laura Samuels, period."

"Detective Brown, were you able to verify if Nicole Wells did get her review from Martin Samuels?"

"Yes. Danny and I got that information from Mr. Rosen, the senior partner at the firm, when we called him later that day."

"And what type of review did Miss Wells get from Mr. Samuels?"

"He gave her an 'excellent' rating."

"Did he give her a salary increase also?"

"She got a $5,000 raise, increasing her salary from $42,375 to $47,375 annually."

"Thank you, Detective Brown. I have no more questions."

Valentine began with a series of questions designed to cast doubt on Tara's ability to conclude if a subject were lying or telling the truth, then he got to the important stuff. "You said, Detective Brown, that you were convinced that Detective Boyland had not met Miss Wells prior to their encounter on Thursday, June 17. Is that correct?"

"Yes."

"But that is only your opinion, is it not? You have no direct, factual evidence to support your conviction, do you?"

"No, I do not."

"And you also stated that Detective Boyland is innocent of these crimes and that Nicole and Marty killed Laura. Correct?"

"Yes."

"But that's also your opinion, Detective Brown, because that's what this jury will determine. They will determine the facts and they will decide if Detective Boyland is innocent, not you. Is that correct, Detective Brown?"

"Yes."

"No further questions," said a satisfied Paul Valentine.

"I have one question for re-direct, your honor," said Jeff.

"Proceed," said Delaney.

"Detective Brown, what did your investigation of the murder of Laura Samuels conclude?"

"That Nicole Wells and Martin Samuels did it."

"Thank you."

"Re-cross, your honor?" asked Paul.

"Proceed," he replied.

"Then why didn't you arrest them, Detective Brown?"

"We didn't have enough evidence."

"Exactly," he said. "You may step down."

"Call your next witness," said the judge as I was mulling over the last couple of questions which hadn't gone well at all.

"Your honor, I plan to call no further witnesses. The defense rests."

Delaney was obviously pleased and asked if Jeff and Paul were ready with their closing arguments. "Ready your honor," said Jeff.

"Your honor," said Valentine, "I was anticipating more witnesses. I'm not quite prepared. Could I have an hour or so?"

"I understand," said Delaney looking at his watch. "It's 11:30 now. Can we resume at 2:00 p.m.?"

"That would be fine," Paul said.

"Gentlemen," said the judge, "I am not fond of long, flowery, closing statements as I'm sure you have heard."

"Yes, sir," they both replied.

"Then I'm sure each of you can adequately sum up your cases in a half hour, forty minutes at most. Am I correct?"

"Yes, your honor," they again replied.

"Keep the time in mind as you sum up. I'm determined to charge the jury and give them the case by four o'clock at the very latest. Court is adjourned until 2:00 p.m., sharp."

I went back to the holding cell leaving Jeff to put the finishing touches on his closing presentation. I hoped and prayed that he would do a magnificent job, because I now knew for sure that Paul Valentine was a damned good prosecutor.

Jeff began at precisely 2:01 and concluded at 2:27. But in those 26 minutes he did a masterful job of concisely summarizing the testimony of all the witnesses and making the best case possible for my innocence—a devious frame-up—and identifying the real murderers of Laura Samuels. He concluded in a thundering voice with, "Ladies and gentlemen of the jury, Daniel Boyland is innocent of these charges. You know it, I know it, everyone in this courtroom knows it—and you all know who the real murderers are. Please bring these proceedings to a justly deserved quick conclusion and let the investigation of Nicole Wells and Martin Samuels commence again with vigor and determination. Let's put the real murderers on trial and stop this miscarriage of justice perpetrated by them against Daniel Boyland. I ask you to stop it—now."

Oh, he was great. Too bad we couldn't have ended right there. Too bad the jury had to listen to Paul Valentine, because he was great, too. So great that had I been on the jury, I probably would have convicted myself!

Valentine tore our defense to shreds emphasizing the physical evidence in the case. He took great pains to have the jury once again pass around the ledger, the fake driver's license, the toluene bottle, the roll and two pieces of duct tape and the cotton batting. "Here are the facts in this case, ladies and gentlemen of the jury," he said. "These items have been positively linked with the defendant. The defense's assertion of a frame-up is ludicrous, a manufactured story in a last ditch attempt to rescue a killer from his deserved fate, the fate that you will shortly determine. There is only one killer in this courtroom and there he is."

He pointed at me and paused in that position for a few seconds. "There he is, the murderer of Laura Samuels. Put him in prison where he most certainly belongs."

He finished at 3:02 p.m. and the judge moved to charge the jury, but first called a fifteen minute recess. I spoke with Jeff as we awaited the jury's return and asked him what he thought. "Danny, I don't know. No one knows, but I believe we threw a lot of doubts on their case and as I said, all we need is one to get a hung jury."

"Is that our only hope here? A hung jury? We'd have to go through all this all over again?"

"Better than a conviction, isn't it?"

"Not better than an outright acquittal though," I smiled.

The recess was over and Delaney went right into charging the jury after Jeff made the obligatory motion to dismiss the case based on the fact that the prosecution had not established a prima facie case. The motion was denied and Delaney was done with his charge in twelve minutes. There were no complications here, no lesser included offenses, no manslaughter or criminally negligent homicide for the jury to consider. Either I had intentionally murdered Laura Samuels, or I had not—either I attempted to murder Marty Samuels, or I had not. Very simple folks—I did it, or I didn't do it. Now, go decide.

The jury officially received the case at 3:17 p.m., Tuesday, November 9. Now all we had to do was wait. I went back to my holding cell in the courtroom in case the jury reached a quick verdict. They did not and called it a day at 7:30 p.m. I was transported back to the county jail to continue the wait. Wednesday passed ever so slowly, and on Thursday morning Jeff stopped in to see me.

"What do you think?" I asked.

"You could argue both ways," he said, "but I choose to believe that the longer they're in there, the better it is for us."

"Or the more time they have to convince the one or two holdouts of my guilt."

"Or of your innocence. Don't be negative. It works both ways."

We chatted awhile and then Jeff's cell phone jingled. We both jumped. This could be it. It wasn't, and we breathed in relief, but we didn't like the news when Jeff called in. Jeff had left an associate from his firm in the courtroom, and he informed him that the jury requested a read back of portions of Nicole's testimony and my testimony, and they also requested to see all the evidence items once again.

"What do you make of that, Jeff?"

"I think they're getting down to the nitty-gritty—your word against hers—and if they can't decide they'll go with their interpretation of the physical evidence."

"Which would be…?"

"Who knows, Danny? Who truly knows? I better get back over there now. Keep the faith."

Thursday moved on to its finish and I tried to sleep. Surely, I thought, tomorrow would be it. The jury wouldn't want to go into the weekend. They were thinking of their Friday night cocktails and I smiled in spite of the circumstances. I thought how wonderful it would be if I were sitting in Mulvaney's tomorrow evening gradually getting shit-faced on ice cold martinis, listening to Tara spouting insults at the criminal justice system and Manny Perez vowing to track down "That weasel and his bitch" and beat confessions out of them. I finally fell asleep thinking of the squad, and Jeanie, and Patrick, and Kelly. I did not dream of Niki.

I was reading the newspaper the next morning when, shortly after eleven o'clock, a correction officer tapped his stick on the bars of my cell. "We have to go, Boyland," he said. "Your jury just came back." The satisfaction that my prediction had come true disappeared. I realized that my fate had been decided. All that remained now was to hear it.

A correction officer opened the door and escorted me to the defense table. I was the last one to enter the courtroom, as it had been a 20 minute drive from the jail. I looked over the crowd as I reached the desk. I glimpsed Jeanie, Ray Roberts, Tara and Manny Perez, but there were no signs of Niki or Marty. No wonder—if I were exonerated they would be targets again. As soon as I took my place at the table Judge Delaney called the proceedings to order and asked the bailiff for the jury's verdict. The foreman of the jury handed the note to the bailiff who passed it on to Delaney. I watched him as he opened it. It appeared his eyebrows raised a bit in surprise. He handed the note back to the bailiff who returned it to the foreman. The judge said, "Please read your verdict, Mr. Foreman."

I stared at them hoping for some clue. A few of them glanced at me. Most did not. The foreman began, "On the count of the attempted murder of Martin Samuels we find the defendant, Daniel Boyland, guilty as charged."

The courtroom erupted and Delaney quickly restored order, banging his gavel loudly several times. My knees got weak and I grabbed the edge of the table to steady myself. Delaney said, "If there are any more outbursts I will hold those responsible in contempt of court. Bailiff, when the foreman is finished reading the second charge, clear this courtroom of all spectators as soon as possible."

"Yes, your honor," he replied.

"Continue, Mr. Foreman," said the judge.

"On the count of the murder of Laura Samuels we find the defendant, Daniel Boyland, guilty as charged."

Despite Delaney's admonition, bedlam erupted as I'm sure he knew it would, but the court officers moved swiftly and cleared everyone out. Within five minutes the room was empty and the doors locked. Jeff put his arm around my shoulders and helped me sit down as Delaney thanked the jury for their service. Jeff requested that he be allowed to poll the jury. Each one, individually, affirmed their guilty vote and then Jeff asked if he could speak with them in the jury room. Paul asked to be present and Delaney agreed. All I could do was sit at the defense table with my head in my hands in shock and disbelief.

Jeff and Paul returned and the jurors went home. Delaney looked at his calendar and said, "I'd like to set Tuesday, December 14, for sentencing. Do either of you have any conflicts on that date? They returned to their tables and punched up their little computers and returned to inform the judge that they were free. "Good," he said. "Ten o'clock."

"By the way Jeff," said Paul. "You did a great job and put up a magnificent defense."

"Thanks, Paul, but it just wasn't good enough was it?"

"Could've convinced me," he said as he walked away.

"What did the jury have to say?" I asked Jeff.

"We'll discuss that tomorrow. Willy and I are coming over to talk with you. He has some ideas."

"About what?"

"He'll tell us tomorrow. All I can say is we're not finished yet—not by a long shot."

We shook hands and he left, and the correction officers put the handcuffs on me and took me away. As they drove me back to the jail the realization of what had just happened began to penetrate my brain. When the jury announced the verdicts I went into temporary shock caused by disbelief. When I recovered, I spoke with the lawyers almost as if it hadn't happened—as if I were planning the next day's testimony, but now it hit me. It had happened. I was found guilty of murder. I was going away for a long time, maybe forever. Delaney could have sentenced me on the spot. There was no discretion involved with these charges—25 to life for murder and 15 to life for the attempted murder—both terms to be served consecutively. My first parole hearing would be in 40 years. I would be 76 years old or already dead, buried and long forgotten.

I started to shake and then began to sob. I was glad that I was alone in the back of the van. Forty years! Would I ever see my kids again? And Niki—where are you now, my lovely Niki? You promised to love me forever—where the hell are you now?

I couldn't believe it, but I slept like a rock that night from 8:00 p.m. right through breakfast. The guard had placed my food tray in my cell and let me sleep on. I didn't awake until after nine. I guess all the tension and sleeplessness of the past two weeks had caught up with me and my body had said, "Enough!"

Willy and Jeff showed up at 10:30 and Jeff filled us in on the juror's comments. "It was as I figured. They convicted you for destroying your family. They didn't know which side to believe, so they went on the physical evidence, or so they said."

"Did they really admit that?"

"No, but I read between the lines. It's pretty obvious when you hear things as, 'What a shame that he did that to his family,' and 'How could he carry on with that woman'?"

"Do we have any recourse? An appeal?"

"An appeal is automatic in a capital murder conviction, but that's for procedural errors only and there weren't any. We need something to re-open the case and get a reversal."

"And I have an idea along those lines," said Willy.

"I'm listening."

"The two lying witnesses—Reggio and Millstein. I'm sure they were being blackmailed. I know it in my bones and Sam and I are going to find out why and try to flip one or both of them."

"Well, if anyone can do it, you can," I said. "How am I going to pay you and Sam? I…"

"Danny, Jeff's firm is paying us. We gave him a good price, a police discount because he's a good guy and you're a good guy. I never want to hear another word about money again. Understand?"

I turned to Jeff and he put his hand up to stop me. "I have eight appoint-ments next week with people who I believe have a lot of money and are looking to retain my services."

"Don't they realize you lost my case?"

"Doesn't matter," said Willy. "All publicity is good publicity. Besides, they probably figure that any lawyer that could concoct that phony frame-up theory for you could come up with an equally good story for them."

We had a nice laugh over that one and it felt good to laugh again. Willy was some guy. He stuck with me all the way and I knew he'd stick with me a whole lot longer, even if the money ran out.

"There's nothing much else to do until sentencing," said Jeff. "Delaney doesn't have much leeway I'm afraid. So let's work on Willy's idea. He's going to bring all the papers over so you can read the trial coverage. Make some notes. Give us some ideas."

December 14 arrived soon enough and Delaney sentenced me as we predicted—40 years to life. They took me back to the county jail pending my custody change to the state system. I sat around in my cell until they found the right place for me. Cops, lawyers and those who sexually abused children get separated from the general population. The wardens don't want any additional assaults and murders on their watch if they could avoid it.

On December 19, a Sunday, they came to get me and drove me to my new home for the next 40 years, the state correctional facility at Wallkill in upstate Ulster County, about an hour and a half from the city. Forty years to reflect on what I had done to myself and my family. Forty years to think of the woman who framed me so beautifully, so expertly, and gift-wrapped me for delivery to the care and custody of the New York State Department of Correctional Services for what would probably be the rest of my natural life.

PART THREE

So now you know what happened—what I did to myself and what I did to my family. When they slammed the gate closed on my new home in cellblock 2B, it was as if it slammed my entire prior existence into another dimension, never to be retrieved. Good-bye Jeanie. Good-bye Patrick and Kelly. I'll never see you grow up, get married, have kids of your own—my grandchildren. My God, can you ever forgive me? I'll never go to work again in the Homicide Squad with Tara and Manny and Francis Finn—never wait in anticipation for another Big One. I had my whodunit, and I screwed it up—royally.

The urgency to write a million dollar best seller has abated somewhat, but I'm keeping up this journal anyway. There's not much else to do here, except read and write. Jeff seems confident he will make a lot of money in the future, so that took a lot of the pressure off. Even though the Son of Sam law prevents me from earning any profits from my "crimes," that's all right. I'd give all the money to Jeanie and the kids since I can't support them any more.

But wait a minute you're saying, this story is over, right? You might think so, but you'd be very wrong. Not so fast there, readers—this story is not over. Not by a long shot. The fat lady has walked onto the stage, the lights have come on and the band has warmed up, but she hasn't even started to sing yet.

Chapter 13

Cellblock 2B contained two dozen inmates. Most of them were disbarred lawyers, disgraced cops and assorted sexual perverts. There was only one other murderer in the block, a guy who had sexually abused, raped and suffocated a seven year old girl. We were a small group and not allowed to mix in with the general prison population. We had to spend 20 hours each day, every day, alone in our cells with only our thoughts and our memories to keep us company. That was fine with me—I had absolutely no desire to associate with any of my dirtbag block mates. They were criminals—guys I spent my career locking up. I was not. I kept to myself in silence at meal times and during exercise periods and rebuffed attempts to engage me in a conversation.

So I suffered by myself in self-loathing and self-pity. My first Christmas away from my family occurred just six days after I arrived. If spending Thanksgiving at the Nassau County Jail had been awful, Christmas here at the Wallkill Correctional Facility was much, much worse. It was depressing beyond words and feelings.

The difference between a local lock-up like the Nassau County Jail and a state lock-up like the medium security prison at Wallkill can be compared to the difference between Purgatory and Hell. Having been raised in the Roman Catholic faith when Purgatory was still in fashion, I well knew the difference. If you were in Purgatory, no matter how much you had to suffer for your sins, no matter how much time you had to spend there in that torment, salvation and the promise of Heaven were always there—the bright, white light at the end of the tunnel.

The Nassau County Jail was Purgatory. It was a relatively pleasant place for those with short fixed sentences for one reason only—you knew if you played by the rules and kept your mouth shut you would be out in less than a year. State prison was a totally different place, especially for those placed here with long sentences like mine. When the doors clanged shut I imagined that there was a sign above them that read, "Abandon All Hope Ye Who Enter Here." That's exactly how I felt—hopeless. No better word existed to describe my condition.

In early January I was sent a copy of the final divorce decree which had been granted to Jean. She got the house, the cars, the kids, and all my pension money—the $22,000 I was going to use to escape to paradise with Niki. I got my clothes and golf clubs which were now in Willy Edwards's house in Bellerose. None of that had mattered—the material things, that is. What did I need money for? Or a car? And for that matter, when I see Willy I'll tell him he might as well sell the clubs and give the money to Jean.

Fortunately, Jeff volunteered to review the divorce papers back in December. He passed them on to the matrimonial lawyers in his firm and they made some changes, the most important of which was visitation. Jean's lawyer had a clause in there that stated I was forbidden to visit or attempt to contact her, Patrick, and Kelly forever. It seemed of no consequence since I was going to be here for 40 years, but Jeff said, "Suppose your conviction gets overturned?" So they changed that to allow visitation in that circumstance. I thanked him, but knew the chances of that happening seemed slim to none.

I finally got up the nerve to do something I had been avoiding since the day I was arrested, but now seemed to be the time. The divorce was final and I was out of her life forever. I took a sheet of paper and wrote,

Dear Jean,

It is difficult for me to imagine the suffering and misery I've caused you and our children. I cannot find the words to express my sorrow and shame for doing what I did to our family. I am not referring to my conviction for murder—I did not commit those crimes and I believe you know that I did not.

But then, I committed worse crimes by getting involved with another woman and thus destroying our family. I guess you could well believe I did commit murder as well, and I wouldn't blame you for that.

I apologize to you and the children for what I have caused. I have no explanation for my actions. Although wrongly convicted, I will spend the

next 40 years paying for what I did to you. I will not ask your forgiveness.
I could never deserve it.

May the future be bright and happy for you, Patrick, and Kelly. I will
think of you always. Danny

Ten days later I received a letter from the lawyer who represented Jean.

Dear Mr. Boyland,

Your communication to your ex-wife was referred to me and is returned,
unopened, with this letter. Please be aware that she does not want to have
any contact, written communications, electronic communications or tele-
phone communications from you to her or the children. These prohibi-
tions are detailed in pages 17-19 of your stipulation of settlement, adden-
dum A, in your divorce decree. Continued attempts at communications
may result in legal actions.

> *Very truly yours,*
> *R.H. Sinacore, Esq.*
> *Cc: J. Levy, Esq.*

Legal actions, Mr. Sinacore? What are you going to do? Have me
thrown in jail?

Willy came to see me for the first time in late January. Although I had
spoken with him and Jeff once in a while on the phone, this was my first
in-the-flesh contact with a person from my former life. The visit, however, cut both ways. It was great to see the old, smiling retired detective and
to spend the time with him. But when he left it was as if part of my life
was leaving forever even though I knew he would be back. But when
would he come back? And how long would he keep up the visits? And
when Willy was no more, who would come to see me then? Or even
remember that I was here at all?

Willy told me that he and Sam Lewis had almost completed their back-
ground investigations into Victor Reggio and Ronald Millstein. "There's
no doubt that Nicole was involved with them in the past," he said. "I
developed a couple of sources in the neighborhood, one of whom is a
paralegal at the law firm—in fact, one of those you and Tara had interviewed."

"What are you going to do?"

"Sam and I are going to talk to both of them and try to convince them to come clean and admit they perjured themselves."

"What makes you think they would do that? Perjury is a felony."

"Sam and I have been figuring that out and we have the beginnings of a plan, but let's not talk about that now until we're certain of how to best approach them."

Willy came again to see me six weeks later. "Any news of Niki and Marty?" I asked.

"They're both still at Keenan, Rosen and Vario and seem to be chummy again. George Stanton told me that the insurance company had no choice but to pay off on the policy. Marty got the million on February 15."

"Did he transfer any to Niki?"

"Nope, he paid off his mortgages and replaced the money in his kid's college funds. That left him with a little over $750,000 which is in an assortment of mutual funds and cash at a brokerage firm."

"I thought for sure they'd split it."

"Maybe they're just continuing to lay low for a while longer. They have to know by now that me and Sam have been nosing around."

"Anything happening with Reggio and Millstein?"

"Ah, yes! The main reason for my visit. Let me relate the stories of our encounters with Victor and Ronnie."

"I don't like the way you said that, Willy. Are you about to subject me to another long-winded caper?"

"Do you have someplace to go?" he smiled. "A hot date perhaps? A tee time at the local golf course?"

"With your stories you never know. This won't take longer than 40 years will it?"

"Now, now, Danny Boy, you hurt me deeply. I'm going to ease your pain because I'm not going to verbally relate these interviews. I'm going to allow you to read them and then we will discuss them. I know I do have a slight tendency to ramble on and stray from the subject at hand when I'm speaking, so here you go."

Willy handed me two bound volumes of transcripts. One was very slim and had the name of Victor Reggio on the cover. The other was much thicker and had the name Ronald Millstein on its cover. I asked Willy how he got these.

"Whaddya mean?" he replied. "They're the transcripts of our interviews."

"I figured that out, but you must have taped them, right?"

"Of course, but they knew that...er...sort of."

"Huh?"

"Danny, just read them, will ya? It's all explained in there. Meanwhile, I'm hungry. I'm going down to the visitor's cafeteria for a long lunch. You should be finished when I return."

He called for the guard and when he left I figured I'd start with the easy one first. I picked up Reggio's transcript and read the preamble.

"This report is the transcript of an interview conducted by Samuel Lewis (SL) and William Edwards (WE) with subject, Victor Reggio (VR), owner of Victor's Lounge, Queens Boulevard, Kew Gardens, NY. The interview began on February 20 at 3:00 p.m. and concluded at 3:29 p.m. We first met Reggio just inside the front entrance to the lounge.

SL: Good afternoon, Mr. Reggio. May we have a few words with you?

VR: Who are you guys?

SL: I'm Sam Lewis and this is Willy Edwards. We are private investigators.

VR: Oh, yeah? Who are you working for?

SL: We represent former Detective Daniel Boyland.

VR: I have nothing to say on that subject.

WE: That's no problem, Mr. Reggio. We will not ask you any questions. All we ask is that you listen. We have information that may be of great value to you.

VR: Such as?

SL: Can we talk somewhere in private?

VR: No, I don't want to talk to you guys or listen to your bullshit. I have absolutely no reason to. Get lost.

WE: How about your life?

VR: Huh?

WE: Is the fact that your life may be in serious danger a good enough reason to listen to us?

VR: Let's go to my office, but this better not be a waste of my time.

(The following occurred in Mr. Reggio's private office)

SL: I'll get right to the point Mr. Reggio. We believe Danny Boyland was framed and we believe your testimony was used to assist in that frame-up.

VR: Hey, what the fuck?

SL: Please, hear me out. We also believe that you did not perjure yourself willingly. We believe you were coerced and blackmailed into doing so.

WE: And what we would like, Mr. Reggio, is for you to give us a written statement admitting to that fact and...

VR: You guys must be nuts! I told the truth on the stand. Nobody blackmailed me. This conversation is over.

SL: Hold on. We said that's what we wanted. We had no expectation that you would admit perjuring yourself, but we had to ask. We believe you and Nicole Wells had an affair and that she possesses certain pictures of the two of you, which if made public, would destroy your marriage and probably your business.

VR: I had no affair with Niki.

WE: Mr.Reggio, Nicole Wells murdered Laura Samuels. Nicole Wells framed Daniel Boyland for the murder. There are only two loose ends to tie up, or better, to eliminate—two loose ends that stand between her eventual discovery and her future with Marty and a million bucks. Those two loose ends are you and Ronald Millstein.

VR: Are you saying Niki is planning to knock us off?

SL: Exactly, Mr. Reggio.

VR: (laughing) Niki kill me? Wait'll she hears this one!

SL: I wouldn't advise telling her about this conversation.

VR: Why not?

SL: It might hasten your death.

VR: Oh, yeah? You're both nuts. You can leave now.

WE: We'll go, but think over what we said. Think it over very carefully and then take a few steps to protect yourself.

SL: Quickly, Mr. Reggio, before it's too late.

VR: Hey, what's that? You're taping me?

SL: Yes, we are, but when we leave you can have the tape. Take it to your lawyer. Cut a deal on the perjury charge. Get the truth on the record and get into the witness protection program—soon.

WE: Very soon, Mr. Reggio. Good-bye.

(End of conversation)

Nice job guys. That should shake up Victor despite his tough guy stance, but was it enough to scare him into confessing to perjury? I didn't think so—and I wondered if he did call Niki. I picked up Millstein's transcript. The initial approach to him was the same one they had used with Reggio. Millstein had not shown any bravado, but threatened to call his lawyer on a couple of occasions before they were able to calm him down and get him into his office at the rear of the pharmacy. They had approached him at closing time on February 22. The only reason he continued the interview was Sam's and Willy's promise not to require him to answer any questions or, for that matter, to speak at all. When they got into the office Sam produced the tape recorder right up front and put it on the desk. I was now sure that Willy had a second recorder secreted in his jacket pocket.

SL: The tape is yours when we're done, Mr. Millstein, a sign of our good faith and seriousness.

RM: The only reason I've agreed to listen to you is your rather startling statement that my life may be in danger. Once you tell me why, I plan to discontinue this interview.

WE: Fine, Mr. Millstein. We believe that Nicole Wells murdered Laura Samuels and framed our client, Daniel Boyland, for that murder. We also believe you and Victor Reggio aided in Danny's conviction by giving false testimony.

RM: I did not…

SL: Mr. Millstein, you do not have to defend yourself or explain your actions. The tape is yours. Just listen as we agreed. Although we would love to have you admit to us right now your perjury in this case, we realize you have no reason to do so.

WE: If I were in your shoes I wouldn't admit to anything either, Mr. Millstein. You have too much to lose—your wife, your family, probably your business.

SL: But on the other hand, your continued complicity could result in your death.

The interview went on with Sam and Willy playing a semi-good cop/bad cop routine. They gave him the 'two loose ends' scenario as well as a few others. For the past twenty pages he had not said a word. When I was wondering how long Sam and Willy could hammer him without a gripe, Sam, who had sensed the same thing said,

SL: We've laid it all out, Mr. Millstein, and we appreciate you listening to us. It's up to you now. We'll leave you alone.

RM: May I ask a question?

WE: Sure.

RM: I'd like to pose a hypothetical situation—purely hypothetical.

WE: Go ahead.

RM: Let's assume something for the moment, hypothetically, as I said. Let's assume that everything you said is true, that I had an affair with Niki, she took compromising photos and she threatened to make them public if I didn't give false testimony. Furthermore, let's assume that she now plans to kill me to tie up her loose ends, as you put it. Assuming all that is true, what would you do now if you were me?

WE: First, I would have to weigh the probability that Niki would really try to kill me. If I were convinced that was a remote possibility and was assured of my continued safety, I'd keep my mouth shut.

RM: I appreciate your honesty, Mr. Edwards, but suppose I did believe my life was in jeopardy?

SL: Then I'd take this tape and go immediately to my lawyer and explore my possibilities, and I'd do it right away.

RM: What possibilities are there?

WE: You know my first thought might be to take the tape, write out your whole story, assemble any evidence you might have and package the whole thing up for your lawyer with a note saying, "TO BE OPENED IN CASE OF MY DEATH," but that's really no good.

RM: Why not?

WE: Well, it helps Danny, but then you're dead. Let's look at an option that keeps you alive.

RM: Such as?

SL: Take all the stuff as Willy said and confide in your lawyer. Have him approach the DA to cut a deal for you—immunity on the perjury and placement in the witness protection program. When Niki gets arrested for the murder you resume your normal life.

RM: Without my wife and family.

WE: Not necessarily. Nicole might not have a chance to release those pictures. The police may find them in the search incident to her arrest. They may never see the light of day.

SL: Mr. Millstein, we know we've put you between a rock and a hard place, but Danny's doing 40 to life for crimes he did not commit. Think it over. Do the right thing. We'll leave you in peace now.

RM: Peace? I don't think so.

(End of tape)

A magnificent interview! Sam and Willy were old pros—two of the best. I had some hopes now. Come on, Millstein, get to your lawyer—now. I had a chance to re-read both transcripts, more carefully this time, before Willy finally returned from lunch.

"So, what'd you think?" he asked.

"Impressive. You and Sam are still super detectives. Anything from Millstein yet?"

"Nada, but we'll keep after him once in a while. It's only been three weeks."

"**You** guys were so convincing that I'd have been to my lawyer's office the next morning."

"He's got a lot to lose if he fesses up, but as I said, Sam and I will keep pushing."

"I know you will. Willy, I don't know how to thank you enough for sticking by me. All I have left in the world is you and Sam and Jeff. I don't know…"

"Hey, Danny Boy, knock that crap off. As Kojak used to say, 'who loves ya, baby?'"

March ended and Millstein and Reggio sat tight. My automatic appeal was denied, as was expected, and my hope that at least Millstein would crack, gradually faded away. I re-read all the newspaper accounts of my arrest and trial, over and over, trying to find something in the reported versions that could offer some slight hope. I found nothing.

Willy called every so often, but nothing had popped. He and Sam tried to approach Victor Reggio again, but he threatened to call the cops and his lawyer. They visited Millstein, but he only said, "I'm sorry, there's nothing more to discuss."

After Willy's visit in March, where I got juiced up by reading Millstein's interview, I again sank back into depression when nothing happened. I was helpless and hopeless. There was nothing to do, but read and keep my journal up-to-date. But what was there to put in it? Every day was exactly the same—Wake up. Breakfast. Read in cell. Lunch. Exercise. Read in cell. Dinner. TV. Read in cell. Sleep. Wake up…The thought of being here and doing this for 39½ more years was not in the realm of possibility. I wished for my gun. If you had ever suggested that

I, Daniel Boyland, would ever consider suicide, for any reason, I would say you were crazy. Not so anymore. I now equated suicide with freedom.

April, May, June and July crawled by. On August 20 Willy came to see me. I asked him if he brought me an anniversary gift.

"What?"

"It's one year to the day that I got arrested."

"You're kidding! Already?"

"Amazing, isn't it? Only 39 to go."

"Sorry, I forgot the gift, but I have some very interesting news."

"I'm listening."

"Guess who slipped out to Las Vegas on the fourth of July and got married?"

"Jean?"

"Nope."

"Well, tell me already, will you?"

"Marty and Niki."

"You're kidding! How did you find out?"

"Remember George Stanton?"

"Sure, the retired Suffolk County cop from the insurance company."

"George has proven to be a very good friend and reliable source of information. All these insurance guys belong to a security association and George had let them all know about the million dollar policy and the fraud involved. So one of the security guys calls George the other day and tells him that a Mr. and Mrs. Martin Samuels of Woodmere, New York have applied for various insurance coverages which will, no doubt, be denied."

"What do you make of it?"

"I guess they feel that you're away for good and their relationship, and now their marriage, can't do them any harm. I took the opportunity to visit Millstein again and I lied a little bit."

"What did you tell him?"

"I told him of the marriage and I fibbed and said there existed a million dollar life insurance policy on Marty and I guessed he could now be considered a third 'loose end.' I wondered out loud who would get knocked off first."

"Any reaction?"

"No, but then I asked him if Niki ever stopped in to say hello or buy some mouthwash, and he answered 'no' much too fast. He's scared stiff.

I think that Mr. Macho Man, Reggio, tipped her off, and that she occasionally visits Millstein to remind him to keep his mouth shut."

"Any hope that he'll come forward soon?"

"I don't know. There's gotta be something more I can do to put pressure on him. I'm searching, you know that."

"I know, Willy. I know."

The seasons changed once more as September arrived, but I couldn't tell from in here, just from the calendar. The only glimpse of nature I ever got was a view of the sky from the high-walled exercise yard. I was a year older and so were Pat and Kelly, growing up without me. Willy came to see me from time to time, basically to just say hello and try to boost my spirits. I think he knew that his visits were the only thing keeping me barely sane. Then, when he came in January, he brought a bunch of newspapers.

"Wait till you read this, my boy. Now there are two."

"What are you talking about, old timer?"

"Here, read," he said, opening the *New York Daily News* to page four.

The headline said: Local Queens Lounge Owner Dead.

The story said: *Victor Reggio, owner of Victor's Lounge in Kew Gardens, was killed last night as he walked on Queens Boulevard after closing his place of business at about 2:00 a.m. He was apparently the victim of a hit and run accident, although a passing witness said the car, which had jumped the curb and came up on the sidewalk, had headed directly for the unsuspecting victim and had made no attempt to swerve to avoid hitting him.*

The force of the impact drove Mr. Reggio into the brick façade of a building instantly crushing him to death. A young man wearing a dark colored ski mask exited from the vehicle according to the same witness and ran to the first cross street where he turned and disappeared. Mr. Reggio left a wife of fifteen years and two young children. Queens Homicide is investigating.

"Holy shit!" I said. "When did this happen?"

"Three days ago."

"Does Millstein know?"

"Why, certainly! I delivered the newspapers personally to him that very same morning."

"And how did Ronnie handle that news?"

"He was trembling something fierce—could hardly keep the paper still enough to read it. All I said to him was, 'Food for thought, Mr. Millstein—only two loose ends to go.'"

"Do you think that guy in the ski mask was really Niki?"

"Can't say. Queens Homicide went over the car with a fine tooth comb. The only prints they found belonged to the owner who didn't even know his car was missing. It was stolen in Brooklyn about two hours before the hit."

"Is Queens Homicide going to look at Niki?"

"Possibly. The stories in the *Post* and *Newsday* both mention Reggio's role in your trial. Sam and I put the bug in their ear, but I'm not hopeful."

"I'm sure Niki's loving hew husband will swear she was right next to him in bed all night long. Are they living in Woodmere permanently?"

"Yeah, Niki gave up the apartment a couple of months after they got hitched. Now they can drive into work together."

"How can they do that?" I asked. "Sleep in the same bed together that they murdered Laura in. It's a desecration!"

"They have a term for people like that, Danny—amoral. They have no conscience. Sociopath might fit, too."

"Jeez, Willy, maybe this will make that fucking Millstein step up to the plate and hit a home run for us."

"I'm hoping so, too. Oh, by the way, some dopey insurance company finally did provide coverage for the newlyweds. One million on Marty's life with Niki as the sole beneficiary, and 250 thousand on Niki's life with Marty as the sole beneficiary. And their wills leave all assets to each other with the exception of the house. If Marty dies the kids get the house to share, but Niki gets all the cash, stocks and mutual funds."

"Plus the million dollars. She sure does like nice round numbers."

"A million always has a nice ring to it, doesn't it?"

"Hey, how do you find out all this stuff?"

"How dare you ask me that? I was an ace detective for over 30 years and now I am an ace private eye. Vee haff our vays."

I laughed along with him and it felt good. I hadn't laughed at anything for a long, long time. "So who do you think is next on the hit parade?" I asked.

"It's a toss-up, but if it's Millstein, I hope the dumb bastard has a package at his lawyer's office waiting to be opened."

•

Willy's visit and the slim hope that something might happen that could get judicial notice of my case temporarily buoyed my spirits and I began to fantasize of rebuilding my life outside of prison. Of course, the main vision was a complete recapture of my home, wife, children and my job. But that vision quickly faded when I faced the facts of the situation— Jeanie had divorced me and would, rightly so, hate me the rest of our lives. My kids hadn't seen me in over a year and no doubt felt the same way as Jean. The Department had fired me and would never take me back, even if I was somehow, someday, acquitted of the false charges.

As I read and re-read my journal, there was one thing that I couldn't shake—a few sentences I could not get out of my mind. On that Tuesday in August of last year, the night I last saw Niki, she had held me tight, looked directly into my eyes and said, "You must know that I love you, and that I will always love you. Remember that, Danny. No matter what happens, I will always love you."

Of course what happened was that she turned me in the very next day. And yet I felt, and still feel, there was more to her words, some hidden meaning, some master plan that was yet to be played out. And on the stand, when Jeff had asked her about those words and said they were just another lie, she looked at me, and answered, "No, not really." And although she would not directly state that she was in love with me, could not state that as it would ruin her deception, her eyes said it all.

But why fool myself. A hopeless man clings to whatever thread might be available to hang onto when all the other threads have slipped away. And yet, I just could not shake those words from my mind. And I could not delete the beautiful face that said those words.

Chapter 14

It wasn't Millstein who had the next "accident"—it was Marty Samuels. He had departed suddenly, and unexpectedly, by drowning while snorkeling with his lovely young wife off the beach at St. Bart's in the Caribbean during their winter vacation. The press release said: *Mr. Samuels had apparently gone into a diabetic coma while snorkeling, and subsequently drowned. Mrs. Samuels, who said she was on the opposite side of the lagoon when the accident occurred, was too distraught to speak with reporters and was expected to return with the body to the United States upon its release by the local coroner.*

I had received a note from a guard to call Willy when it was my time to access the telephone and that's when he had given me the news. "I guess Ronnie Millstein is on the verge of a breakdown by now," I said.

"It seemed that way when I told him about the 'accident.' I thought I smelled a faint odor of diarrhea emanating from behind the counter, especially when I reminded him that he was now the last 'loose end.'"

"The only diarrhea I want him to get, Willy, is diarrhea of the mouth."

Back in my cell I pondered this new turn of events. What was going on here? Why would Niki murder Marty? For the insurance money again? Wasn't one million enough for the both of them? Didn't they have what they wanted? They had gotten away with murder and should have lived happily ever after. Maybe it was an accident. In either case, if I were Ronnie Millstein right now I'd be one scared druggist.

And then, finally, on March 17, good old St. Patrick's Day, Ronald Millstein could suffer no longer and went to see his lawyer. What put him over the edge we later learned—the one additional shove he needed—was that he had recently discovered his wife had been cheating on him. When he confronted her she told him she didn't care, she no longer wanted to be married to a stuffy, old pharmacist. She wanted excitement in her life and she wasn't getting it from him. And that was the last hurdle Ronnie had in front of him to clear and he now actually hoped his wife would get to see the pictures of him and Nicole. "Screw you, you bitch!" he had told her. "I beat you to it!" And I whispered aloud, "Thank you, thank you, Mrs. Millstein, wherever you are!"

The deal-making between Millstein's lawyer and the establishment dragged on. Ronnie wanted complete immunity from prosecution and a spot in the witness protection program. The first response from the DA had been no immunity, but a reduction of the felony perjury charge to a misdemeanor and some jail time. Also, the protection would end when Nicole was apprehended and convicted. Millstein balked and the wrangling continued. He stuck to his guns, claiming he had a lot to offer, and I thought he certainly did. He was willing to testify that he perjured himself at my trial and that he had given the toluene, duct tape and cotton to Niki about ten days prior to the murder. But his biggest ace in the hole was the original ledger—he had not destroyed it but hid it with the pictures of him and Niki! He would testify to the authenticity of this ledger and describe the painstaking hours he spent copying each entry into the second ledger, at the insistence of Nicole, to falsely add the "Arthur Davis" transaction.

The negotiations continued for two weeks as I sat in my cell waiting in agony. All the parties involved were going to meet on Friday, April 1, to hammer out the final deal—Millstein, his lawyer, Judge Delaney, Jeff Levy, Barry Walsh and Paul Valentine. But, April Fool!—one person didn't show up. He couldn't attend the meeting because the night before, as he was closing up the Boulevard Pharmacy, two ski-masked stick-up men robbed him for the money and for the drugs and left Ronald Millstein sprawled in the pain reliever aisle with four slugs in his head and chest. Apparently, the last 'loose end' had been neatly tied up.

Now a new round of bargaining began. The chief sticking point was paper testimony versus live testimony. Were Millstein's written affidavits and verbal admissions sufficient to overturn my conviction without him being able to testify in person? Later on Jeff told me they all agreed they were, but they wanted to make sure they had all their ducks in a row before submitting their findings and recommendations to the appellate court.

More weeks dragged on as I suffered in silence, then on Tuesday morning, April 19 at 10:45 a.m., Willy Edwards appeared at my cell with a correction officer in tow and a big smile on his face. "As they used to say in the old gangster movies," he said. "Pack up your things—we're blowing this joint!"

"This is really it? I'm free?"

"Yup, yesterday afternoon a three-judge panel of the appellate court handed down a unanimous decision overturning your conviction and vacating your sentence. Sam Lewis is waiting in the car and Jeff is in with the warden serving him a copy of the order. They're bringing your clothes up shortly, but if they don't fit I brought pants and a shirt that are a size smaller."

I got dressed—I had to use the clothes Willy brought—and the officer escorted us from cellblock 2B to freedom. I had spent 16 months here in Wallkill, and as I walked out I said good-bye to no one, and did not look back. With the four months in the Nassau County Jail I had spent a total of 20 months behind bars for crimes I had not committed. If I had lived a nightmare, what about those occasional cases you read about where innocent guys spend 20 years in jail? I considered myself fortunate and, as we met Jeff and walked to the car, I breathed in deeply of the mild, spring air and the tears rolled freely down my cheeks.

Willy got in the front seat with Sam and I got in the back with Jeff. When I stopped crying they all congratulated me on my release and I thanked them profusely for their tireless efforts in getting me out. Most of all I thanked them for their faith in me and my innocence. Right now, these were the last three friends I had in the whole, wide world.

Sam meandered through some scenic country roads as he headed for the New York Thruway. I drank in the beauty of nature—the horses and cows in greening meadows, the flowers beginning to bloom and the trees beginning to show their leaves. I saw a gorgeous patch of bright pink hyacinths and I asked Sam to pull over for a minute. I got out and walked over to the flowers and knelt in front of them to inhale their fragrance. My hands dug into the loose black earth and then I rose, lifting my face to the midday sun. When I returned to the car I said, "Ah! The winter of my discontent is made glorious by the bright spring sunshine of New York."

"Shakespeare?" asked Jeff.

"Paraphrased from *Richard the Third*," I replied.

"Wow, an intellectual is in the car," said Willy.

"In addition to writing my memoirs of this case, I read a lot of books back there including all of Shakespeare—twice."

When we got back to Nassau County we stopped for lunch at Mulvaney's.

"We figured you might want to dig into a big cheeseburger and wash it down with a beer," said Willy, "and do so in a friendly, familiar place."

"You figured right," I said.

I devoured the burger, and naturally it was the best tasting, most satisfying burger I had ever eaten. After 20 months of jail food it had to be. Even with the burger and fries in my stomach, the alcohol in the Heineken's went right to my head before I was halfway finished with it. I guess that was to be expected since I hadn't had a drink in a long time. I looked around Mulvaney's recalling the good times, but only memories now. The party was over and the good times would never return.

We all went back to Jeff's office, and saw his desk was covered with pink paper messages. He scanned them rapidly and said, "Most of these are inquiries from the media. I guess I'll have to call a press conference tomorrow morning. Want to attend, Danny?"

"Hell, no! You know I rank reporters one rung below lawyers, present company excluded, of course."

"No problem, I'll handle it."

"Hey, Jeff," said Willy, "if business got better after the trial, just imagine what will happen now that you got Danny's conviction overturned? You won't be able to handle the case load."

"You can double your hourly rate," said Sam.

"Wear your best suit and smile for the cameras," I said, "I'll watch it on television..." And then it suddenly hit me—I had no place to go and that's what I blurted out. "Oh my God, I have no place to go. I have no home."

"Sure you do," said Willy. "You will be living with me and Edna. We have two spare bedrooms and one of them is waiting for you with your clothes hanging in the closet and your golf clubs in the garage. Edna's shopping for your homecoming dinner right now."

"Willy, I don't know what to say, I..."

"Say nothing. Stay as long as you need to."

"Oh," said Jeff, reaching into a safe underneath his desk, "this is for you."

I took the envelope and recognized it at once. "For Danny" it said, and the note was still there wrapped around the money—"Danny, from your friends in the squad."

I said, "Jeff, I can't take this money. It's yours for all your…"

"Danny," he said, "there is no legal bill. You are paid in full."

"Keep it," said Willy. "It's a start to your new life."

Jeff had me review and sign some papers and then we all said our good-byes. Willy drove me to my new home and I finally started to believe the nightmare was over.

The local cable TV all-news channel carried Jeff's entire press conference live. It was bedlam and lasted well over an hour. The stories in the papers before, and especially after the news conference, centered on Nicole. Some enterprising young reporter had coined her the "Dragon Lady," and it stuck like glue. "Where is the Dragon Lady?" a headline shouted. "A string of bodies in the Dragon Lady's path" said another. The press concluded that she had murdered Laura Samuels, Victor Reggio, Ronald Millstein and Marty Samuels, although no proof existed for those conclusions. They also speculated—"Who's next? Will the Dragon Lady's next victim be ex-Detective Daniel Boyland? Is he in danger?" I got a big laugh out of that one. In retrospect, I shouldn't have laughed at all.

I settled in with Willy and Edna and they insisted that I relax for as long as I wanted before I looked for work. "I work only two days a week, so you can use my car if you want," said Edna. "And Willy can drive me on the other days."

"Yeah," said Willy, "drive around, go hit the golf ball, go to the beach, and when you get bored then go looking for a job."

I thought of driving Edna's car to my old neighborhood in Franklin Square to catch a glimpse of Pat and Kelly getting off their school bus. I desperately wanted to see them, but that idea was put to rest by a telephone call from Jeff the next day.

"Danny, I received a letter from Sinacore, Jean's attorney. I'll send you a copy, but in essence it says they want support and maintenance payments from you as soon as you begin to work. They want the payments to go to Sinacore's office and he will forward them to Jean. It seems Jean and the kids have re-located out of state and that her last name is no longer Boyland, although Sinacore wouldn't divulge what it was."

As I was absorbing this blow I was wondering where they would have gone. Her parents were in Virginia and her brother was in California. I asked Jeff about visitation. "Jeff, my conviction has been overturned. Can she continue to prevent me from seeing my kids?"

"In my opinion, no. I'm not an expert on family law, but she may fight it vigorously."

"What do I do?"

"Find out where she lives, and then hire the best lawyer you can find in that area and go after her."

"Expensive?"

"Yeah, no free counsel in the civil justice system. I would guess 20 grand, minimum, if she fights you."

"Thanks for the good news."

"Sorry. I'll send you the letter, and if you find where your kids are living, I'll see if I can find a lawyer for you in that area."

"Thanks, friend, I appreciate your efforts, as always."

This depressing news was followed by more that evening. "Danny," said Willy, "I didn't want to tell you sooner, but Edna and I went to contract on our house about two weeks ago."

"You're moving?"

"Yeah, and there's something else I didn't tell you—I have a bit of a problem with the old ticker."

"But Willy, I thought you checked out perfect when you had your medical exam right before you left the job."

"I did, but they never pick up everything. I was having chest pains a few months back and the tests showed blockages in two of my coronary arteries. I had a couple of stents put in. No big deal, I'm fine."

"No big deal? Why didn't you tell me?"

"You had enough problems in your life up there in Wallkill without me burdening you with mine."

"You are too much, old man. You should have told me. I would rather have worried about you than cried in my own beer."

"Thanks," he said.

"So, tell me more about this."

"First, I'm packing the private investigator career in, short as it was. The doc says it's time to slow down, enjoy life and smell the roses. He wants me to have as little stress as possible. Now with no job, me and

Edna figured it was the time to move down near where my son, Bill, lives."

"Is he still in Atlanta?"

"Yes, and probably will be there a long time. They have a three-year old boy and another child on the way. Do you know Edna and I have seen our grandchild only three or four times? That's gonna change. We're pushing 60, Danny. It's time."

"You're damn right it is. I'm happy for you and Edna. Get out of New York and enjoy your golden years with your family."

"Willy, when are you actually moving?"

"We're tentatively going to closing in about a month."

"Well, that gives me time to get a room somewhere and find a job."

"Edna and I are going down for ten days or so to check things out. We're considering building an apartment extension on Bill's house or getting our own place, maybe a condo, or maybe a small house. We don't know, but we have to do something pretty soon. Bill is letting us stay with him until we decide, but we don't want to put him out for too long a time."

"When are you leaving?"

"Next Monday, out of JFK, and we need a lift to the airport."

"No problem," I said. "I am available."

"Good, use the cars and keep an eye on the place while we're gone— but no wild parties or exotic women allowed."

"Yes, Daddy, I'll be a good little boy."

"I know you will, son, and as I said a few days ago, get out in the air. Relax, golf, get your head together."

They took off for Atlanta on the first Monday in May. The early morning clouds were burning off and I got back to Willy's house by 10:00 a.m. The forecast was for a warm, sunny day with the temperatures approaching 70 degrees. I checked the garage and found my golf bag resting in the far corner. I pulled it out and checked my clubs. They were dusty, and the grips had traces of green mold on them. I got some rags and paper towels and some spray cleaner from the kitchen and had them looking like new in a half hour. I found my golf shoes in my bedroom closet and threw them and the clubs in the trunk of Willy's car and headed out east on the Long Island Expressway to Bethpage.

I hit a full bucket of balls at the driving range, starting out with the short irons and swinging easy. By the time I was done I had a little of my rhythm back which surprised me since I hadn't swung a club in two years. I joined a threesome of retired guys and we chose to walk the 18 holes. I played without worrying about the score and was surprised when the scorekeeper in the group announced I had broken a hundred, coming in with a 97.

I stopped at McDonald's for a fast food fix, and by the time I got back to Willy's house it was past six o'clock. I showered and shaved and went into the kitchen for a glass of water. I noticed the answering machine blinking with two messages. The first was from Willy announcing they had arrived safely and leaving me his son's address and telephone number which I wrote down on a slip of paper and left on the counter next to the phone. The second message was from Jeff's secretary telling me that they had received a FedEx envelope addressed to me and wanting to know if I wanted to pick it up or have them forward it to me at Willy's house. I figured the office was closed for the day by now, so I'd return that call in the morning.

I slept well that night and I dreamed of Niki. It was a pleasant dream of the time I was crazy in love with her, but the details were vague. I had toast and coffee for breakfast and called Jeff's office and told them I'd pick up the package in half an hour. It was probably another missive from Jean's lawyer threatening me with some more legal mumbo-jumbo.

Jeff's secretary handed me the envelope. It was addressed to me, care of Jeff, and the return address was a FedEx drop off center in Miami. "Lucy, is Jeff in? I'd like to say hello."

"Are you kidding? He's never in. This morning he's in Brooklyn. This afternoon it's the Bronx and the rest of the week, Manhattan."

"I guess he's really in demand now."

"That's putting it mildly," she said. "The firm hired three assistants for him, and the rumor is he'll be made a partner before the year is out."

"Good for him," I said. "He's a great lawyer and a great person. He never lost faith in me and I'd still be rotting away upstate if it wasn't for him. Tell him I said hello, will you?"

"Sure, you take care."

I got back in my car and the thought crossed my mind that as long as I was near Mineola I would go over to see Barry Walsh and Jake Ellison to thank them for their support in the appellate court. I figured I should also call or visit Paul Valentine in Queens to do the same. I zipped open the FedEx and withdrew a sealed, letter-sized white envelope marked, "For Daniel Boyland, Private and Confidential." I opened it and saw a wad of cash, an airline ticket, and a letter. I read:

Dear Danny,

Congratulations on your release from prison! You can thank me in person next week. Use this money to get yourself some beachwear, shorts and sandals. I'll meet you at the airport and drive you to paradise. Remember what I said on our last night together? I said, "No matter what happens, I will always love you." I meant every word then, and still do. With all my love, until the Twelfth of Never.

Niki

P.S. Don't even think about not coming. Where else will you go?

There was $1,000 in hundred dollar bills and a one-way first class ticket to St. Martin out of JFK for next Tuesday, May 10, with her note. To say I was in total shock and disbelief would be the understatement of the century.

When I snapped back to reality I couldn't organize my thoughts. There were just too many options and possibilities, with the pivotal ones being—does she really believe I still love her after what she did to me? Why would she think I'd actually go to St. Martin to meet her? And what the hell did she mean that I could thank her? For what? For 20 months in jail? I forced myself to stop thinking and I put the envelope in the glove compartment. I now had a very good reason to visit Jake and Barry other than to just say thank you.

A different secretary, obviously new, was at the reception desk on the second floor. "Do you have an appointment with Mr. Walsh or Mr. Ellison?" she asked.

"No, I don't. I'm an old acquaintance. Please buzz one of them and tell him I'm here."

"Are you a detective?"

"I used to be. Now I'm just Mr. Boyland."

"What's your first name, sir?"

"Daniel, uh...Danny."

"Danny Boyland...Oh... oh! Yes. I'll buzz Mr. Walsh right now."

"Thank you, young lady."

She buzzed Barry and announced my presence. She said, "Mr. Walsh said to go right down to his office."

I walked down the hallway and shuddered as I passed the conference room where the cuffs were placed on me an eternity ago. Barry greeted me warmly and poured coffee as usual without asking. Jake came in smiling, and shook my hand in both of his. "Guys," I said, "I basically came here to thank you for your efforts in helping Jeff get me released and my conviction overturned."

"We were happy to do it," said Barry. "How are you doing?"

"As well as expected being I have no wife, no kids, no home and no job." They shuffled in their chairs, embarrassed. "Hey," I said, "I'm not blaming you guys or even the system. I've come to terms with this and I know I have no one to blame but myself. I got involved with a murder suspect—the height of stupidity—and I brought the house down on my own head."

"If it's any consolation," said Jake, "I never believed you were guilty."

"And you, Barry?"

"I was unsure. I'm glad I wasn't on the jury."

"Me, too," I said. "I was set up beautifully by Niki and Marty—a frame-up worthy of an academy award. Even the jury couldn't decide on the facts, so they basically whacked me for my disloyalty and betrayal of my wife, family and shield. I can't say I blame them."

"Well, it's all over now," said Barry. "You're free and you have a whole new life ahead of you."

"And," said Jake, "I'm here to help you make that fresh start—in whatever way I can—financial, references, anything."

"That goes for me, too," said Barry.

"I really appreciate that guys, but I don't really believe that it's all over. What about Niki? What about the woman the newspapers call the 'Dragon Lady'?"

"Yes, Niki," said Barry. "She's been the subject of much discussion."

"She put me in jail for 20 months. I'd like to return the favor—in spades. Who's got the case?"

"Apparently the consensus maintains that there is no case," said Jake.

"You gotta be kidding! She's a multiple murderer!"

"Is she? Can you prove that?"

"No, not me. I'm not a detective anymore, but somebody should be working on this."

"Let us give you the thinking of all us on this," said Barry. "And by all of us, I mean the Nassau and Queens Homicide Squads, and the Nassau and Queens District Attorney's Offices."

"Right before we arrested you," said Jake, "we were moving to arrest Niki and Marty for conspiracy and we probably would have done so."

"But," said Barry, "a conviction was far from certain. The only evidence we had was Whitey Messina's testimony—a convicted gambler looking to cut a deal. His motives for coming forward were suspect and self-serving. And don't forget, one of the two co-conspirators is now dead."

"Then you get convicted," said Jake, "and the case appears closed—until Ronald Millstein finally came forward and told us what really happened."

"So that has to be a crime," I said. "She coerced him to perjure himself."

"Correct," said Jake. "Coercion and subornation of perjury. Two felonies, but Mr. Millstein is now dead. No witness to confront in court. A conviction based on his affidavit alone without the opportunity of the defense to cross-examine him would not be forthcoming."

"And remember," said Barry, "he previously testified differently at your trial. How do you get the real truth if he is unavailable to testify?"

"Naturally," I said. "That's why she had him killed."

"Oh?" said Jake. "Can you prove that? Can you prove that she also had Reggio killed?"

"What's Queens Homicide doing about those murders?"

"The Reggio death is a hit and run accident and is still open, but I'm sure you know that it's in the back of someone's file drawer by now," said Barry.

"And," said Jake, "Millstein's death is a robbery/homicide investigation that's also unsolved and gathering dust."

"What about Marty? You can't believe that was a fucking accident? Another million dollar murder?"

"Danny," said Barry, "that one's out of our jurisdiction and the authorities down in St. Bart's ruled it an accidental drowning due to diabetic shock."

"She tampered with his meds. I know it," I said.

"You know it?" said Jake. "Then prove it."

"Are you telling me that there is nothing to go after her for? Nothing?"

"Maybe perjury during her testimony against you," said Barry, "but then our lovely Miss Wells is among the missing. She has disappeared from the area and left no forwarding address."

"How long has she been gone?"

"About a week after she got the insurance settlement. We went looking for her the day after Millstein first came in. She was long gone. Quit her job, vacated the Woodmere house and has not been seen or heard from since."

"Let me tell you our 'loose ends' theory," I said, and explained what Willy and I reasoned was Nicole's plans to eliminate all witnesses whose testimony could send her to jail.

"Interesting theory," said Jake, "and if true, they're all tied up nice and neat now."

"I wonder," I said, "if the only possible charge still hanging out there is her perjury at my trial, could I be considered a 'loose end'—the real last loose end to eliminate?"

Barry and Jake looked at each other and Barry said, "It's possible, but let's look at a completely opposite scenario, one just as plausible. Maybe Niki murdered no one at all."

"What? You have to be kidding!"

"Not at all," said Jake. "What if Marty hired someone to help him kill Laura and that accomplice left the scene with the evidence that was later planted in your garage?"

"And what if Marty just used Niki to get the tape and toluene from Millstein?" said Barry. "And suppose Reggio's death was an accident as was Marty's? And suppose Millstein was just the victim of a routine stick-up?"

"Do you guys really believe that?"

"It's a possibility," said Jake. "We're not saying she didn't help set you up to take the fall. She knew you were getting close to nailing her and Marty for conspiracy at the minimum. For crying out loud, you passed on enough confidential information about the investigation to her during your affair."

That hit home, hard, and I quietly said, "Yes I did, fool that I was. So where do we go from here?"

"There is no active investigation being conducted on Nicole Wells at this time," said Barry.

"She may be innocent of murder," said Jake, "or guilty of four—none of which we can prove."

"Unless," I said, "she confesses."

"Now I say Danny, you have to be kidding," said Barry.

"You want her bad, don't you?" said Jake. "Well, go find her and obtain her admissions of murder on tape in clear, unmistakable language, and then we'll talk."

Jake was right—I wanted Niki bad, but for what? To arrest her for murder? Or to live with her in paradise?

I said good-bye to Barry and Jake and headed back to Bellerose. I spread the money out on the table and looked at the ticket again. I re-read Niki's note several times, wishing that Willy were here to help me figure this out. She was right about one thing—where else could I go? Was she seducing me all over again? Was she enticing me to St. Martin to tie up her last loose end? Or to love me until the twelfth of never? And if I went, who would greet me from behind the closed door? The Lady or the Tiger? The beautiful Nicole Wells or the evil, ugly Dragon Lady? I had a lot to think about, didn't I?

Chapter 15

And think hard I did over the next few days. I thought and I pondered over everything—from the moment I first met Niki on the street in Queens until the last time I saw her on the witness stand. I read her note at least 50 times during the week. I again wished Willy had been here to talk it over. I thought of calling him in Atlanta, but didn't want to upset him as he and Edna began their new life. And deep down I knew that no matter what Willy advised, and no matter what Barry and Jake had told me, this decision was mine alone. Willy was right—I needed a new direction in life—a new start somewhere else.

After four days I finally reached my decision—not on an objective evaluation of all the evidence, but on a gut feeling that centered on the words that had haunted me in prison, "No matter what happens, I will always love you." I had to find my destiny, whatever that might be. But, however things would turn out, I knew the answer had to be with Niki.

During the week, I used Willy's computer to type my "best seller." I had over 300 pages written in longhand and it was getting bulky. I typed it single spaced and got it down to 200 pages which I hole-punched and placed in a three-ring binder. I backed up the copy on a disk and slipped it into the binder's inside pocket. I had the feeling that there remained only a few more chapters to be written, so I added a package of loose-leaf paper after the last typed chapter. Maybe only one chapter remained to be added to this story, and I wondered who would write it.

I went shopping as Niki had suggested. I bought two pairs of swim trunks, three pairs of shorts and half a dozen short-sleeved tropical looking shirts. Then I bought a 26 inch wheeled suitcase and a matching carry-on and packed up the new stuff with some of my old clothes that still fit me. The rest of my old stuff I bundled up and dumped in a Salvation Army clothing bin.

On Sunday evening I called Willy to tell him I was leaving for a while. We chatted a long time before I could get up the nerve to tell him and finally I didn't tell him at all. All I said was, "I'm going out of town for a week or so to look at an opportunity. I'll leave you a note with all the details."

"Good for you. I hope it works out just as things seem to be working out for us down here."

"Have you and Edna reached a decision?"

"Yep, we put a down payment on a two bedroom condo that's being built now. It should be ready in two months. It's only four miles from Bill, and the price is right."

"That's great, I can't wait to visit you guys down there."

"We'll see you when we get back to Bellerose, right?"

"Er...I'm not sure. I don't know how long I'll be gone. You may have already closed on the house and moved to Atlanta by then."

"Yeah, that's getting close. You take care. We'll see you soon, no matter where it is."

"Okay. Oh, since I won't be here to pick you up on the twelfth, I ordered a limo for you and Edna—my treat. Look for the guy holding up a sign that says 'EDWARDS.'"

"Danny, you didn't have to go to that expense. We coulda grabbed a cab."

"Nonsense, it's the least I could do for all you and Edna have done for me. Enjoy a bit of luxury."

We said good-bye and I composed a long letter to him. I told him about the note from Niki, and the money, and the ticket to St. Martin. I summarized the discussion I had with Barry Walsh and Jake Ellison and the uncertainty concerning Niki's guilt or innocence. I asked Willy to find a home for my golf clubs and promised I would call him as soon as I found out my situation. I took $1,000 from the squad money for him and Edna, explaining that it was to cover my room and board for the last couple of weeks. I knew that would be the only way he would take any money from me. I concluded,

Willy, as I said many times before, thank you for standing by me. I don't know if the course I'm taking now is the right thing or the wrong thing to do, but I have to go. All the questions I have can only be answered by

Niki, and I'll never have peace or closure until she tells me those answers. Until we meet again in Atlanta, old friend—Danny

Monday morning was overcast and chilly. Tomorrow I would be on a plane to a place 1,500 miles away and there was definite uncertainty when, or if, I would ever return to New York. I took Willy's car and drove through Brooklyn, Queens and Nassau on a nostalgia tour of sorts. I went through the neighborhood I grew up in, past my house, my schools, my hangouts, past the church I attended, then the church where Jean I were married and finally back to the house in Franklin Square where we had settled and raised Patrick and Kelly.

The trip back in time had not been a good idea. Although the memories were mostly of good times, they depressed me. I drove down to Jones Beach and walked the boardwalk in slow silence for an hour, then stopped at a diner for an early dinner. When I got back to the house I locked up the cars and put the keys next to the telephone with my letter and the money for Willy. I noticed the slip of paper with Bill's number on it and I took it and put it in my wallet. I picked up the phone and ordered a taxi to pick me up at 6:00 a.m. for the trip to JFK—a trip that I knew I had to take, but a trip whose outcome was yet to be determined.

If good beginnings foretold good conclusions, I was in luck. American Airlines flight number 667 scheduled to depart at 8:00 a.m. for the four hour flight to St. Martin lifted off at 8:17, which was "on time" by any standards at a New York airport. I was already on my second scotch and soda and relaxed in the luxury of the first class cabin as the plane became airborne. The captain promised a smooth flight and an on-time arrival. He delivered, dropping us quietly down on the runway at Princess Juliana Airport in Dutch St. Maarten, precisely at noon.

I had watched out my window as we made our descent. The sun reflected off the brilliant blue-green waters as the island came into view. I saw white beaches, dark-green mountains, clear lagoons and white sailboats. Then the high rise resorts appeared and then the airport. I had only been to the Caribbean once before when Jeanie and I honeymooned on Paradise Island and I was looking forward to this return. But my anticipation was tempered by dread as I neared my reunion with Niki. What would she say? How would she look? What was really going to happen here in "paradise"?

I followed the crowd to immigration and customs. Ten minutes later I was walking to the baggage carousel when I heard her call out, "Danny!" I turned as she approached me. A wide smile was on her tanned face and she hugged me and kissed me on the lips. When she released me she said, "Oh, Danny, I knew you would come! I'm so happy! Let me look at you."

"Well," I said, "it's good to see you again, Niki. You look wonderful."

That was an understatement—she looked gorgeous—long, tanned legs, a healthy, radiant complexion, and those sparkling blue eyes. She was oozing sensuality, and memories of our past intense love affair flashed through my mind.

"And you, Danny, you look…not so good."

"That's what 20 months in jail does to a person."

"Oh, I'm so sorry for that, but I'll make it up to you for sure. I'll have you tanned and healthy and up to your fighting weight in no time."

"Niki, I have a lot of questions…"

"Hush, I know you do and I'll answer all of them in due time. I promise. But now go find your luggage and go out those doors over there. I'll be at the curb cranking up the AC in my jeep."

She hugged me again and headed toward the doors. Niki had certainly seemed thrilled to see me. I couldn't wait to hear what she had to say. I retrieved my bag and walked out the doors into a blast of heat and bright sunshine. I began to perspire immediately in my New York clothes—a long-sleeved shirt and jeans. Niki was just pulling up to the curb about 20 feet away and I hurried over. She got out and helped me put the heavy bag in the back of the jeep and we got in the front seat. "That cold air feels good," I said. "No wonder you don't have the top off this thing."

"Only after the sun goes down." she said. "You'll fry your fanny on the seat otherwise. Reach over into the back seat for the cooler and pop open a couple of cold ones for us."

I did just that, and we both took a long swallow of the ice cold, golden Carib beer. She pulled away from the curb, beer in hand, and headed toward the airport's exit.

"Drinking and driving?"

She laughed and said, "One of the great things about St. Martin is there are very few rules. You can drive where you want, as fast as you want, and park where you want. You can walk down the street drinking a beer or a guavaberry colada. You can swim at beautiful beaches and eat scads of delicious food."

"Sounds like my kind of place."

We stopped at a light and she reached over and kissed me. Then she raised her beer to mine and we tapped bottles. "Welcome to paradise, Danny. It's so good to be with you once again."

She drove through Maho and Mullet Bay on the Dutch—St. Maarten—side of the island, pointing out the hotels, casinos and beaches. She took the road up to Marigot which she informed me was the capital city on the French—St. Martin—portion of the split island. "My place is on the French side," she said. "It has better restaurants than on the Dutch side, but no casinos. However, you can swim nude at Orient Beach. The Dutch don't go for naked much."

"Interesting. And what do you like to do?"

"All of it. Swim nude during the day, party and gamble at night."

"Not self-conscious about being naked in front of strangers?"

"My place has its own private beach. There's no one to see me, except for you now."

Private beach? She must have some place, but then she had come into some big bucks, hadn't she? We drove off the main road after we passed through Marigot and Niki twisted and turned the jeep up and down hills and through narrow dirt roads. Then all of a sudden she braked hard in front of a wrought iron gate which quietly slid open when she touched a button on the remote control clipped to her sun visor. We drove several hundred yards down a winding gravel road with manicured shrubs and flowers on either side, and then finally pulled up in front of a low, wide stucco home.

"This is it," she said. "I rented it for six weeks and got a great deal—only $20,000. It's owned by some rich businessman from Europe who comes down here in January and February. The rest of the time it's rented or left vacant."

"Only $20,000?"

"Wait until you see it, and the grounds. We can afford it now."

I picked up on the *we* and said, "For twenty grand the freezer better be stocked with porterhouse steaks."

"Oh, it is, and the wine cellar is stocked with vintage reds to go along with them."

The home was truly magnificent and furnished tastefully in what I guess could be called "Caribbean casual." It was set on a hill overlooking the turquoise sea, and the entire rear of the house consisted of floor-to-ceiling glass panels. A pair of French doors opened up onto a patio with a huge built-in swimming pool. Beyond the pool, stairs led down to a dazzling, secluded white sand beach. I stood there in awe as Niki handed me another beer. On the sides there were verdant gardens and thick jungle beyond.

"Well, what to you think?" she asked

"It truly is beautiful. Exactly what I imagined paradise to be. Just how big is this place?"

"About 20 acres, I think. Hey, are you about ready for a swim?"

"You bet," I said, "let me get my trunks out of my suitcase."

"Trunks? You don't need no stinkin' trunks! It's just you and me here, lover boy."

We stripped in a hurry and Niki grabbed a couple of beach towels from a pile by the pool. I looked at her body and began to get an erection. She was completely tanned. Her firm breasts and bottom were the same golden color as her face, arms and legs. By the time she turned back towards me, I was at full-mast and she said, "Oh, my goodness, you can't swim with that poking out of the water. I'll take care of that right now."

She led me into the large bedroom and we were at each other in a flash. I hadn't had sex in almost two years and suddenly realized that the last time was with Niki, in her apartment, the night before she betrayed me. That thought didn't dampen my enthusiasm, however, and we both quickly climaxed.

"Come on," she said, "we'll take that swim and then we'll be ready for round two. Only let's make it last longer than three minutes."

Niki ran right into the gentle emerald waves and I tentatively stepped in expecting the cold shock of the Atlantic Ocean's 60 degree waters that I was used to on Long Island. I was surprised to feel the warmth of the Caribbean and plunged in after her. We swam and dove and hugged and kissed.

"Isn't this just beautiful, Danny?"

"Paradise, indeed," I replied. "Truly paradise."

"I have snorkel gear if you want to give it a try. I can show you how to do it in a jiffy. You can practice in the pool. There are beautiful tropical fish all around those rocks at the end of our beach."

I wondered if that's what she had planned for me—a snorkeling "accident" reminiscent of her late husband's. I put that thought out of my mind and reasoned that my paranoia could be misplaced. The problem was that I was falling in love with Nicole Wells all over again—if I had ever truly fallen out of love with her in the first place. I said, "I'd love to do that. Show me how."

"Not now. We have to get out of the ocean."

"Huh? So soon?"

"Danny boy, you are in the tropics," she said as we walked out of the water arm in arm. "Get under these palm trees now."

We dried off and spread our towels under the shade of the trees. Niki got a bottle of SPF-30 sun block lotion from a wooden chest by the stairs.

"After I get this rubbed into every inch of your body you can go back in the sun for thirty minutes, fifteen on each side—and that's it for today. By the end of a week you'll be able to stay out for four hours."

She began to rub the lotion onto my shoulders and back. Her hands felt wonderful as she kneaded the tension from my muscles.

"Do I get to rub your body, too?"

"Sure, as soon as I finish with you, then you can oil me up to your heart's content."

By the time I rolled over I was hard as a rock again and Niki said, "My goodness, that thing just won't stay down, will it?"

She went down on me, and I enjoyed every second, even though a vision of Whitey Messina flashed through my mind saying, 'and then she proceeds to give me one of the best blow jobs I've ever had in my life...'

When she was done she grabbed the lotion and said, "Now let me finish you up."

"I think you just finished me up fine."

"You're wrong there. We won't be finished for a long, long time. We'll never be finished with each other."

"Until the twelfth of never?"

"At least," she said. "Perhaps beyond."

After I oiled Niki's smooth body we moved our towels out from under the trees and into the sunshine. The heat felt wonderful on my back, as if it were burning out all my cares and concerns. I started to nod out, but Niki poked me, saying it was time to turn over. I lay on my back thinking how wonderful it was to be here with her. It felt as if the healing sun were melting away the memories of the last 20 months—the arrest, the trial, and the iron bars of cellblock 2B. Good-bye to the past. I'm here now and for the first time in recent memory, I'm happy.

She prodded me on schedule saying, "Enough, you beach bum, I don't want a lobster in bed with me tonight."

We grabbed our towels and went up the stairs where we showered off the salt water and suntan lotion and took a dip in the pool. I was feeling drowsy when I finished toweling off and Niki picked up on that. "You look tired. What time were you up this morning?"

"Four a.m."

"Well, that's not going to happen here. We get up when we want, depending on how late we stay at the casino or the clubs."

"Sounds good to me."

"I'm going to put on some soft music and you're going to take a nap on this comfy lounge chair. I'll wake you up in time for cocktails."

"You're too good to me,"

"Why shouldn't I be good to you? I love you. I told you that on our last night together, remember? I said I will always love you. No matter what happens, I will always love you."

"Yes, Niki, I remember it well."

"And I want you to tell me, right now, that you will always love me, but I understand that would be difficult—after all I put you in jail for almost two years. But you will tell me that, I know you will, and you'll tell me soon. Now take your nap."

Despite the conflicting emotions that little speech aroused in my brain, I drifted off into a deep, untroubled sleep.

"Hey, sleepy head," I heard a voice say from far away. "It's cocktail time!"

"What? What time is it?"

"Five on the dot. You had a nice two hour nap."

I sat up and Niki was standing there smiling with a cocktail tray in her hands. On it were two of the largest martinis I had ever seen. Moisture was dripping down the outside of the glasses and she handed one of them to me. She took the other one and raised her glass to touch mine. "To us, Danny," she said. "To us. Until the twelfth of never."

"The twelfth of never, and beyond," I said.

We moved over to a small table and sipped our ice-cold drinks. The sun was going down in the west directly in front of us and Niki said, "The sun will set as we're halfway through our second martini, then you can shower and shave while I start dinner. I'm already done."

"Yes, I can see that. All fresh and made up and smelling great."

I leaned over the table and kissed her softly on the lips. She was wearing short shorts, a halter top and no shoes. She noticed me looking her over and said, "Standard outfit around the house when I'm not naked. When I go out I usually dress a little more formal, even wear panties and a bra on rare occasions."

"Not that you need them. Are you planning to go out tonight?"

"No, I know we have to talk. I can't put it off forever. Let me make that second drink now."

We watched the sun touch the water as we stood at the top of the stairs, drinks in hand and arms around each other. The colors shot up and across the sky as the sun melted into the ocean on this, my first day in paradise.

After I showered and shaved, I opened my suitcase and put all my things away in the dresser and walk-in closet. I selected a wild tropical shirt and a pair of white shorts and went into the kitchen looking for Niki. She called out to me that she was on the patio. I followed my nose toward the aroma of steak grilling on the barbecue and found her just turning two thick T-bones. The table was set for two and plates of salad were already waiting. "You can pour the wine. I have to go get the potatoes."

She returned with two large baked potatoes and we took a sip of an excellent cabernet. "The steaks will be ready in four minutes," she said. "We can start our salads now."

"You're amazing—beautiful, sexy, smart and able to cook a man's meal."

"I owe you this and a lot more. From the looks of you, there weren't many meals served like this in prison."

"You can say that again."

"Well, you're not there anymore. You're with me now and I'll never desert you again."

After dinner we moved into the house and relaxed with an after dinner drink of 30 year-old tawny port wine. "Where do you want me to begin?" she asked.

"I usually begin at the beginning," I said, thinking of my manuscript tucked away in a compartment of my suitcase, "but your note intrigued me. Just why in hell should I thank you for putting me in jail for almost two years?"

•

"Because I told Ronnie Millstein it was all right to tell his story to the DA and cop himself a plea, that's why, Danny—and thank God he came forward before he got killed in the stickup."

"You forced him to testify against me, and then you told him to re-cant that testimony? I'm a bit confused."

"Let me begin at the beginning as you suggested, and I'm sure it will all become clear."

"I'm all ears."

"Marty killed Laura for two reasons—me and the money. He did it by himself, without any assistance from me, or anyone else."

"How could that be? The ME said…"

"Danny, listen. Here's how he did it. He first administered the toluene slowly for several minutes until he thought she was unconscious. He then placed the plastic bag with the toluene-soaked cotton in it over her face and taped her mouth closed. He panicked when he thought she started to move, so he choked her until she was dead. Then he inhaled some of the toluene himself. After he woke up, and before he called the police, he put a piece of tape on his mouth and removed it a minute later. He wanted traces of his saliva on it in case it was tested. Then he took the roll of tape, plastic bag, toluene bottle and cotton batting out to the garage and hid it all in the trunk of Laura's car, in the wheel well."

"What about the ski mask?"

"He had used that to administer the toluene to himself and he forgot to retrieve it when he awoke. It had fallen out of view into the space between the bed and the night stand where you later found it. He really sweated it out until the tests on it came back negative. He was so relieved that it had all evaporated."

"And it was yours?"

"Just as I told you; I gave it to Marty for the kids."

"How do you know it all happened this way for a fact?"

"I didn't know at first. He stuck with the burglar story with me, too. He told me much later, after we were married, and when he feared he was close to death."

"Close to death?"

"Yes, his diabetes had gotten much worse. He became insulin depend-ent, needing shots twice a day. I tried to get him to confess Laura's murder to me on tape so that in the event of his death I could use it to get you out of jail."

"But he drowned before you could get it?"

"Yes, and I was distraught thinking that you might be in jail forever. That's when I went to Millstein to talk him into confessing. He was my last hope since Victor was dead from that hit and run accident."

"Why did you and Marty set me up for the murder?"

"You were too damn good a detective and we knew you were closing in on us, although you were wrong about me being in on it with him. So, to protect ourselves from arrest, and to be able to collect the money, we framed you."

"And did a beautiful job of it. Who planted the evidence in my garage?"

"I did."

"Who borrowed my license and had the phony one made and put in my wallet?"

"I did."

"Who coerced Reggio and Millstein to testify against me?"

"I did."

"Had you had affairs with them?"

"Yes, I blackmailed them with pictures I had taken from the hidden video cam in the bedroom of my apartment. I did the same later with you in case I needed to produce them at the trial to prove our affair."

"How could you have anticipated the use of Reggio's and Millstein's compromising photos at a future trial?"

"I was blackmailing them for money all along. Then when this situation arose, I promised to leave them alone forever if they came through on the testimony."

"Is money that important to you, Niki?"

"Yes, I hate being poor and always struggling to make ends meet. I want the good things and the good life that money can buy."

"So you get me convicted and out of the picture, and Reggio, Millstein and Marty are dead. You're home free with a million and a half? Why not just live the good life? All your loose ends are tied up."

"Oh, Danny, how could you say that? I fell in love with you at first sight. You were the big complication in the whole plan. The complication I couldn't shake. Remember my words…"

"Of course I do."

"What I wanted to add, but couldn't, was, 'tomorrow I'm going to go to the DA and frame you for murder, but don't give up hope. Whatever happens, I'll make it right, I promise.'"

"What happened was 20 months in jail."

"I hope you can forgive me for that someday, but let me tell you this—I was following the trial in the papers every day, and I never thought that jury would convict you. I had my bags packed and a cab waiting to take me to the airport as soon as they came back with a not guilty verdict."

"Was Marty going with you?"

"No, he thought he could tough it out by continuing to remain silent, but I told him he was foolish. I said as soon as you were found not guilty the Homicide Squad and the DA would come after us right away."

"But then I got convicted."

"Yes, I was in shock and vowed to find a way to get you released as soon as possible, but I couldn't think of a way to do it. Then Marty got the money from the insurance and re-kindled our romance and I married him, really just for the money. I was still in love with you."

If you were so in love with me why didn't you come forward yourself and admit the perjury? Didn't love me that much, did you? Didn't love me enough to give up the million dollar good life, hey Niki?

"So Reggio gets killed, Marty dies, and then you go to Millstein. Why did you wait so long?"

"I really thought Marty was going to die sooner than he did and the tape I was trying to get would have gotten you released."

"Please tell me, Niki, that you had absolutely nothing to do with the deaths of Laura Samuels, Victor Reggio, Ronald Millstein and Marty Samuels."

"Absolutely nothing at all and I'm horrified that you would ask me that question. I may be a blackmailer, but I am not a murderer."

"I believe you," I said, "but the cop in me made me ask that question."

"I understand. Thank you for believing in me. Now, let me continue to make up for what I did to you."

She moved next to me on the sofa and kissed me passionately. We went into the bedroom and made love once more. As I lay next to her waiting for sleep to come, I ran her story through my mind several times looking for holes and inconsistencies. I couldn't detect any. The story was plausible and I so desperately wanted to believe every word of it. But then, I remembered, she had 20 months to prepare it and make it airtight—didn't she?

Chapter 16

We slept until eight the next morning, and ran right into the Caribbean for a dip. As we hugged in the warm water, I resolved to myself to accept Niki's version of the events as 100 percent factual—and why not? She was going out of her way to make up for what she had done to me, and she loved me. And I loved her just as I had during those weeks we were together back in Queens. After another on-the-beach love session, we showered and dressed and got in the jeep.

"Today, I'll show you around the French side of the island, tomorrow the Dutch side," she said as we moved down the driveway.

We went to Marigot and strolled through the waterfront market and peered in shop windows and Niki said we would come back soon to do some "serious" shopping. On the way back to the jeep she pointed to a sign on a restaurant that said La Vie en Rose. "Best French restaurant in Marigot, but a bit pricey. We have reservations for seven tonight."

"Niki, I have $2,800 with me, and that's all the money I have in the world."

"Let's talk about money now for a few minutes and then never again, okay?"

"Okay."

"I ended up with $1,600,000 after Marty died. I invested it, and fortunately, the stock market went on a huge tear. With all the spending I've done, I have more than when I started. My accounts are pushing two million. I can't spend it fast enough, so all future spending is to be with my money, period. Are we clear?"

"I feel like a gigolo."

"Nonsense. Consider it reparations for the twenty months I stole from your life."

"Thanks, but I've been wondering about something—how and why did Marty get a million dollar policy on his life?"

"He knew that his diabetes was getting worse and he managed to get the policy while he was still on the pills—before the needle was necessary. He paid a higher premium, but they wrote the policy. As I said, he was really afraid that he was going to die soon and he wanted to take care of me."

"He must have really loved you."

"Yes, he did. I was sorry I couldn't love him in return. He wasn't strong as you, Danny. As I once told you, he was weak-willed, a whiner—basically a wimp."

But the wimp got up enough courage to kill Laura? By himself?

Niki continued the island tour and we stopped for lunch at a beach shack for a burger and fries and a guavaberry colada, the local island drink. We then drove south on the east side of the island and, from a rise, we saw the Dutch capitol, Phillipsburg, and its harbor. Three huge cruise ships were in port and the view was worthy of a postcard.

"We're not going near Phillipsburg today with all the boat people in the streets. Tomorrow those ships will be gone and others won't arrive until Friday."

She cut through unpaved roads and made a right turn back towards Marigot and we pulled into our driveway twenty minutes later. "So what do you think of St. Martin so far?" she asked as we sat by the pool after an afternoon dip in the sea.

"Beautiful," I said. "It is truly an island paradise."

"I'm so glad you're enjoying yourself."

"That I am—the island, and you, Niki. I'm enjoying you most of all."

"Oh, Danny, I do love you so."

"But what happens when we leave paradise? When the six weeks are up, where do we go?"

"I was thinking about Ireland because they have no extradition treaty with the United States."

"Why should that be a consideration?"

"I can't go back to New York. They'll probably arrest me for murdering everyone involved in the case, even Laura."

"Let me tell you the current thinking of the district attorneys of Nassau and Queens," I said. "I think you will be pleasantly surprised."

When I finished, she jumped into my lap and hugged me and kissed me until I was breathless.

"We can go back! To Manhattan! We'll get a big apartment and live the high-life. Isn't that wonderful? Oh, Danny, isn't it just wonderful?"

"For you maybe, but not for me."

"Why? What's wrong?"

I explained about being blackballed in the only profession in which I was qualified to earn a living. She said, "There you go again, thinking as a civil servant. Your former life is gone forever. We have two million dollars. You don't have to work."

"Believe it or not, two million might not last forever."

"Then we'll buy a business that makes money. You can run it part-time if you want, or hire a full-time manager. We can buy whatever you desire—a liquor store, a Starbucks, a dry-cleaners, a cocktail lounge—anything."

A cocktail lounge? I wondered if Victor's joint on Queens Boulevard was still available.

"You're right," I said. "Old habits are hard to break, and old life styles are harder yet, but I'll do it."

"Now you're talking! Come on, one quick dip then we have to get ready for dinner."

The Caribbean lobster special at La Vie en Rose was outstanding and we walked around Marigot once more to help digest the sumptuous meal. Niki resumed the tour the next day on the Dutch side, pointing out more beautiful scenery, casinos, night clubs and better restaurants.

Our tour ended in Phillipsburg and we strolled along Front Street, Back Street and the waterfront, checking out the stores. "There must be 40 jewelry stores here," I said.

"It's because of the great prices. Come with me into this one."

She steered me into a jewelry store and the proprietor greeted her by name and offered us both a Heineken which we gladly accepted. "Rashid," she said, "I want to buy a nice watch for my gentleman friend. What do you have?"

"How nice do you want it, Miss Niki?"

"Very nice. As in Rolex nice."

"Niki, I…"

"Be quiet. Do you want the gold one or the platinum one?"

I accepted the gold one. It was only $10,500 compared to $15,000 for the platinum. I was still protesting as we walked out of the store and she shushed me and directed me into the Guavaberry Emporium for a large, tall colada. "Niki, that wasn't necessary. I feel like a kept man."

"You are, Danny. You're my kept man—so lay back and enjoy it."

We ate a light fish dinner in Phillipsburg and got back to the house at seven. It dawned on me that it was Thursday and Willy and Edna should have gotten home by now. I figured I'd better give him a call to let him know I was still alive. "Niki, can I use the phone to call New York?"

"Sure, it's part of the package. Who do you want to call?"

"Willy Edwards, an old pal of mine."

"Do I know him?"

"I don't think so. He retired from the squad six months before I met you. He's really the only one, except for my lawyer, who stood by me during the whole ordeal."

"Good for him. I like him already."

I dialed their number and Willy answered on the third ring. "Welcome home, Willy," I said.

"Danny! How the hell are you? Are you all right?"

"I'm fine. In fact, I'm wonderful. St. Martin is a beautiful place."

"Are you with Niki?"

"Yes."

"Is she there now?"

"Yes."

"That was some letter you left for me. We have to talk—soon. Get some place private and call me, any time of the day or night. I have some serious concerns about what you're doing."

"Sure old-timer. How was Atlanta?"

"As I said, we're getting that condo and I had a message on the machine that we're going to closing on this house the middle of next week. We'll be packing and such. You call me—understand?"

"Sure, sure, that's great news."

"What the hell was that thousand dollars you left us? You know…"

"Be still. The money is yours. You and Edna deserved it for what you did for me. I pay my debts."

"Yeah, I know you can't talk, so I'll say good-bye—you call me, got it?"

"Sure," I said. "Talk to you soon."

"What's with Atlanta?" asked Niki.

I told her of Willy's plans and how he had helped me so much. "You know, I'm going to miss that old white-haired guy something fierce."

"Atlanta's a two hour hop from JFK. We can visit him as often as you want to."

"I guess we can."

I lay awake a long time wondering what Willy was so concerned about and I thought of a plan. The next morning after our swim and breakfast I said, "Niki, would you mind if I took the jeep into Phillipsburg?"

She looked at me quizzically and said, "Of course not, I'll go with you."

"No, I want to go alone. I want to get you something. What was the name of that store where you bought me the watch?"

Caribbean Great Gold, but Danny you don't have to…"

"S-s-sh!" I said, "I have almost three grand just burning a hole in my pocket and I want to get you something. Please let me."

"Go ahead, here are the keys."

"Can you point me in the right direction?"

"Make your first right after you leave the driveway, then two lefts followed by two rights and you're on the road to Phillipsburg. Lunch is at one o'clock," she said. "Will you be back on time?"

"I sure will. See you later."

I found Phillipsburg and the jewelry shop with no difficulty and ordered a platinum necklace and pendant with "NIKI" spelled out in diamond chips and sapphires to match her blue eyes. I didn't know jewelry prices, but at $1,700, Rashid assured me it was a "special bargain." He said it would be ready early the following week, but told me not to come on a Wednesday, Friday or the weekend. "The ships are in port those days and I have to make my money from the boat people," he explained.

I left the store and walked down the crowded street. I found a pay phone in a relatively quiet spot near a waterfront café. I didn't have a calling card, so I called collect and Willy picked up right away. "Hi, Willy."

"Hi, yourself. Now just what the fuck do you think you're doing?"

"What do you mean?"

"You damn well know what I mean—that letter you left me!"

"What about it?"

"What about it? I've never read such bullshit in my life! Those DA's are assholes and you know it—or should know it if you weren't blinded by those big blue eyes and long legs of Niki Wells."

"Willy, I don't…"

"Be quiet and listen to me—it's my dime. I'm telling you, you're shacked up with a murderer, a real Dragon Lady, and you could be next on her hit list."

"How can you believe that? The other scenario is just as plausible. Will you listen to me for a minute and let me tell you her side of the story as she told it to me?"

"Go ahead," he said reluctantly.

I told him as she had told me a few days before, word for word, to the best of my memory. "Now tell me, isn't that a possibility?"

"That story is worse than the DA's version. It has more holes in it than a block of Swiss cheese. Walsh, Ellison and Valentine want these murders, or 'accidents' as they classify them, to go quietly away. They don't have a case to prove against Niki, so murders become accidents and stickups stay stickups. Now you want to believe the same bullshit. I can't really believe it. Are you the homicide detective that I broke in? Didn't I teach you anything?"

"I'm listening."

"The first thing I learned when I was new in Homicide, and I know I told you the same thing, was that there is no such thing as coincidence. Now you're telling me that not only two but three fucking deaths of men intimately connected with your trial and conviction—three deaths—are mere coincidences? Are you brain dead?"

"Well, it could be."

"No, no, no, it can't be! Wake up and face the truth! She murdered Marty's wife and then later she murdered him. Then she murdered two witnesses who she had been blackmailing, to tie up her loose ends. Now only you remain."

"There's no proof she did any of that. She encouraged Millstein to testify to save me."

"Yeah, then she had him killed in a phony stickup."

"I can't believe you. She's a wonderful person and…"

"And you love her, right? Danny, you are a hopeless case. You are in the web of a black widow spider and when she's done fucking your brains out, she's gonna eat you alive and spit your bones into the Caribbean."

"Willy, I think I'd better hang up."

"Don't you dare, not yet. Please hear me out."

"Go on."

"I know I'm not making headway, so I'll back off—but I want you to do two things for me."

"If I can."

"Good, first I want you to put on your old detective's thinking cap and carefully go through all the conversations you had with Niki during your initial investigation—the ones where you concluded she was lying. Then go through all those conversations you had with her since you met her down there. Then compare her stories, the body language she exhibited, the nuances of her voice and eye contact. Compare all of it and come to a conclusion of her truthfulness only after you've thoroughly analyzed everything. Will you do that for me?"

"Yes," I said, as a queasy feeling rolled through my stomach.

"And the second thing—and this is a must. Call me at least once a week; no make that once every five days, so I know you're doing okay. I fear for your life. I truly do."

"Well, calm your fears. I'm in no danger at all, believe me."

"Regardless. Make an old man happy and call me, promise?"

"I promise."

"Good, now go think things out. Oh, tell me where you're staying."

"On some guy's estate on the French side. Niki rented it for a few weeks."

"What's the address?"

"I don't think it has one."

"The phone number there?"

"I don't know."

"Get that for me the next time we talk, okay?"

I said I would and we said good-bye. I had time to stop and get a couple of guavaberry coladas which I had developed an extreme fondness for. I cranked up the AC in the jeep and drove back to the house arriving at 12:30. I handed her the colada and she said, "Is this it, a half-melted guavaberry colada? You went all the way to Phillipsburg for that?"

"No," I smiled, "that's just a little extra treat. Your gift will be ready next week, or so Rashid told me."

"Oh, Danny," she squealed, "I love jewelry. I hope you didn't spend too much."

"Hey, we're in St. Martin! I got a great deal."

•

I thought about Willy's concerns and, the longer I thought, the more uncertain I became about Niki—and my concerns were not of her alone. I worried about my future with her—did I really want to live the high life in New York?

I realized that I had a written record to help me get things straight in my head—my almost completed manuscript. On Saturday morning Niki announced that she wanted to shop for some clothes in Marigot and also do the grocery shopping. "Care to join me?" she asked.

"I'm not a shopper," I said. "I don't mind joining you in the supermarket, but clothes shopping? No thank you, my dear."

"Then stay here and bake in the sun."

"Enjoy yourself and don't spend too much, and don't buy anything for me."

"We'll see about that," she said as she grabbed the keys to the jeep and walked out the door. When I was certain she was gone, I got the manuscript from my suitcase and brought it to the pool. I went right to the page where I first met Niki and the interview the next day with Tara Brown. Body language indicated she was lying to critical questions. Said Marty was a wimp. Said she liked the good life. Said Marty only placed a few bets. Refused to take a polygraph for dubious reasons. And then the kicker at the end of the interview when Niki had left and I had asked Tara Brown what she thought. "Lying bitch," she said. And I said, "My conclusion exactly."

Then there was the ski mask with the two, long, dark brown hairs inside it and her explanation of how it had gotten there. Weak story. Then when all the evidence came in from the Lab and the ME, we had all concluded that the most likely scenario was that Laura was murdered by Niki and Marty together and, other than Niki's denials to the contrary, nothing had changed to alter that original opinion.

As I re-read those passages a picture emerged, a factual pattern that I could not objectively refute—Niki had actively participated in the murder of Laura Samuels—without a doubt. Then she set me up for the murder. I found the pages where she testified against me and I remembered her face and body movements as she brazenly told lie after lie. She had acted exactly as she had when Tara and I interviewed her. I took the interview and the testimony and closed my eyes and focused on this past Tuesday night when Niki had told me her version of things, her story that she had 20 months to polish to perfection. I focused on her voice, her inflections, her movements and it didn't take long for me to objectively conclude that, as in the interview and in her testimony, she was lying all the way. Well, that was one thing we had in common—we both were not good liars, but she was a helluva lot better at it than I was.

I checked my watch, my new gold Rolex, and discovered it had taken only 90 minutes to figure things out. I returned the book to my suitcase and poured myself a double scotch on the rocks in the kitchen and headed for the beach. After I finished the scotch I swam for a while then lay in the sun on my back, thinking the whole thing over. I was shacked up on a beautiful island with a beautiful woman who had murdered four people. The question now loomed—did it matter? I drifted off into a troubled sleep and was awakened by a foot gently prodding me in the ribs. I opened my eyes to a naked Niki standing over me, smiling and saying, "Come on sleepy head, into the water!

On Monday morning Niki said, "Get dressed, we're going shopping and you're coming with me this time."

"Why?" I asked. "I don't like shopping."

"Everybody comes in today—the gardener, the pool guy and the maid. I want to stay out of their way. They'll be done and gone by four o'clock."

In Phillipsburg we stopped in Caribbean Great Gold where Niki wanted to buy me a diamond ring, but I absolutely refused, telling her that I was not a jewelry person—the watch was more than enough. Rashid whispered to me that the necklace I ordered would be in later that afternoon and I said I would pick it up the following morning. It would be a good reason to get away to phone Willy again as I had promised.

After our morning swim the next day I told Niki, "Now it's your turn to bake in the sun. I have to go see a man about a horse."

"The man wouldn't be Rashid, would it?"

"I say nothing, but I'll bring you back a guavaberry colada."

Niki headed down to the beach and I headed out the door and drove to Phillipsburg. I paid Rashid for the necklace and admired its beauty, staring at the sparkling blue letters that spelled out the name of my lover in paradise—"NIKI." My conflicted mind suggested I should get another necklace spelling out her alter-ego—"DRAGON LADY."

I had accepted a Heineken from Rashid and drove down to the wharf. It was a Tuesday and the pier was devoid of cruise ships. I got out of the jeep and called Willy. When he answered, I heard obvious relief in his voice. "Danny, it's good to hear your voice."

"Yours, too. Are you still set for the closing this week?"

"Yep, at two p.m. tomorrow. The big truck's coming the next morning bright and early and then we're on our way to Atlanta."

"Wonderful," I said. "I hope everything goes smoothly."

"Thanks. How's it going down there?"

"Going fine."

"Did you do what I asked you to do?"

"Yes."

"And?"

"And you were right, of course. Niki's a cold-blooded murderer."

"Thank God you've seen the light. Now tell me, what the hell are you still doing there?"

"I don't know what to do."

"What do you mean? Get away from her now."

"It's not that easy. Get away from Niki to what?"

"Are you telling me that you are considering remaining with her? A fucking quadruple murderer? Have you lost your mind? Are you still in love with that…that Dragon Lady...that black widow spider?"

"Willy, please listen. Where do I have to go to as an alternative?"

"To Atlanta with me and Edna, that's where."

"I appreciate the offer, but Jean and my kids and the Homicide Squad are not in Atlanta. I've done a lot of thinking and I have only two possible courses of action—either I try to get my family and job back, or if I can't get them back, I'll stay with Niki be she a murderer, dragon, spider, whatever. I don't care."

"Do you have any ideas on how to accomplish that? Getting those things back without tipping off Niki?"

"Yes. In reviewing the case I remembered what Barry and Jake told me about Niki—that they had no case for murder against her. But then Jake said if I really wanted to get her, I had to find her and get her to admit, on tape, all the murders in clear, unmistakable language."

"Well, you found her. Now how do you propose to do get those admissions?"

"Maybe I could convince her that I've figured out that she is a murderer, but that it doesn't make any difference. However, I'll say I can't tolerate living with a liar, so tell me the truth once and for all and I'll accept it, and we'll live happily ever after."

"Or she'll smell a big rat and tie up her last loose end by killing your ass, increasing her total to five."

"Forget my ass for a minute and answer me this—if I did get her admissions on tape and brought it to Jeff and he told the Department and the DA's, and then if she was arrested and convicted based on those admissions, could I get my job back?"

"Possibly, but it would be a long legal uphill battle"

"And could I get my family back?"

"That would be up to Jean," he said, "but as Jeff told you, she can't prevent an innocent man from seeing his own kids. By the way, I know where they are."

"What? How? Why didn't you tell me?"

"I'm telling you now. I worked on it and Sam completed it while I was in Atlanta. We are ace investigators you know, and skip tracing is one of our specialties."

"Where are they?"

"Roanoke, Virginia. A small house about two miles from Jean's parents. Your kids go to Roanoke schools and Jean works for the city in the budget office."

"How far is Roanoke from Atlanta?"

"I figured you'd ask me that. It's exactly 460 miles."

"So, what do you think?"

"You're treading on dangerous ground. I still feel you should blow out of there, but I know you, you have to make your own decision—and you should also know that whatever you decide, I'm still here for you all the way."

"Thanks, Willy, I know that, but I was beginning to wonder the way you were yelling at me."

"Only because I love ya, kid. You have my son's number?"

"Yeah."

"And you got the number for me where you're staying?"

I gave him the number and he said, "So you'll call me again in five days, right?"

"Right. So long till then."

I took a walk down Front Street and soon spotted a consumer electron-

ics store. They were almost as numerous as the jewelry, liquor and clothing shops. I bought the smallest tape recorder with the longest tape time
that I could find, and I got it to start up on voice activation. I didn't want
to fumble with a switch if I got her to confess, but I had to admit that right
now I still had no idea what I would do after that. I would have to wres-
tle a long while with that decision.

Chapter 17

Fortunately, when I got back to the house Niki was still down on the beach, so I was able to hide the microrecorder in my suitcase. I stripped off my clothes and took the coladas I had picked up and the box containing the necklace which Rashid had gift wrapped for me. She was sleeping soundly and I prodded her in the ribs as she had done to me a few days earlier.

"Ah," she said, sitting up and stretching, "my lover returns bearing gifts."

We sipped our drinks and she opened the jewelry box and withdrew the necklace. "Oh, Danny," she said, "it's beautiful. I love it."

She put it on and it looked great on her nude golden body. She fixed me with those big blue eyes and said, "I do love you so."

We made love and her enchantment took me in its grip once more. Did I really want to leave this beautiful woman who was so in love with me? And had two million dollars? And who was a murderer and a liar?

The days passed and I hadn't found the time or place to pop the question to Niki. During that time I came to a decision that really was not a decision. I would attempt to get Niki's confession on tape and then I would make the final decision to turn her in or stay with her. And if Niki did not confess and stuck to her story, I really didn't know if I would stay or leave. I just didn't know.

Another week went by and our time in St. Martin was reaching its end. I called Willy every five or six days as promised and he prodded me to "shit or get off the pot." He didn't have to remind me—my stress was increasing every day and Niki began to notice. She asked me on two occasions if something were wrong to which I replied, "No, just maybe getting depressed that we'll be leaving paradise soon. What do we have, two weeks left?"

"Twelve days actually," she said. "I'm going to go into Marigot to book our flights and shop for some New York clothes. Want to join me?"

"No way," I said. "I'm going to get in as much beach time as I can before I leave."

"You do that and have an ice-cold vodka martini waiting for me when I return at cocktail time. Oh, and take a couple steaks out to defrost. I'll cook them up later."

I did go down to the beach and then came up to sit by the pool with my newest crime thriller, but I couldn't concentrate on it. As Willy said, it was time to "shit or get off the pot." I got the tape recorder and tested it. It worked fine as it damn well should since I paid $300 for it which was with a 40 percent discount. It was very slim, no more than a half inch thick, and measured about two by three inches. I dressed and slipped it into the front pocket of my loosest fitting shorts. I examined myself from various angles in the full-length mirror and could hardly detect a bulge. To be on the safe side I put on a tropical shirt and let it hang outside of my shorts, covering the pocket.

At 4:55 p.m. I mixed the martinis and, true to her word, Niki walked in the door at 5:02 with an arm load of packages. We had our drinks by the pool and she said, "Make us another one and I'll start getting dinner ready."

I returned to the pool with my second drink and picked up my novel, but again I couldn't read a sentence as I planned my approach to Niki. I decided to go for it after dinner was over while we were still seated at the table. When I had tested the tape recorder earlier in the day, I had placed it on the chair I would sit in at dinner and covered it with a dish towel. Then I sat in Niki's chair and spoke in a normal tone of voice. The recording was loud and clear and the volume had been only set a bit above half-way.

My appetite was not great as I had a knot in my belly in anticipation of the forthcoming conversation. I ate most of the mashed potatoes, but only half of my steak and hardly touched the broccoli. I finished my cabernet and poured another glass of courage. The two martinis and the wine had made me a little woozy and I was about to take the plunge when Niki smiled and said, "Something the matter, Danny? You look a little green."

"My stomach's not feeling too good," I said. "And my head is spinning a little from the drinks." I yawned, and raised my hand to my mouth with some difficulty.

"It's not only the drinks, Danny—it's also the drugs."

"Huh, what drugs?" I yawned again.

"The ones I put in your mashed potatoes and broccoli—chloral hydrate and a short acting barbiturate. And the ones I put in your wine—thorazine and two long acting barbiturates."

"Niki, I…"

"You what, Danny? You want me to confess? All right, I will. Can you handle it? Can you deal with it?"

She reached under the table and came up with my manuscript in her hand. She slammed it on the table and shouted, "I read your book! Is your tape recorder on now? Is it? Are you getting this all down?"

I was really feeling groggy now and I couldn't lift my arms from the table. I spoke and my voice came out in a harsh whisper. "Niki, what are you doing to me?"

"Putting you to sleep for a long time, and when you wake up, I'll be long gone and so will the tape and this story of yours. One thing that Ronnie Millstein was good for was his shelves full of all those wonderful goodies in his drugstore which he willingly gave me when I couldn't get to sleep. And he was very knowledgeable about how they worked."

"Niki…"

"Shut up and listen to me you stupid cop—you foolish, foolish man. You're just like the others—stupid, stupid, stupid! I thought you were finally the one Danny, the real thing. Oh, what a disappointment you are! For God's sake, I killed four people for you, you ungrateful son-of-a-bitch! I killed Laura—that wimpy weak-willed Marty couldn't do it—and then I killed him, too, of course, by substituting water for the insulin in his last two needles. And the other two jerks—Victor and Ronnie—those murders cost me ten thousand each. The same guys killed both of them. You can buy anything when you're rich, you know. But no, you don't know, do you? Oh, Danny, why couldn't you have just let it be? Why couldn't you have loved me as I loved you?"

I was really dizzy now and couldn't stop it when my head fell forward into my dinner plate with what I imagined had to have been a loud crash. But I hadn't heard a thing.

•

By now I'm sure you realize that I wrote the last chapter of Danny's book. He sure as hell couldn't have done it himself laying face down in his mashed potatoes, could he? I was fairly certain I gave him enough drugs to kill him. I had to do it in order to tie up the last "loose end" as Danny so aptly described himself.

I know I told him he was just going to go to sleep for a while—I mean that old guy Edwards may think I'm the Dragon Lady, but I'm not totally heartless. But I think Danny knew that I killed him anyway from the look on his face before it crashed into his dinner plate. And I do feel really bad, believe me—just awful. But it had to be done. I'm sure you understand that it just had to be done. I didn't come all this way to end up in prison for the rest of my life or, more likely, to get a lethal dose of my own in the needle chamber in Sing Sing.

I still can't get over him thinking he could go back to that stupid little ex-wife of his and get his menial job back. He was deluding himself if he really thought that could happen. As I said, just another stupid, foolish man. He had it all. I gave it to him and then he threw it all away with his civil service mentality and his misguided sense of someone else's values.

I stripped off Danny's clothes and packed them away in his suitcase with the rest from his closet. I put his book, the tape recorder and the Rolex I had given him in there as well. I'm going to take all that with me and dispose of everything a little at a time when I get back to New York. Maybe I'll someday find a real man who I can give that watch to, if such a man exists. I'm not holding my breath on that one.

I retrieved a wheelbarrow from the gardener's shed and put a shovel and Danny's naked body—that wonderful handsome body—into it. It was a struggle, and the 90 degree heat certainly didn't help. I pushed the wheelbarrow through the thick foliage and over the roots and rocks to a far corner of the property and dumped him on the ground. The spot was densely overgrown and looked as if no person had ever been there. It took me a couple of hours to dig a very shallow grave what with all the tough roots and rocks hampering my efforts. I should have dug much deeper but dark storm clouds were approaching and the sun was getting low on the horizon. I had to finish the job now as I had an early flight back to New York in the morning. My arms ached and the sweat poured off my body as I eased Danny into the grave. I took one last look at that beautiful face and shook my head, thinking of what could have been, as I covered him up.

There were only a couple of inches of loose earth covering his body and I added some light branches and large leaves on top of it. That was the best I could do under the circumstances, and I thought it might be actually better this way. His naked body would decompose rapidly in the heat and humidity, and the worms and insects would finish the job in short order. Even if the police figured out where he had been staying on the island, they'd probably never find him way back here anyway, and the next renter wouldn't be here until October, over four months away.

I was a bit surprised when the tears began to roll down my cheeks and, as I wiped them away, I recalled reading in the book of his desire to have that old tear-jerker, Danny Boy, sung at his funeral. Danny Boy would have also been a great title for his book. He did exhibit a bit of talent in his writing, I give him that. Maybe I could re-write it myself someday and turn into the best-seller he wanted. After all, as Danny had said, two million won't last forever.

I'm not a great singer, but I can carry a tune. As the tears began to flow once more, I bowed my head and softly sang, "Oh, Danny Boy…Oh, Danny Boy, I…loved…you…so."

Epilogue

I dreamed I was floating in cool, wet cement in complete darkness. A dim light slowly passed over me, grew brighter, then faded to dimness again. The blackness returned. Something was on my face, and when I tried to move my hand toward it, I found my arm was firmly frozen in the wet cement which now seemed thicker and colder.

The dim light returned again and this time I managed to free my right arm from the cement. It made a loud sucking sound as it came out, and the effort caused my head to explode with pain. The light was still there when the sound of my stomach gurgling came into my awareness. Suddenly I panicked as the thought of what was happening to me burst into my mind—I was drowning in a pool of quicksand, and I had to get out of it now.

Ignoring the pain I pushed my arms down with all my strength and rose to a sitting position with a loud splash as leaves and twigs fell from my face. I opened my eyes to the bright sunshine filtering down through the tropical trees and foliage, and surveyed my surroundings. I crawled from my mud hole like the creature from the black lagoon and out of the jungle toward the smell of the sea. I was naked, weak, filthy and ravenously hungry and thirsty. My bones, and especially my head, were infiltrated with pain. I entered the warm water on shaky legs and carefully washed off the mud, insects and worms, then completely submerged myself for a few moments.

When I stood up in the water I spied the big house on the bluff 500 yards in the distance and the events of my last waking moments came back to me—the confrontation with Niki, the drugs she gave me—My God! How long had I been out? And why had I been in a hole in the jungle, naked, and not on the sofa with my clothes on?

I reached the back of the house and turned on the outside fresh-water shower gulping down great mouthfuls of the cool, life-giving liquid and rinsing the sea and the remaining traces of mud from my body. I crept up the stairs to the pool deck and cautiously peered in the windows. Then I recalled that Niki had knocked me out to give her time to flee the island, and the house should be vacant. But why had I been in a hole—a grave—if she wanted to only put me out for several hours?

I broke a window pane in the French doors and reached inside to unlock and open them. I quickly walked to the alarm panel in the kitchen and punched in the code to prevent a signal being sent. I looked around. There were no traces of our last meal. The dishes and glassware had been washed and stored away. The refrigerator had only a few beers in it and I prayed that the freezer downstairs still held some steaks. The bedroom closet and bureau drawers were empty. No traces of my presence there seemed left, nor that of Niki for that matter. I picked up the phone and dialed Willy Edwards.

"Hello," he said, with a trace of apprehension in his voice.

"Hi, Willy. It's Danny," I said, with a weak, scratchy voice.

"Danny! Jesus, are you all right?"

"Yeah. No…Willy, please get down here right away. And you better bring Tara with you."

"What the hell happened?"

"The Dragon Lady tried to kill me. She's gone. Please, come quick. And, Willy, you better bring some clothes for me. Uh, underwear, shoes and socks, too…"

Printed in the United States
134782LV00002B/17/P